ANDRE

Bad Faith

First published by M4L Publishing 2019

Second edition

ISBN: 978-1-951762-01-8

Editing by Stephanie Cohen-Perez
Cover art by ebooklaunch.com

This book was professionally typeset on Reedsy.
Find out more at reedsy.com

For my Auntie Chris. You helped me through a dark and confusing time of my life. Thank you for helping me see the road ahead more clearly.

"Breaking someone's trust is like crumpling up a perfect piece of paper. You can smooth it out, but it will never be the same again."

—Unknown

Contents

GET EXCLUSIVE BONUS STORIES!

Connecting with readers is the best part of this job. Releasing a book into the world is a truly frightening moment every time it happens! Hearing your feedback, whether good or bad, goes a long in shaping future projects and helping me grow as a writer. I also like to take readers behind the scenes on occasion and share what is happening in my wild world of writing. If you're interested, please consider joining my mailing list. If you do so, I'll send you the following as a thank you:

1. A free copy of *Revolution,* a prequel story that goes back in time before Chris Speidel ever knew about the mysterious world of time travel.
2. A free copy of *Road Runners,* a prequel story that visits the origination of the Road Runners organization.

You can get your content **for free,** by signing up HERE. https://www.andregonzalez.net/Wealth-Of-Time-Bonus

1

Chapter 1

Martin Briar sprawled in the mud, a generous gash oozing blood over his exhausted legs, his arms screaming in protest, sweat rolling down his mud-caked face, his entire body numb with pain.

"Pain is weakness leaving your body!" Staff Master Collins had barked at least 200 times over the past two months in his sharp, intimidating growl. Martin particularly enjoyed when the belligerent staff master would drop to the ground as he completed his 150th push-up, shouting that same line in his face while demanding fifty more.

Martin had put on a few pounds during his twelve-week recovery and rehab from Sonya blasting his legs into uselessness, but the Road Runner Training Program was simply a nice way of phrasing "boot camp." With the calendar flipping to 2019, Martin shed all of the extra weight, and for the first time since his twenties, sported actual muscles.

"I'm too old for this shit," he had muttered under his breath on the first day, wondering how the hell he'd make it to the finish line. Staff Master Collins had promised to destroy the body and psyche of all those in attendance, a group of Martin and six others recently recruited to join the Road Runners. Only one had dropped out after the first week, leaving the rest to form a bond and push each other through the ten-week program.

"You people don't know true hell," Staff Master Collins had calmly explained one day after training ended. He stood exactly six feet tall, with muscles bulging from every centimeter of his dark-skinned body, a heavy brow line keeping his face in a constant frown. *Even his muscles have muscles,* Martin noted before the first day of training.

Collins liked to give his version of motivational speeches at the end of each day, always while the group panted for breath, hands on knees as they listened. "I've been to hell and fought the demons. You need to be strong, mentally and physically, because they will try to break you."

Part of the program was learning to survive. Each trainee was given a specific amount of water to drink each day, decided by their weight and age to determine the bare minimum needed to not faint during the rigorous workout.

"What happens if you travel into the future and get captured by the Revolters? Do you think they're going to give you a bottle of water? Maybe order a pizza and fix a soft bed for you? Hell *no*!" Whenever Collins shouted, spit flew from his mouth in messy droplets.

"These people will leave you to starve, leave you to thirst, and leave you to die. If they don't kill you right away, they'll take you hostage, wait until you can barely stand up, then beat you to death because you're defenseless and can't even lift your hand to wipe your ass! Do you understand, Briar?"

Martin nodded at the crazy bald man two inches from his

face, bulging brown eyes burning into his spirit.

"Good. Especially you, Briar." Collins paused and crossed his arms, taking a step back from Martin. He lowered his voice and continued. "They want you bad, Briar. You're not the kind of man they'll kill at first chance—they will torture you. They want that sweet, sweet gift you have, and if they have to rip it out of your organs, then that's what they'll do."

This moment ten weeks ago had forced Martin to dedicate his life to the training program. He didn't know if the things Collins said were true, but he did know Chris wanted him, whether out of revenge for fleeing, or for being a Warm Soul.

Today was day 70, the final day of the training program, as Martin lay in the mud. They expected him to maintain his new figure, and he had every intent of doing so. Martin felt the best he ever had in his life. He slept better, ate better, was never tired, and no longer craved alcohol. He was now a middle-aged man with a chiseled physique and the skills to murder a man with his bare hands.

"Everybody up!" Collins grumbled, intentionally kicking mud in the faces of those slow to rise. Despite the cramping spread across his entire body, Martin jumped to his feet within two seconds. His mental strength had developed even more than his body, in his opinion. "To the rifles!"

The group of three men and two women dragged themselves out of the mud pit where they had just completed a twenty-minute round of army crawling. At least the rifles didn't require any further physical strength, but rather mental will.

A gazebo housed the rifles one hundred feet away. Martin ran to it, grabbing his rifle and a bandolier to sling over his shoulder. Every day ended with a quick session on the shooting range.

"Start us off, Briar," Collins shouted. They all had to watch each other shoot, a way to practice in the spotlight.

"Learn to shoot under any circumstance. There will be times you feel like you're dying, maybe you *are* dying, but you have to shoot on. Kill every last Revolter until you no longer can." Another inspirational line from Staff Master Collins.

Martin obliged and took his post. Ten rubber dummies stood across the open field, ranging from fifty to five hundred yards in distance. He focused on his breathing, inhaling deeply through his nose and exhaling steadily out of his mouth. He dropped his head to see into his scope and started firing.

He shot the first nine in rapid succession, his hands gliding from side to side as each dummy rocked in its place. The tenth and final shot required extra concentration as it stood 500 yards away. He'd heard the stories of Andrei Morozov's long distance shot on Chris in Alaska. Even though the shot didn't end up deadly, it was still touted as the greatest shot in the history of the Road Runners. Martin had the opportunity to meet Andrei at the beginning of their training program and received a few tips from the pro, including the breathing technique used when lining up the long distance shots.

He drew his breath and fired the shot, watching the dummy's head rock back. His fellow trainees ruptured into applause at witnessing his performance. Maybe once a week someone would have a perfect outing and hit all ten targets; this week was Martin's turn.

"Nice shooting, Briar," Collins said in the closest tone he had to a normal voice.

Martin stepped back and joined the rest of his team, who all offered slaps on the back and fist bumps for his stellar performance.

"Can I have a word with you?" Collins asked as the next trainee stepped up with their rifle.

"Sure."

They dropped back a safe distance where their voices couldn't be overheard by the others. Collins spoke in a low voice, just above a whisper. "They want me to report back what I think your best role would be. Now, by the looks of it, you have all the tools of a front line soldier. That would mean you'd barge into Revolter hideouts and kill everyone in sight, help with ambushes, and kick ass in general. But I get the sense that doesn't really excite you—you don't have the killer mentality that most soldiers have."

Martin nodded. "I'll go wherever I'm needed."

"Get off your high horse, Briar. Just tell me what you want to do."

"I honestly don't care. I just want to get this medicine for my mom. Whatever happens after that I'm fine with. I do want to kill Chris."

"Well, get in line. We already had a task force assigned to kill him, and they failed."

"The mission failed; they did not. Andrei landed that shot."

"Precisely. You may not have all the knowledge of someone who's been with the organization for years, but I feel you have the smarts to figure out a way. Combine that with your Warm Soul, and you might be the person who brings down Chris."

Martin had never thought of himself as smart. He got by in high school, never went to college, and bounced around jobs as a mid-level manager for various companies. Now with the Road Runners, more and more people had been praising his thinking ability, when all he thought he was doing was giving honest feedback.

"I don't even know what my ability means—I've never even seen it in action."

"There'll be a special session for you with some of our scientists. I think you'll be heading there the day after tomorrow."

"Can't wait."

"Don't be a smart-ass, Briar, I'm trying to help you."

"I know, and I appreciate it." Collins had never shown his compassionate side, and Martin wasn't sure what to do with it as the others in his group howled and cheered for each other on the shooting range. "I have my sights set on one thing at a time, and for me, it's getting that medicine."

"I respect that, but you can't lose sight of the future. Especially around here – you have to be ten steps ahead."

The two men stood in silence as an ugly gray cloud moved above them.

"I know. Honestly, I'll trust your recommendation for whatever position you think is best."

"I only recommend, but Commander Strike has the final say. She's checked in with me every day about your progress."

"What have you told her?"

"I told her there's something burning inside you, something that's pushing you to do the impossible." Collins paused and kicked the dirt with his heavy boot. "I'll be honest with you, this program is not meant for fifty-year-old men. It's designed for kids in their twenties, in their physical prime—like them." He nodded to the rest of the trainees. "I didn't think you'd make it past day one, but you've proven all of us wrong. That's how I know there's something driving you; I've never seen a transition like yours."

The Road Runners had put Martin through a rigorous rehab for his legs before starting the training program with Collins.

Through that, he felt a motivation to not let Sonya's cowardly actions define the rest of his life. They thought he'd have a new limp after coming out of his cast—he didn't. They said his knee would never bend the same way again, leaving him no flexibility—they were wrong. The weakness in his shot knee tried to creep up at times, but he followed the rehab program to the last detail. The Road Runners' doctors may have not had medicine from the future, but they had knowledge from it, and applied it to his rehab to make his legs stronger than before.

"I appreciate the compliment, and I'm sure Commander Strike will have a talk with me before deciding anything. I assume a lot will depend on how these tests go with the scientists."

"I suspect that, too. Either way, it's food for thought. If you ever need to talk about things, just let me know. I'll be here."

Collins stuck out a hand for Martin to shake. He had never shown his human side, and by doing so, showed Martin how highly the Road Runners thought of him. Collins thanked him for working so hard over the last ten weeks and wished him the best in whatever he'd end up doing for the organization.

An hour later, Martin was officially free to return home after living on the training base for the last ten weeks. Granted, it was only ninety minutes away from his house—and had all the luxurious accommodations he'd come to expect of anything hosted by the Road Runners—but he wanted to sleep in his own bed and see his mother in person instead of the brief phone calls they had at night.

He'd have to drag himself to the car to begin his long drive, but the prospect was enough to spark a new wave of energy as he left the hardest chapter of his time as a Road Runner in the rear view mirror.

2

Chapter 2

Martin's stay at home would be short-lived. During his drive, Commander Strike called to inform him that the group of international scientists had arrived in Denver and were expecting Martin in the office first thing the next morning.

He agreed to arrive at eight, citing a night of deep sleep that awaited him. The Commander was also flying in to witness the experiment, hoping to learn of a breakthrough in how Martin could best be utilized.

Martin didn't know what to expect of a gift that was foreign to even himself. They claimed he had remained mobile while the world was frozen through earlier tests, but he had no recollection of this happening.

During the rest of his drive home, soaking in the breathtaking nature of the Rocky Mountains, Martin reflected on his life. He never imagined ending up an integral part of a secret society trying to stop another secret society from taking over the world. Only, the Revolters couldn't be too big of a secret if they end up rising to power in the future.

Thinking about the future made him uneasy. Was it really

as bad as everyone claimed? People tended to make things a bigger deal than they actually were.

It can't be too bad if they're sending others with me. Why put Road Runners at risk to save my mom?

As the sun set, casting an orange glow across the horizon, Martin tried to push the future from his mind to think about the past. Even though he had a fresh take on life, he still felt the same inside: helpless and desperate for the end.

Sure, he had a lot going for him, but he was back to square one with no Izzy, no Sonya, and a future where his mother's brain would slowly but surely deplete, unless he secured a miracle medicine in the future.

Not exactly winning at life, Martin thought most nights before falling asleep. His body had undergone a transformation, but he had no use for it. Part of him hoped to join the front line soldiers just to increase his chances of being killed.

"You can't die," he said to his empty car. "There's a woman who needs you. She brought you into this world, and now she needs you."

A tear rolled down his face as he sped down the freeway.

* * *

The next morning's sunrise came quicker than expected. Martin had arrived home late after stopping at a diner for a burger, finally strolling in to his house at ten and immediately going to bed, his body drained.

His mom was already asleep, and was still snoozing when he woke—she'd been sleeping a solid ten hours each night since moving in, and that apparently hadn't changed while he was away.

Martin dressed and was out the door by 7:15, leaving him just enough time to get from Littleton to downtown Denver by eight.

When he arrived to the office, he made his way through the main level that served as their front as a marketing company. Martin nodded at the many familiar faces as he crossed toward the stairs and descended to where the Road Runners conducted their official business.

The basement was filled, as usual, with the brains of the operations scattered about, sitting at their desks and watching monitors that changed every second. Tarik's office was immediately to Martin's left, its door open with a handful of people packed inside.

Martin assumed these to be the scientists and knocked on the wall to get their attention.

Tarik and Commander Strike both stood behind the desk, while the group of four scientists all turned in unison. Two men and two women, all young and fair-skinned, watched Martin in amazement.

"Good morning, Martin," Commander Strike welcomed him, taking a sip from her coffee mug. "Thanks again for coming in so soon after completing your training. I'd like you to meet the team – please introduce yourselves."

A short woman stepped to Martin with a hand extended. She had piercing blue eyes that complemented her strawberry hair and wide smile. "I'm Megan Privvy. We've heard so much about you."

"Nice to meet you."

"I'm Steffan Privvy," said the man behind Megan, who

sported equally good looks with his chiseled brow and jaw, and wavy brown hair.

"That's my husband," Megan said. "We met studying time travel thirty years ago and have been together ever since, still studying."

Thirty years? They don't even look thirty years old.

Martin grinned at them and shook Steffan's hand. Thirty years could mean a variety of things when discussing time travel.

"And I'm Leigh Covington," the other woman said. She appeared slightly older than the rest, perhaps in her mid-30's, and lacked the natural warmth that Megan had radiated. Leigh had long brown hair that framed her high cheekbones.

Martin shook her hand and turned to the final man on the right.

"I'm Brigham Kelley," the man said in a strong British accent.

"Nice meeting you all," Martin said to the circle.

"Our scientists come from Europe," Commander Strike said. "Their advances in medicine in the future are way beyond what we have in the future, and they're actually accessible."

"Why didn't you just have them bring the Alzheimer's cure instead of sending me into the future?"

"We don't actually have that cure, Mr. Briar," Brigham said. "I'll be staying here while you go on your mission to get it. We're interested in studying it and replicating the medicine, if possible." Brigham adjusted his glasses as he spoke, his black hair spiked in every direction.

"So I need to get more than just for my mom?" Martin asked, puffing out his chest to show off his new strength. He felt much older than everyone else in the room, being the only one with streaks of gray on his head and early wrinkles forming below his eyes.

"Yes," Commander Strike said. "We figured since you'll already be there, we can use the opportunity to get some for ourselves and rightfully distribute it in different times throughout the past."

"Fair enough."

"We can discuss those details later. I know these fine folks are excited to start the experiment with you, and I don't want to waste any of their time. Shall we?"

The scientists nodded and filed out of the room, strolling by Martin with wide grins. Commander Strike and Tarik joined the back of the procession and followed behind with Martin.

"What are they going to do to me?" Martin asked Strike.

"It's not much," she replied, brushing a hand through her blond hair. "They're going to draw some blood to examine in their labs, run some tests on your brain, and film you with time frozen to see how the experience is for you."

"They can freeze time?"

"Steffan can. It's why he's in this group, trying to figure out how someone could resist it."

"Does that mean he's also warm?"

"Sort of. Anyone who can freeze time is warm, but not everyone who is warm can freeze time. The latter is more rare, which is why we need to figure it out."

"And use this to kill Chris?"

"Exactly. Imagine a scenario where all of his guards are frozen while we send in someone like you to kill him."

Martin knew they wanted to use his ability to their advantage in the war, but having him be the one to personally kill Chris? Yes, he wanted the old bastard dead, but he couldn't even kill

Sonya. How was he supposed to become the biggest hero in Road Runner history?

They went to a conference room in the back of the office—the largest one they had—where a camera stood on a tripod along the front wall. The room had been cleared of the tables and chairs that normally filled it, leaving a lone table pushed into the corner, out of sight from the camera. Chairs were positioned for each person, seven in total.

The scientists filed in, taking their seats around the table, leaving the middle chair open. "Please sit here, Martin," Megan said.

Martin obliged, all eyes studying him.

"Today will be fairly simple," Steffan said. "We're going to run some tests, and then you and I will go for a little spin in the frozen world, right in this room. I expect we'll be done within an hour, not counting the frozen time, but that doesn't count anyway."

Steffan spoke to Martin as if he already understood how this worked, so he offered an obligatory nod in return.

Tarik and Commander Strike sat on the ends of the rectangular table, clearly here to observe, as they lacked the pens and notepads like everyone else.

"Let's begin," Leigh said, plopping a briefcase on the table and flipping its latches in one fluid motion. Wires jumped out, which she pushed aside. "First, we're going to take some blood from you. We'll study it back at home to see what our machines say." She pulled a syringe from the briefcase along with four empty vials, each three inches in length.

"Go right ahead," Martin said, sticking his arm out and pulling his sleeve up to his shoulder.

The others took out papers and scribbled notes while Leigh

drew the blood. Strike and Tarik looked around, possibly bored, possibly anxious. Martin couldn't tell for sure. Having his blood drawn had always made Martin a bit woozy, and this time was no exception. Tarik recognized this and left the room to bring back bottles of water for everyone.

As soon as she packed away the full vials, Leigh pulled the wires in front of her and separated them from the tangled mess they had formed. She flattened them across the table, creating what looked like a tree with bare branches spreading out. She stood, wires in hand, and shuffled behind Martin. "You can stay seated. I'm going to strap these to your head so we can measure your brain activity before, during, and after time is frozen."

Martin noticed a slight elevation in her voice as she spoke this final line. Her fingers danced around his head, pushing down in random places as she pressed the wires into position. All of the wires converged at the base of his neck and twisted into a thick bundle that connected to a small black box.

"What does that thing do?" Martin asked after Leigh had sat down.

"That records everything going on with your brainwaves. The technology is the same in terms of *how* we measure, all that's different is where that data is stored and sent. We have a laboratory full of scientists back in Europe waiting for this data to be transmitted so they can start analyzing. The video feed you'll be on with Steffan will also be sent their way as soon as we wrap up today."

"And when will you analyze it? I assume you're the best if you came all this way."

"We're boarding the jet immediately after we wrap up here today, except for Brigham, of course. He'll be staying back for the medicine. As soon as we arrive home, we'll join our teams and analyze all of this data."

"This is a huge deal, Martin," Strike cut in. "This is the first test of this kind. We once had a chance to draw blood from an enemy who we learned was warm, but he died before we could run him through an experiment like this. We have no expectations, only hopes of learning something new."

Martin nodded. *So I'm the lab rat for Warm Souls. Be sure to put that in my obituary.*

"I see," he said. "Why haven't you just studied Steffan, then?"

"We have. He's not actually warm—just someone who can freeze time—so we didn't learn anything valuable from his tests."

"How do you know I can't freeze time?"

"Can you freeze time, Martin?"

"Well, I don't think so."

"That's how we know. It's not an ability that lies dormant."

Steffan nodded and stood up. "It's more like a sixth sense, you could say. Enough with the questions. Let's start!"

Megan strolled to the tripod, pushed a button on the camera and stood in front of the lens to speak. "Today is Monday, February 4, 2019. We're in Denver, Colorado, at the Road Runner offices with Commander Strike, Tarik Sadi, Steffan Privvy, Leigh Covington, Brigham Kelly, and myself, Megan Privvy. Our test subject is Martin Briar, who we have confirmed is a Warm Soul. Blood samples have been drawn, and the pre-examination tests are complete on his brain activity." She checked her watch. "I have a current time of 8:52 a.m., Mountain Standard Time."

Megan returned to her seat and gestured to Steffan to begin.

"Martin, please stand and go to the back of the room," Steffan said, his voice turning suddenly serious. "And take the black box with you."

Martin rose, a slight tremble working through his legs as he grabbed the box off the table. A palpable tension hung in the air as everyone inched forward in their seats, watching Martin cross the room. He stopped about forty feet away from the group of scientists and the tripod.

"You're good there," Steffan shouted. "I'll commence the freezing of time on my count of three. You will all be frozen, except for myself and Mr. Briar. You will not realize you're frozen, as your current perception of time will be temporarily halted until I unfreeze it. Since I'll be in direct contact with the camera, it will roll and capture our interaction. Are we all ready?"

He looked down the table of his colleagues, and each returned a silent nod, still not breaking their stares from Martin in the distance.

"Okay. On my count. Three . . . two . . . one."

3

Chapter 3

Martin expected a rumble of some sort, but apparently the freezing of time was as uneventful as the passing of regular time. He watched Steffan place his hands on his head, eyes shut, giving his entire concentration to the task of stopping time in its tracks.

No rumble. Just the blank stares of three scientists and two leaders of the Road Runners.

Steffan put his hands down and stood, slightly wobbling.

"How are you feeling?" Steffan shouted across the room.

"I'm fine," Martin replied. "What am I supposed to do?"

They could have been playing a prank on him by how fake they all appeared, looking like a panel of gawking judges on one of those shitty televised talent contests.

"Walk this way," Steffan said, coming out from behind the table. He positioned himself in the camera's view and turned to speak to it. "I can confirm that time is frozen. My colleagues are sitting at the table, unable to move. As you can see, Mr. Briar is mobile." He looked over his shoulder as Martin approached.

Martin took cautious steps, feeling like he had magically stepped into a photograph. Even though the others were in the room, it seemed more that he and Steffan were the only two people in the world. Gooseflesh broke across his body at the thought. He reached Steffan's side and joined the scientist in front of the camera.

"Martin, how are feeling?"

"I told you I feel fine."

"I need you to elaborate. Are there any kinds of side effects you're experiencing? Light-headedness, dizziness, wooziness?"

"No. I feel completely normal. How I always do."

"I see doubt in your eyes."

Martin pursed his lips, his brows furrowed at Steffan's accusatory tone. "This is hard to imagine as real, but I thought the same thing about time travel when I first experienced it."

"Is your memory still intact? Do you know where you are, what you're doing here, et cetera?"

"Yes. I'm in Denver, at the Road Runners' office, and we're testing my warmth."

"Very good. I want to take the camera out to the office, and perhaps out of the building. Martin, I want you to go out and interact however you see fit. Let's take these wires off your head so you can roam more freely."

Martin looked at Steffan with a cocked brow as he reached over and started tugging the wires off, stashing them next to the black box on the table.

"It's fine," Steffan assured him, and grabbed the camera from the tripod. He held it in a shaky hand and gestured for Martin to exit the conference room. "We'll put them back on when we return."

Martin shuffled by his frozen colleagues, reminding him of those wax museums where you can hang out with Elvis and Michael Jackson, only these were people he actually knew. And they definitely weren't wax.

As he passed them, he swore Tarik's eyes followed him, but chalked it up to paranoia. The pictures of Jesus Christ in his mom's old house had the same effect and always made him walk a little faster down the hallway. He did the same thing now and leapt toward the door, pulling it open to reveal the rest of the office.

Martin stopped in the doorway.

The office looked exactly the same: monitors flashing, Road Runners at their desks, knee-deep in work. But no one was moving, and a deafening silence blanketed the room. Martin's heart raced a tad quicker at the sight.

"It's okay, go ahead," Steffan said from behind, camera held high to record Martin's first interaction with the frozen world.

The scene reminded Martin of a haunted house around Halloween time. They often had several characters set up that looked fake, but there was always one who was real, waiting to jump out and scare the shit out of you. He waited for someone to make a sudden head turn and send him running back to the conference room, but it never happened. Everyone sat or stood exactly as they were.

"Did they know they were going to be frozen?" Martin asked over his shoulder, refusing to break his gaze ahead.

"No. There's no need to tell someone they're being frozen. They don't realize it, and when I unfreeze them, they just continue with what they were doing, unaware they ever stopped."

Martin stayed against the wall as he shuffled toward the kitchen. A man had apparently been speaking with a woman, pouring a cup of coffee from the pot, the brown liquid frozen in mid-air.

"So this is all normal?" Martin asked.

"Sure is. Pretty cool, don't you think?"

Martin didn't think it was cool, but rather disturbing.

"How many people have this power to freeze time?"

"Twenty-three that we know of for sure."

"And how many are warm like me?"

"You are the fourth known instance of someone being warm *without* the capability of freezing time."

"I still don't understand how the abilities are different."

"Those who can freeze time remain mobile when *they* perform the action. If someone else freezes time, that same person is not immune. If a Revolter were to freeze time, I'd be frozen right along with everyone else, unlike how I'm mobile now because *I* caused this."

"Doesn't this seem kind of dangerous? Does Chris have the ability to do this?"

Steffan nodded and shrugged his shoulders. "We don't believe he can freeze time, but he can certainly resist the freeze. It has its frightening parts, but that's why we're trying to figure this all out."

"How did you do it—freeze time?"

"It's hard to explain. It's sort of a telekinetic power, I guess. I have to completely concentrate on it until it happens."

"And you were born with it?"

"I dunno. It didn't start until I was in college. Fortunately, that's when I met Megan, and she was already a Road Runner."

"Right. You guys said you've been together for 30 years?"

Steffan cackled. "Yeah, that always gets a good reaction from people because we're both only 27. We met in 1987. I became a Road Runner, and we've been traveling through time ever since, never aging."

"So you never go back to your original time?"

"Rarely. We both lost our families to Victor—he's Chris's counterpart in Europe—so we don't have any reason to go back. We've built a life together trying to keep the world safe and wouldn't have it any other way. So, yes, it can be scary knowing this capability even exists for our enemies to use, but we suspect they're also figuring out how to use it to their advantage. I know Victor once made an attempt to assassinate our leader, Commander Blair, by freezing time, but failed because he is also warm—one of the four that we know of."

"Who are the other two?"

"One is a Revolter in Africa, and the other is an ex-Revolter who now lives in the middle of a forest in China. We tried recruiting him, but he swears to a life of neutrality and doesn't want to be bothered. He sleeps with guns in both hands, waiting for anyone to try and tell him otherwise. And there's also Chris, but we don't count him, for obvious reasons."

"So I'm the only one in the U.S. that has this ability?"

"You're the only one on this side of the ocean that is warm. That's why Chris won't stop until he gets you. Your ability is something he's only ever heard of."

"But isn't he hiding?"

Steffan snorted laughter. "Please. He's probably in Denver as we speak. I'm not convinced one bit that he's still in his house. He probably froze time and walked out the front door. And now everyone is in a panic. There's an infinite number of places to hide if you're Chris, and his silly mansion is at the bottom of that list. Enough with all of this talk – let's go for a walk outside."

Martin didn't realize how long they had been talking, and had no way of knowing for sure, either, as the clocks on the wall remained still, not ticking the day away. They had an entire conversation in the middle of the silent office, their words falling on literal deaf ears.

Steffan pushed by Martin and led them to the stairs. They went up, crossed through the marketing office that held a similar scene of employees mid-conversation, and rushed out the building.

A short flight of four stairs descended from the building to the sidewalk below, but Martin stayed at the top, keeping his back to the building as if it protected him. The scene outside reminded him of zombie apocalypse films where the roads were filled with cars, either abandoned or occupied by corpses.

Vehicles always lined the streets for metered parking downtown, but seeing dozens of cars in the middle of the road, drivers staring out the windshield, was both chilling and surreal.

"What the fuck?" Martin whispered under his breath, as Steffan jumped down the steps and ran into the middle of the street.

"Isn't it fun?" he shouted, twirling the camera in circles to capture the frozen world. A group of pedestrians, clearly all downtown office workers, filled the sidewalk. Some had their cell phones to their ears or held in front of them as they looked down. Others had grins on their faces as they enjoyed the fresh air. "Come down here!"

This is your reality now, Martin thought before going down the steps with the caution of tiptoeing through a minefield. The back of his mind still waited for one of these frozen people to jump at him.

When he reached the sidewalk, Martin looked up to a flock of birds frozen in flight, their dark V-shape contrasting against the bright blue sky. The nearest tree on the sidewalk stood slightly tilted, and he could only assume there was a strong morning breeze blowing its way through town.

"Wanna play hide-and-seek?" Steffan called from across the street, a cheesy grin on his face as he ducked behind a car.

The air was silent, so Martin heard him cackling like a teenage boy telling dirty jokes. As uptight as everyone in the Road Runners seemed, it was refreshing to see one of them enjoy life with childlike wonder. Steffan may have been alive for 50 years (or however the hell he calculated it), but he knew how to bask in the small pleasures in life.

I wonder how often this guy freezes time and goes playing in the middle of the street.

The thought of Steffan dancing in the middle of the cobblestone roads in Europe forced a grin.

"I'm not gonna come find you," he shouted back. "But you're right, this is pretty cool."

Martin approached a car in the middle of the road, noticing the driver through the rolled down window. It was an older man with a cigarette pinched between his lips, his left hand on the wheel, and his right hand on the radio dial, the gray clouds frozen still from the orange embers on the cigarette's tip. He debated plucking the cigarette from the man's mouth, but couldn't find the courage to do it. All of the people looked eerily dead with their lifeless stares and eyes that never blinked.

But they also looked so alive. This wasn't a zombie apocalypse; these were people on their way around town.

Steffan came out from behind the car, grin still splattered across his face, camera pointing at Martin. "So what do you think?"

"It's definitely weird, but I can see why you like to have so much fun with it."

"Yeah, I suppose it's like any great gift. It can be used for good and fun, but others will use it for evil and selfish reasons."

"I can see that. So what exactly are we trying to figure out here?"

Steffan flipped the lid over the camera. "I don't know, man. It's a total shitshow. All of the Forerunners are losing their mind over Chris. They don't know if he's home plotting some great massacre, or hiding in an underground tunnel waiting for the search to die down. They've done some digging—literally—around the mansion, but have come up empty. And now they have you to consider, and everyone has an opinion on how to best utilize your skill. Commander Blair wants to send you into Chris's house with loaded guns and shoot everything in sight while it's all frozen. Commander Guang—from Asia—wants us to freeze time and have you infiltrate the Revolters' hideouts one by one and take whatever information you can gather. And Commander Strike is clueless. I think she's still losing sleep over the whole Sonya debacle. Maybe we should have just frozen time and let you slip that poison into her drink. She would've never known you were there."

"Why didn't you suggest that?"

"I did. I spoke with Julian while he was out in Europe for a trip. He thought it was brilliant and said he'd take the idea to Commander Strike. I never heard anything back, so figured she vetoed it, or he never told her."

"I don't see how she could veto that. She made the choice to move forward with the assassination, and never presented that as an option."

Steffan looked around as if one of the frozen people might be eavesdropping. "Look. Between you and me, Commander Strike isn't exactly the best fit for her position."

Martin's eyebrows shot all the way up to his slowly receding hairline.

"Don't get me wrong, she's an incredible woman, confident most the time. But when it comes to difficult decisions, she's extremely indecisive. It's like she waits for someone to make a choice for her, or wait for matters to play themselves out. You haven't been in the closed-door meetings since we arrived. She has no input, just defers to Tarik and lets him guide the discussion."

"Interesting. I don't get that impression at all."

"Of course not. She's charming and can radiate her authority over those who don't know better. You should hear the way she's perceived over in Europe."

"How's that?"

"Let's just say when news broke out about your gift—keep in mind, the first of your kind on this side of the pond—almost all of leadership started making jokes about how Strike would blunder the situation. We were all watching the footage of Chris getting shot by Andrei. We all saw him rise like he had only been punched in the chest. But we all had a feeling, in the back of our heads, that there wasn't going to be a different outcome. No way Strike would ever be the one to end Chris."

"Is that why you all came out here together?"

Steffan nodded, brushing a hand over his chin. "I'm afraid so. There are plenty of capable scientists here who could conduct this experiment, but we were afraid Strike would try to lead the way with them. With us, she's happy to take a back seat since we're the visitors who came all the way from Europe. She doesn't want to do anything to step on our toes and warrant an angry call from Commander Blair."

"So then what's really the plan?"

"We're going to keep running experiments. We want to know *why* you are able to resist time freezing, but I'll be honest, I think it's sheer luck. There's nothing concrete that stands out about you compared to this old man smoking his cigarette." He gestured to Martin's friend playing with the radio. "Commander Strike has one year left of her term. We're going to try and wait her out and hope that someone more decisive can get elected and set a plan in stone."

Martin crossed his arms and stroked his chin. "I didn't realize this was so political."

"Oh yeah, more than you know. All of our leaders are elected by the people, for the people. Everyone is on a one-term, two-year limit to ensure ideas are kept fresh. That alone cuts all the nonsense out of the politics; no one really bothers campaigning extensively for such a short term and never has to worry about re-election."

"Are you ever going to run?"

"Nah, it's not for me. I like conducting my research and contributing to the big picture that way." Steffan looked around again at the frozen cars in the middle of the road. "We should head back in. Not nice leaving everyone frozen while we have all the fun."

Steffan howled laughter to the sky and turned to go back up the stairs to their office.

Martin followed, still trying to figure out how all of this Road Runner business worked. Apparently, Commander Strike wasn't taken seriously by her peers, something he'd need to keep in mind in his future interactions with her.

4

Chapter 4

Returning inside, Steffan had unfrozen time as they walked back down the stairs to the office. The bustling floor of Road Runners remained oblivious that they had just been frozen, and continued with their work as normal, paying no attention to Martin and Steffan as they strolled back to the conference room.

The scientists asked Martin what he thought of the experiment, hanging to his every word as he explained the experience. They had a brief chat about the next steps, which included them all returning to Europe to analyze the data and review the video footage. Aside from Brigham, they all wished Martin safe travels into the future, and offered him a place to stay should he ever end up in Europe. They left with hugs and handshakes before departing.

Strike, Tarik, and Martin returned to Tarik's office, where the space felt welcoming again with the large crowd gone. Brigham posted up in another office down the hall to work on research.

"We need to swear you in under our official oath," Commander Strike said as they settled in. "If you plan to go to the future with other Road Runners, you need be an official member of this organization."

Martin agreed to the terms, and mentally pushed away all of the negativity Steffan had said about Strike. Was she really as clueless as he made her sound? From his personal experience, she seemed a savvy leader with all the traits of a demanding presence and powerful voice that one would expect of her position.

Maybe she was different in certain situations, but that didn't have to discount the work she had already done. She *did* authorize the mission that would've killed Chris; it wasn't her fault Sonya was already three steps ahead of everyone else.

"When should I expect to leave for the future?" Martin asked when Strike closed the office door.

"As soon as you're ready," Tarik said, sitting down behind his desk, his brown eyes studying Martin.

"Let's execute this oath, and you can head there right now if you want," Strike said, remaining by the door. "Please stand and face me, and hold your right hand over your heart."

Martin obliged, standing in the middle of the room like a schoolboy ready to recite the Pledge of Allegiance.

"Please answer my questions," Strike said. "Do you, Martin Briar, vow to uphold the integrity of the Road Runners by never putting yourself above the greater good for your own personal reasons?"

"I do."

"Do you swear to use your abilities for the improvement of the world, and not for the collapse of modern society as we know it?"

"I do."

"Do you vow to kill Chris Speidel, should the opportunity ever present itself?"

"I do."

"Do you vow to do as instructed by the Road Runners, no matter how difficult the task?"

"I do."

"Last, and most importantly, do you vow to keep the secrets of our operations from anyone outside of the organization, with the exception of immediate, household family?"

"I do."

"Perfect. With that said, welcome—officially—to the Road Runners. You are now cleared to go on missions on our behalf." Strike stuck out a hand to officially seal his membership with the team.

"Thank you."

"Normally we have a small celebration, but we can postpone that until you come back," Tarik said. "Now that you're ready, let's discuss the year 2064."

Tarik gazed at Strike as she crossed the room to stand beside him.

"Martin," she said. "I need you to understand that everything we've mentioned about the future is not an exaggeration—it's a dangerous time. We suggest you always cover as much skin as possible. Wear gloves, hats, scarves, whatever you need to make sure no one can see the glow of your skin. They will shoot any known Road Runner without hesitation. We suspect they have orders to not kill you, seeing as Chris wants you to himself, but we can't afford to assume that is completely true."

"Why is it so dangerous?" Martin asked, sitting on the edge of his chair.

"Between now and 2064, Revolters infiltrate the government, both locally and nationally. They spark fear into their supporters. Fear of anyone not like them."

"Fear of who?"

"Poor people, minorities, handicapped people. Basically anyone who isn't rich or prominent in society. Every government program that was designed to assist those in need has been erased by 2064. The country basically runs on the wealthy and leaves the rest to kill each other in the streets; they literally deliver crates of guns to the middle of these poor neighborhoods just so everyone can shoot each other."

"That's sick."

"It's a war zone. You need to always be wary of your surroundings. If you walk down the wrong block, and they recognize you as an outsider, they'll jump you and likely kill you for your wallet. No police patrol these areas; no one cares."

"You're going to give me something to protect myself, right?"

"Yes. Protection is always provided. We'll give you a handgun to travel with, but when you get there you'll want to head over to one of our weapons warehouses—they're in discreet locations just like our offices. You can go there any time for more ammunition or if you want a new weapon."

"I'd recommend the most powerful gun they have," Tarik said. "In the areas that do have police, you'll see them with fully automatic Uzis."

"Don't have any run-ins with the police," Strike said. "They will throw you in jail for any reason, and if you have to face a judge, you're toast. The legal system has also been overtaken by Revolters—they actually started there before moving to the political stage."

"So what *can* I do?"

"We'll have someone with experience in the future lead you. Save any specific questions for them, as they'll have a more concrete answer."

"Okay. I get it, but are we going to talk about an actual plan for getting the medicine?"

Strike looked to Tarik, who returned an uneasy stare.

"We don't really make plans for missions this far into the future. Plans require research, which require Road Runners to spend time in that era," Tarik said.

"We don't send Road Runners to any time period after 2050 unless they specifically request it," Strike said, a hint of irritation floating beneath her voice.

"So then who's coming with me?" Martin asked.

"We put out an offer for volunteers. There are still plenty of Road Runners who *want* to conduct research in the future and know the risks associated with it."

"You'll be fine, Martin," Tarik said. "You'll be with a group of experienced Road Runners who are prepared for this mission. Stay aware of your surroundings, confirm your decisions before doing anything, and you'll make it."

"What if Chris finds me?"

Strike paced around the desk and faced the door, her back to Martin and Tarik as she seemed to look for words to fall out of the sky. "I don't want you to worry about Chris. We have our eyes on him. He's in his mansion. If we think you're in any danger, we'll send word for your return."

Martin remained silent, remembering everything Steffan had told him about how no one actually knew where Chris was. He thought he heard doubt in Strike's voice, but chalked it up to the new knowledge he had just learned.

"I'll have to trust you on that. Is it possible he's hiding in the future if we have no presence there?"

"He's in his mansion," Strike snapped.

Martin knew Chris could time travel through simple mind power—the old man had admitted as much. But was Strike in so much denial that she thought everyone else was too dumb to know that as well? Her adamance frustrated Martin, so he dropped the topic before he said anything he might regret. Besides, he didn't have any proof of Steffan's claims. When did trusting gossip ever work out for anyone?

"When will I get to meet the people I'm traveling with?" Martin asked.

"They're in town already. Whenever you're ready to go, we'll call them all in for a brief meeting and you'll be on your way. We have very specific instructions about traveling into the future, and we need to make sure everyone is on the same page. For safety reasons, of course."

"Well, I'm ready. I have nothing else to wait for."

Strike looked to Tarik with her eyebrows raised, tossing her blond hair behind her head before returning her gaze to Martin. "Look, Martin. We know you're anxious to get there, but we really need to advise you to tie up loose ends here at home. Do you even have a written will for all the money you have? Have you said goodbye to your mother?"

"I don't see how that's any of your business."

"It's not our business, but we've witnessed enough instances to know that these types of matters should be addressed before going into the 2060's."

"It's like you're going off to war," Tarik chimed in, his fingers rapping nervously on his desk. "This isn't some glory trip back to the 1920's to experience prohibition and try all the underground moonshine. There is no glory in the future, and you'll see that within five minutes of arriving."

"And we're not saying you'll get killed," Strike added. "But you should understand that the odds of that will increase dramatically."

Martin's fingers started to fiddle on his leg. All *he* wanted to do was get the medicine and come home. And all *they* wanted to do was provide him a never-ending list of reasons to not go. *My mind is made up, people. I'm not backing out.*

They watched him juggle his thoughts, face scrunched into what probably appeared as confusion, but was actually anxiety trying to blow through his head.

"I don't want my mom to worry. I've already told her I'm going to get this cure for her. Why is this such a concern for you?"

"Because if she doesn't know, then it falls on us to deliver the news. We're adamant about providing support to the family members of our team. In a distant way, they're a part of us."

Martin imagined a world where he dies in 2064, leaving his mother alone to care for herself while her mind fades to darkness. The final days of her life would be spent in a confined room, staring at the walls, having no memory of her son, her family, her life. She would've lived an entire life—a full life—only to have no recollection of any of it by the time the reaper came to escort her to the abyss.

"Give me three hours," Martin said. "I'll go home, and I'll be back here in three hours. I don't want to waste another second."

"We can do that," Strike said. "We'll place the calls to those joining you on this trip and make sure we're all ready to meet here."

"Thank you. I'll see you then."

Martin stood and left Strike and Tarik in the office without another word.

5

Chapter 5

Martin pulled into his driveway half an hour later and scrambled into the house. His mom lay on the living room couch, a romantic comedy playing on the TV.

"Marty," she said, jolting up, clearly startled. "I didn't know when I'd see you again. Are you already back from your special trip?" Martin watched his mother stand, her body frail and thin, her left arm twitching as she dragged her feet toward him. She still managed a smile, though, and he recognized the beauty he'd always remember her for.

"Sit down, Mom," he said, meeting her and helping her back to the couch.

Her mind had already taken a turn for the worse by the time Martin checked in to the Road Runners' training program. He had told her where he was going and that it was all so he could get her medicine. He explained this numerous times, as she forgot everyday leading up to his departure. She was still functional, simply an extremely forgetful mind. He had no plans of stopping home until he had the medicine in hand, but here he was having to explain himself once more.

"Not yet. I'm leaving in a couple hours."

"Oh. Did you forget something?"

Martin feared she hadn't even realized ten weeks had passed since they last saw each other. She spoke relaxed, as if he had just left the house this morning.

"Not really. I just wanted to come back and say goodbye. Everyone has assured me that this is a dangerous trip and that I should come say goodbye in case anything happens to me."

Tears immediately welled in her eyes, giving them a glossy coat over their redness. "Marty, if I'm the only reason you're doing this, then please don't. It's not worth it."

"You're worth it; I don't need any other reason."

"Marty, I'll be fine. There are medications that slow the process down."

"All that does is drag out the inevitable, Mom. I can't sit by and watch you fade, knowing I could've done something to stop it. I'm going, and I didn't come here for a discussion about it."

The tears that had pooled in her eyes now streamed down her face in moist trails. "Can I tell you something, Marty?"

He nodded and sat down next to her on the couch.

"You sound just like . . . " she continued.

"Like who?"

"Your father."

Martin's heart skipped a beat; she had rarely spoken of his father since his death.

"How do you mean?"

"He had that same look in his eyes that you have now. Now that you've lost weight, you *look* like him."

As blank of a mind as she had shown over the past weeks during their phone conversations, a new tone took over as she spoke about her late husband. In it, Martin heard years of familiarity, as if his father was someone her mind would never forget, no matter how bad the Alzheimer's advanced. Her voice came out confident and strong.

"Mom, I don't understand why you're saying all this. Dad's been gone for over forty years and you've never told me anything about him."

"There's plenty I can tell you, but none of it matters anymore. Your dad was two different people. There was the man I fell in love with, and the man I didn't know. I have a confession that you should probably know before I forget it all."

Martin subconsciously sat on the couch next to Marilyn and inched closer to her, a fruity stench oozing from her freshly washed hair. "What is it?" The thought of traveling into the future now seemed so distant. His mother had wrapped him in the claws of a story he thought he'd never hear.

"Your father didn't die from a heart attack, Marty. The truth is, I don't have any idea what happened to him."

"Wh-what do you mean? Is he still alive?" Martin's throat suddenly felt as if it were being clenched shut by a heavy fist.

Marilyn shrugged. "He could be. I have no idea. But what you said, Marty, is the same thing he said to me before he left forever."

"What did I say?" he asked in a defensive voice.

"The medicine. The last time I saw your father, I had a bad cold: runny nose, fever, all the bad you can think of. He insisted to go out and get me some medicine. I argued with him for a bit, but I didn't have the energy. So, he left. Off to get me medicine, and I never saw him again."

Martin's jaw hung open. "I don't understand. Why did you tell us he had a heart attack?"

"I couldn't bring myself to admit the truth, especially at your young age. I battled a lot of demons in those following days. I felt like a complete failure for marrying someone who would just walk out on his family like that. I figured pretending he had died was easier to explain. If I didn't, it would have been nothing but a life of questions and doubt for all of us."

Martin sat back, not quite slouching into the soft couch, but needing a moment to gather himself. The truth, a lifelong truth, hit him on the head with the force of a speeding diesel truck.

"I'm sorry, Mom, I can't handle this right now. I really do have to get your medicine, and I *will* be back."

Martin stood, hot anger filling his gut that he wasn't sure was directed toward his mother or his father. The new revelation made him dizzy with confusion, and somewhere in the deepest, most intimate fibers of his being, he already knew he wanted to travel back to this particular night of his father abandoning the family, and learn what exactly happened.

Yeah, and we all saw how well that turned out this last time.

He shook the idea out of his head, the thought overwhelming his already flustered mind.

"Do what you need to do," Marilyn said. "But if you claim this could be the last time we speak to each other, I just thought you should know the truth."

With tears welling in his eyes, Martin leaned toward his mother. "I love you, Mom. And this truth doesn't change anything. You raised me and I'm happy with how my life turned out." These last words were ones he never thought he'd hear leave his lips. While he had suffered incomparable pain throughout his life, he had no regrets. "Now. I'm leaving, I'm getting your medicine, and I'll be back here within two hours at the latest."

Marilyn nodded, keeping her lips pursed as Martin kissed her one final time on the forehead before turning and walking out of the house.

When he closed the front door, he stood on the top step of the porch and ran a hand down the smooth stone walls that lined the mansion's main entrance. He had his new life waiting for him right here in 2019, and it would always be there. All he wanted was to make sure that his mother would be there with him, too.

6

Chapter 6

Martin drove like a maniac, weaving through the traffic that had formed during his quick hour at home. He had intended to draft a document to serve as his last will and testament should he die on this trip, but didn't foresee this elephant of a revelation being dropped on his head by his mother.

He thought back to the morning of his childhood when his mother had sat at the kitchen table in their small ranch home, crying with stacks of papers spread out across the table.

When he and his brother had entered the kitchen, she sat them down and told them their father had suffered a heart attack in the middle of the night. She hadn't mentioned that he was dead, forcing Martin to ask the dreaded question.

Marilyn had refused to say it aloud, only nodding her head in confirmation, and now it all made sense knowing it was a lie. It ended up as the main turning point in Martin's life, losing his father as a child just starting middle school, but his mother had stepped up in a heroic way, ensuring nothing skipped a beat in their household.

He watched the sky and prayed this mission would end within

a day. He had no desire to study the future and see what a shithole the world would one day become. *Just give me the medicine and get me the fuck back.*

When he arrived to the office, Martin parked and waited in the car. His stomach throbbed with anxiety, and his legs turned to mush as they bounced beneath the steering wheel. He hadn't felt nerves like this since his first trip to 1996. A sense that death was waiting for him on the other side of this trip had swelled within. Death or failure now seemed more plausible than success and a happy life.

For the first time, Martin considered turning around and dumping the Juice down the sink. The Road Runners certainly moved with an uncanny urgency, a trait that was already rubbing off on Martin, and kept pushing him into rushed decisions.

You were already thinking of the next mission after this. You're hooked. And since when? What happened to the old Martin who was content with a glass of whisky and a cigar?

"He died when Izzy was murdered and thrown into the lake," Martin said, pushing open the car door and stumbling onto the sidewalk. He faced the building with his hands on his hips, as if he were about to enter the old Colosseum for battle. "Just take it one day at a time. One hour at a time. And everything will be okay."

He entered the building and marched to the back of the office where the stairs led down to his upcoming fate.

* * *

Strike and Tarik were gathered in Tarik's office, the door open as they carried on with an apparently casual conversation. Tarik saw Martin and waved him in. No one in the office paid him any attention.

"Well, that was quick," Strike said, standing up to meet Martin at the doorway. "Your team is here, in the main conference room. Let's head down and meet them."

She pushed by Martin and led them to the conference room where he had just experienced his first freezing of time with Steffan a couple hours ago. When they entered, the room was restored to its typical setup of scattered tables and chairs.

A group of three men gathered around a table beside the entryway, the same area where the scientists had sat while Steffan and Martin danced around on camera.

The three men turned their heads in unison as the group entered the room, and Martin was taken back by a massive dark-skinned man who stood and approached them.

His bald head gleamed under the lighting, and Martin noticed a horrific scar that ran from the man's left eye to his jaw. He towered over Martin, standing damn close to seven feet tall, and stuck out an arm that looked bigger than Martin's entire torso. "You must be Martin," he said, gripping Martin's hand. "I've heard a lot about you and your training. Impressive for an older man coming off an injury like yours."

Is this gigantic man actually complimenting my physical abilities? Martin thought the man could easily pick him up and chuck him across the room like a sack of potatoes.

"My name's Gerald. Gerald Holmes."

"Nice to meet you, Gerald. I'm not sure what you mean about training. I don't think I did anything that remarkable."

"I'm good friends with Staff Master Collins. Don't underestimate how well you did. He raved about you and your dedication. Working hard is ninety percent of the battle."

"I'll take your word for it."

"Gerald here is the one I mentioned who has been to the future before," Strike added.

"That's where I got my scar, but we can talk about that later."

"He'll sort of be the one in charge since he knows his way around and knows what to expect."

Sort of?

Now Martin picked apart every word spoken by Commander Strike. Her last statement sounded unsure of herself, revealed her to be lacking confidence in her decisions. Wasn't she supposed to be in charge of everything? If she wanted Gerald to lead this mission, then she should just say it.

The two others had gathered behind Gerald, hidden behind his massive frame that reminded Martin of poor John Coffey from *The Green Mile.*

"Brigham?" Martin asked, seeing a familiar face. "You're coming with us now?"

The scientist nodded. "I figured why not take advantage? We never really get out and study in the real world. I'm terrified and excited."

The other man, who stood eye-level with Martin and boasted a slight potbelly, stepped to the front. "I'm Webster Baldwin, but you can call me Web. Or Baldy. Doesn't really matter to me." Webster had ruffled black hair and droopy brown eyes that looked depressed.

"Web is our brains," Gerald said. "He'll be the one suggesting our best courses of action, as he has studied the geography of the area."

"I know the places to avoid, the places to relax, and the secret ways into places we shouldn't be," Web added. "Think of me as working in the background to keep us all safe. On that note, shall we begin?"

Martin's stomach drained of all fluids as he looked at this group of men he'd be going into the future with. Someone thought it was a good idea to incorporate Martin and Gerald as equals, at least in terms of fieldwork.

This has to be a mistake, Martin thought. Sure, he had felt accomplished throughout training, even strong and confident, but how would this work with him being Gerald's right-hand man in a gunfight with Revolters? He had the skills to hit a target when there was no pressure aside from a handful of people watching, but to be thrust into the nastiest part of this war with no prior experience seemed ludicrous. He expected to be going with a whole team of Geralds.

This has *to be a mistake. A clerical error.*

"Yes, let's gather around and get started," Strike said, and everyone returned to the table.

"Commander Strike?" Martin asked. "Can I have a word with you?"

She nodded. "One moment, everyone," she said to the group, and pulled open the door to step outside the conference room. When the door clicked shut, she asked, "Is everything all right?"

"Yeah, I'm fine. I'm trying to understand this team I'm going with. It seems Gerald is the only one who's physically capable of . . . battling Revolters."

Strike scrunched her face in confusion. "This is a standard squad that we send into the future: two combat-savvy Road Runners, and two scientists or researchers."

"I'm the other combat person?"

"Do you not think you are?"

"Well, no."

"Martin," she sighed, her blue eyes swimming back and forth. "I don't know why you think so lowly of yourself. Have you not looked in the mirror lately? You are just as physically capable as Gerald. You're not even going into war—this is more a stealth type of mission—but you still need to be strong and agile, which you are."

The truth was Martin hadn't looked in the mirror for quite some time. Sure, he'd catch a glance in the morning when brushing his teeth and washing his face, but he no longer examined himself, terrified to see more gray hairs and wrinkles than he'd like to acknowledge.

"It just seems weird to me that you make the future sound like this horrific place and want to send in Gerald with three people who probably shouldn't be there."

"You wouldn't be going if you didn't pass your training." Strike crossed her arms and furrowed her brow. "You do remember this is *your* mission, right? *You* asked me for this as a favor. I warned against it, but *you* insisted. What were you expecting, for us to just go do this for you?"

"Well, no. I—"

She raised a finger, once again flashing her authority that Martin had originally known. Like Steffan said, she was a great leader in one-on-one situations. "I don't want to hear another word about this, Martin. I put this mission together for you as a thank-you for almost dying in the Sonya debacle. I'm not undoing it." She kept her finger raised while her stern words hung in the air for a few seconds. "Now, can we go back in there and discuss this mission with the rest of the team?"

Martin nodded and followed Commander Strike back into

the conference room.

7

Chapter 7

"Let's get to business," Strike barked as she stormed into the room, Martin trailing behind.

Everyone was seated and looked down to the table as they sensed an immediate shift in Strike's mood. Martin sat between Tarik and Brigham.

"Gerald," Strike said, nodding to him.

Gerald had a notebook that he flipped open and ran a finger down.

"Okay, lots to cover," Gerald said in his booming voice. "To start, we'll be driving over to the location of our weapons warehouse and transporting from there. The building is located in Watkins, about a thirty-minute drive east of downtown in the plains. It's underground and will be considered the safest place to return should you come into trouble in 2064."

"Is there something wrong with this office in 2064?" Brigham asked.

"Yes, it doesn't exist." Gerald said this matter-of-fact. "It was raided and eventually bombed by the Revolters when they learned it was a Road Runner office. I think that happened in

2048." Gerald looked into the air as if he were reliving the event.

Strike glared across the table to Martin.

"Now as far as the actual mission," Gerald continued. "We know the medicine is housed at three separate hospitals in the city. Web, you'll need to find which hospital is the best one for us to try and take it from. The meds are stored in the basement of each facility, with two armed guards at each door. The guards are Revolters—not hospital staff—so we'll also need to figure out how to get by them without causing any gunfire—they will shoot any of us on sight if they find out we're Road Runners. On that note, special attire will be provided when we arrive to help us blend in around town."

"How are we getting around?" Brigham asked.

"We have a car, but need to be wary of where we park it, because it can be stolen if we have to leave it in a shady place. Minor detail, but plan to do a good amount of walking once in town."

Gerald referred to his notebook before speaking again.

"One thing to note is that you will always be on camera once you step outside. Cameras cover every inch of space—this government likes to watch its people closely. There are areas that even have hidden microphones, so it's imperative to not speak about any Road Runner business out loud, or anything negative about the New Age Revolution, for that matter. If the microphones pick up any key words, there will be a squad of Revolters hunting you down. Is that understood?"

Everyone nodded, shifting in their seats.

What the fuck kind of world is this? Martin wondered.

"To further build off this," Gerald continued. "If we're out in public, avoid striking up conversations with random people.

The Revolters go undercover to talk with people in coffee shops, grocery stores, wherever, in an attempt to learn of their political leanings. They'll try to get you to admit you don't like the current administration. If you say anything along these lines, they'll either arrest you or shoot you, depending on the severity of what you say. It's best to just not say anything. The right of free speech has been replaced by the right of silence."

Brigham and Web both nodded excitedly at the revelation. While it terrified Martin, they clearly wanted to learn more.

"Is it President Poe who's running the country in 2064?" Web asked.

"Yes. President Poe. And it's an election year, so the crazies are out even more than normal. President Poe is running for his fifth term in 2064, and he'll easily win. He was elected in 2048 under the official political party known as The Revolution. Halfway through his second term, Revolters had taken control of the Supreme Court, the House, and the Senate. He had zero resistance to abolishing the Twenty-Second Amendment and has been in power ever since."

Brigham and Web went from nodding to scribbling notes in their own notepads.

"Question," Martin said, not sure if he was allowed to speak up. "Are there any *good* people in the future?"

Strike smirked as Gerald answered. "Of course. There are Road Runners, and there are lots of people who stayed after the Revolters came into power. They just can't speak of any of it. There are even people who appear to be hardcore Revolters, but it's just an act to survive."

"How do we know who's who?"

"We don't. That's why you don't talk to anyone about it."

"The future sounds like pure chaos," Brigham said, running

his fingers in circles over the table.

"That's a good way of putting it," Gerald said.

"Where are we staying?" Brigham asked.

"Just outside downtown. I'm not allowed into the city because I'm black, unless I were to go undercover as a janitor. We'll figure those details out later."

"Isn't outside of the city dangerous?" Martin asked, not fully processing Gerald's previous statement.

"Yes, but as long as we stick together, we'll be fine. People don't really mess with me, and if you're with me, they'll leave you alone, too. Never go out by yourself, especially at night. Does anyone have any questions?"

Everyone shook their heads as Commander Strike stood up. "I don't have a question, but I'd like to say something."

Gerald nodded at her to continue.

"I want you all to know that Sonya was spotted last night in 2064, and she's apparently under the protection of the Revolters. We believe this is purely a coincidence that she's in this year, but we may have a new mission for you when you arrive. Research is still being conducted, and we've commissioned a team of scouts to the area for the sake of tracking her down. She's in downtown Denver and will likely never step foot outside of it."

"Are you talking about having us hunt her down?" Martin asked.

Strike stared at Gerald as she responded, sure to avoid Martin's eyes. "It's possible, but I can't confirm that yet. It depends what information our team comes back with. If it's plausible to capture or kill her, we may have your squad carry out that mission."

"Commander Strike," Gerald cut in. "I don't know if this is

the best squad for such a task."

"It's not. But you'll be there. Don't worry, we won't put you into a position for failure. If we decide to move forward with a new mission, it'll be one that fits within your qualifications."

Silence hung in the room as Gerald wrote in his notebook, a frown on his face that clearly showed his displeasure with the news.

"You will all do great," Strike finally said. "I wouldn't have brought this up if I felt differently."

The rest nodded, but Martin remained still. He wondered if this was a desperate ploy to right her wrongs from the previous botched attempt. Would the highest ranking official of the Road Runners really put four of her own people at risk for the sake of correcting a mistake?

A day ago Martin wouldn't have believed it to be true, but now knowing how political everything functioned behind the scenes, he saw no reason to doubt it.

"I know we'll do just fine," Gerald said. Tarik had stayed quiet throughout the meeting, examining his fingers and nodding on cue when appropriate. "We have one final matter of business, and that is our weapons to travel with."

Gerald nodded to Tarik, who pulled out a briefcase and set it on the table, flipping the latches to swing open the lid and reveal four black pistols. Tarik grabbed each pistol and slid them across the table to the four men.

"These are your pistols," Gerald explained. "We're only taking these with us in case something happens during our transfer into 2064."

"I thought we were transferring to and from our weapons warehouse," Brigham said.

"We are. It's just better to be safe than sorry. You never

know what will happen in the future. Now, with these in your possession, we're ready to go to 2064. Are there any more questions?"

Everyone looked around the table, realizing there was no turning back.

"I'll get the car ready," Gerald said, and left the room.

8

Chapter 8

Chris sat in his office and clicked through the different camera angles on his computer screen. While they hadn't approached his house in a week, they still watched him from the woods.

"Cocksucking Road Runners," he said, knowing they'd go away soon. How productive was it for them to spend six hours each day staring at his barricaded mansion? It had been particularly entertaining when they tried knocking down the barricade. They tried sledgehammers, drills, and even dynamite. Outside of that effort, it had remained an uneventful series of days that seemed to run on the same loop.

The barricade was designed to withstand any form of attack. When his team designed it with a stronger steel from the future, the lead engineer had told Chris, "They asked what happens when an unstoppable force meets an immovable object. Well, this here is the immovable object, and I'd hate to see what happens to anyone trying to move it."

They had laughed about this during the test run when they ran a bulldozer into the steel, and howled when it simply rolled its way up the house before tipping onto its back.

He wished they would've tried more, but what could you expect from the lazy Road Runners? With one click of a button he could raise the barricades and expose his house for all to see again, but that would take all the fun out of the game. He knew Commander Strike was having fits trying to figure out where he was, when in reality he hadn't left the place for one second.

If they truly thought I was hiding here, they'd keep coming back and trying to find a way in.

This exact situation was planned for. Food lined the pantry, enough for an entire two months to supply the twenty-five Revolters and fifty prisoners. Five Revolters were dead, meaning they had a couple extra days of supplies.

Chris had no plan. He could've gone to another time, but knew there were thousands of eyes on the lookout. Duane, his closest confidant, had advised the same approach as soon as the barricades had gone up. "This will all blow over," he said.

Duane remained in the mansion with the other Revolters who were fortunate enough to not get shot down by the Road Runners hiding in the trees. He visited with Chris at least three times a day in his office, ensuring the old man had kept what remained of his sanity intact. It had been a week and a half that they were trapped in the house, and while no one had quite yet cracked under the pressure of cabin fever, Duane informed Chris that the general mood was growing antsy among the Revolters.

"You've brainwashed them into machines who love to get work done, and right now they can't. They have pent-up energy that will need to be released." Duane had reluctantly explained this a day before, creating a new problem that Chris didn't have the energy for at the moment.

He slept on the matter and decided to open the mansion in the next five days to let his soldiers out to perform their duties. They'd be ready for whatever Road Runners awaited in the woods, and the more rabid they became with anxiety, the better chances they'd have at killing some of them.

Chris leaned back in his chair, hands crossed behind his snowy head, and watched the monitor that showed the mansion's front entrance. A small black figure appeared in the distance, and Chris bolted upright. He watched it grow bigger as it walked through the open field toward the mansion. His finger dashed across the desk and planted on the small intercom button.

"Duane, to my office please."

Chris rapped his fingers on the shiny oak desk, watching the figure grow bigger with each step it took. When the barricades had first gone up, the Road Runners sent over some of their people to study the unbreakable steel. But a week had passed since they last sent anyone, leaving Chris to wonder who would come knocking on the door after so long.

The office door swung open to reveal Duane, dressed in his usual stay-at-home attire of sweatpants and a baggy hoodie. "Everything okay?" he asked, closing the door behind him, and running a hand through his flowing black hair, his gray eyes bloodshot with fatigue.

"I think so. We appear to have a visitor. Have you checked the cameras?"

"Not in a few hours. What's going on?"

Chris pointed to his screen and waited for Duane to come around the desk for a look.

The figure was still 100 yards away, but close enough to see its hands held up in a typical "don't shoot" position.

"Who's that?" Duane asked, eyes bulging at the screen.

"I'd assume it's one of our friends, but why come back after so many days?"

"They could know you're still here."

"How?"

"Because you're not anywhere else."

"Don't be a smart-ass."

"It's true. They're not exactly stupid. You do know their entire purpose now is to kill you—they don't care about anything else."

The figure reached the front steps, hands still held in the air. The presumed Road Runner on their front porch was dressed for the weather: a heavy jacket, a thick knit cap, and a neck cover that hid their face up to a pair of ski goggles. The person waved a hand, while keeping the other elevated and still.

"Do they want to talk to us?" Duane asked.

"I'd assume so."

The figure twirled in a slow-motion circle to show that they had no weapons on them. Even if they had, their current attire would make it extremely difficult to pull out a gun and start shooting, especially with the thick mittens over their hands.

"What do you want to do?" Duane asked.

"We can talk to them from here, right? Without having to drop the barricade?"

Duane nodded, as if he should've remembered this. The design had been constructed over two decades ago, and it was impossible to remember all of its features, especially with this being their first time using it.

"Hold on!" Chris shouted at the screen, as if the person could hear him.

Duane ran to the nearest cabinet and rummaged through

files of paperwork. He muttered to himself as he flipped through them, pulling out a handbook the size of an old encyclopedia. He flipped open the book and ran a finger up and down the pages until he found what they needed.

The visitor remained a statue with both hands in the air.

"Do you have a headset?" Duane asked. "The kind with the microphone attached."

"Of course." Chris opened a desk drawer and pulled out the headset he used to place calls with his counterparts around the world.

Duane explained what Chris needed to click on the screen, within the security system software.

As soon as the connection was made, the crackle of white noise mixed with wind filled Chris's ears. He looked up to Duane and nodded.

"Now you just talk," Duane explained.

"Hello?" Chris said, not moving his eye from the monitor.

"Chris!" a man's voice cried out, youthful in its tone. "Chris, I just want to talk with you. I have no weapons, just need a word."

The volume was loud enough in the headset that Duane could hear the response.

"Who are you?"

The man lowered his arms, probably exhausted from holding them up for so long.

"I'd rather not say my name, but I am a Road Runner."

"Obviously you're a Road Runner. I must say it's pretty brave of you to come this close with no protection. I can have you shot dead in seconds."

"I know that, sir. But I don't know how else to show you that I'm here for a peaceful visit. Can I come in to speak with you?"

Duane frowned and shook his head so hard Chris thought it might fly off.

"No," Chris said. "We can't let you in here, I'm sure you understand."

"That's fine," the Road Runner said. "This will have to do. I have a proposition for you."

Chris looked to Duane with his eyebrows raised. Duane twirled a finger in a gesture that said *keep him talking.*

"Let's hear it," Chris said coldly.

"We know you have our people held hostage in your basement," the Road Runner said. "We also know we're reaching a crossroads in this war. I can give you something valuable to us, if you release those you're holding hostage."

"Spit it out already. Tell me what you're offering." Chris rose from his seat and subconsciously slammed his fists on the desk.

"I can give you our leader."

Chris sat back down and rubbed his forehead. Duane returned to his studious frown as both men stared at the monitor in shock.

"Are you referring to Strike?" Chris asked, sitting forward.

"The one and only," the Road Runner said, and Chris was sure he heard a smile in the man's voice.

"What's your angle?" Chris asked. "I thought you people were sworn to loyalty."

"My angle is simple: I want our people back. And we are loyal. I'm loyal to the Road Runners and everything we stand for. That doesn't mean I need to be loyal to Commander Strike."

A traitor? Chris wondered. In all of his time learning about the Road Runners and their rapid growth, he'd never heard of such betrayal. He supposed it was only a matter of time before corruption worked its way into their system. The more people you involve in an organization, the more likely it becomes a bad apple will find its way into the pack.

"What do you think?" the man outside asked.

"Part of me doesn't believe you. This could be a bluff."

"I know you're a man of your word. And I assure you I am as well. A gentleman's agreement is all I'm proposing."

"How can I believe you when you won't even tell me your name?" Chris felt he was losing control of the conversation, causing a bubble of frustration to inflate.

"Who I am doesn't matter. I don't want you to think we're friends—I just want to make what I think is a fair trade. I have access to Commander Strike's schedule and can let you know exactly where she'll be at any given time."

Chris looked to Duane, who had remained a statue with his brows furrowed and his hand cupped over his chin, keeping his stare to the floor as if the secret of life were written down there.

"I need a minute," Chris said. "Don't go away."

He removed the headset and dropped it on the desk. Duane finally looked up, looking like someone had just shot his mother.

"What do we do?" Chris whispered.

Duane shrugged before saying, "Part of me believes him—scratch that, I *do* believe him. I just can't figure out *why* he's doing this, and that's what's keeping me skeptical."

"It seems too good to be true, right? We just hand over these 50 useless prisoners we have, and we get Strike in return? Does this guy even know the possibilities that arise from us having Strike?"

"I know that, and that's why I'm trying to think of any

advantage they could gain from having the prisoners back. They don't have any knowledge of our operations and have only seen the front entrance and basement of this house."

"Do you think he's just trying to get the barricades down? Maybe planning an attack that way?"

"Possible, but not necessary for him to come here and make this offer. They could've just waited for that to happen—we'll have to drop the barricades eventually, and I'm sure they know that."

"Then what the hell is he really up to?"

"I can't say, but I think we should do it. I'm trying to think of the worst thing that could happen by us releasing these prisoners, and it simply doesn't hold a flame to what we'd be gaining by having Strike in our possession. You should accept this offer."

Chris watched the screen, the Road Runner standing patiently in the cold, awaiting an answer to a question bizarre in every shape and form. He grabbed the headset and slipped it back over his head.

"I accept your offer," he said. The man on the screen showed no emotion to the response. "To keep this honest, I'll agree to release half of the prisoners before we receive Strike, and the rest after she's in our control. Can we agree on that?" The man didn't move, and Chris adjusted his headset to make sure his voice was carrying outside. "Did you hear me?"

"I heard you. I'm thinking," the Road Runner snapped.

He stood in silence for what felt like an eternity as Chris watched the speck on the screen ponder his decision. The man had come this far and risked his life to make this offer; there was no way he was leaving without some sort of agreement.

"I can agree to those terms," he finally responded. "As

soon as I see the first group of people released, we'll need a couple days to make sure they're healthy—we don't want any damaged goods. If everything checks out fine, I'll be back the following day with Strike's schedule and can help you plan a way to capture her. When can I expect to see my people freed?"

"I'd rather not share that information with you. I still don't trust something about this situation, and I'm not going to tell you when my barricade will be down. It'll be done within the next three days, but you need to ensure me you'll have your men in the trees back down."

"I can ensure that if you do the same. I don't want to see another dead Road Runner on the edge of your property as soon as you let them go. If you do that, I promise you'll stay hiding in that shell of yours forever."

"Deal," Chris snapped. He hadn't considered doing such a thing—Strike was too valuable of an asset to risk.

"Perfect. Like I said, when we get our men back, give me forty-eight hours to return. I can't guarantee a certain time. Would it be okay if I have to come back in the middle of the night?"

"Fine with me."

"Perfect. I'll see you soon."

The Road Runner turned and disappeared back to the woods where he had come from.

"Well, this just got interesting," Duane commented.

"Yes, indeed," Chris said. "Very interesting."

He watched the monitor as the man shrunk to a small black dot in the distance before disappearing for good.

9

Chapter 9

Martin crunched into the back seat of the crowded car as Gerald drove them out of downtown Denver, heading east to the town of Watkins.

Gerald had tried to keep the mood light with small talk, but when no one responded, it became clear that all of their minds were elsewhere, likely wondering what the future had in store.

While the anxiety stabbed Martin in the gut, his mind kept wandering to his mother. On the other side of this trip was a better life. A life with no Alzheimer's. A life with no worries. And hopefully, a life with no more war. He decided that when he returned, he wanted no more of the Road Runners, Revolters, Chris, or any of the bullshit that came with his magical liquid. He'd dump that shit down the drain and never look back, and if Commander Strike couldn't respect that, then she was full of shit about how accepting the Road Runners were.

The sun reached its peak and beat down on the world. Martin thought about Lela and what she might be doing on this beautiful day. Even though she was behind bars, she had managed to remain in the forefront of his mind at the most random of times. She had, after all, hurled the frying pan that changed both of their lives forever. Would things have played out differently if she confessed to the accident from the beginning? Absolutely.

But she didn't. And now they were in their current situations of a prison with bars and a prison of time travel and war.

When they reached the freeway and Gerald sped up to 70 miles per hour, Martin glanced around at his peers, wondering what kinds of journeys had brought them to this point in time. Every Road Runner he met had joined the organization out of a hunger for revenge on Chris. Somewhere along the path, the old man had wreaked havoc on their lives, pushing them to think they had no choice but to dedicate their lives to finding a way to end him.

These men in the car seemed completely content with their lives. But Martin also knew how easy it was to fake a smile when the pain became buried deeper in the past with each passing year. Odds were that these men had an equally painful story that drove them forward, but were they as committed as they appeared on the surface? Or did they each have a selfish motive, like Martin?

The engine hummed as they moved along I-70 and Martin pondered. Perhaps they'd all bond and develop a brotherhood during this trip. If they did, they'd surely get to know each other's stories.

The car pulled off the freeway, taking the exit for Watkins. Gerald led them down a frontage road that twisted into the middle of nowhere. "We're here," he called out. Everyone looked around at the open fields that stretched to the horizon.

"You sure about that?" Brigham asked, a giggle caught in his throat.

Gerald grinned as he turned around in his seat. "Positive."

The rest of the men shot puzzled looks at each other.

"You do know there's nothing here, right?" Brigham asked.

Gerald pulled the car to the side of the road and stopped it completely, dirt, tall grass, and tumbleweed the only things visible.

"We set up different warehouses throughout time. In this era, this is just an open field. But, in 2064, this is home of the Road Runners. Let's all take our sip of Juice to 2064, think of the current day and time, and I'll see you on the other side."

Gerald pulled out his flask and took a quick swig, leaning back in his seat to wait for the trip into the future.

Everyone else pulled out their flasks and twisted the caps off.

"Cheers," Brigham said, and took an amount that looked more like a gulp than a drop on the tongue.

Martin nodded to Web and they took their sips in unison. There was less fear doing this act with others. Each time before—except for the time Chris had busted him out of the Oxford Hotel—Martin had gone at it alone, always wondering where he'd wake up, and if somehow his soul would get lost in the shuffle of time and never return to his body. This time, however, he sipped his Juice with confidence, knowing exactly where he'd be waking up and who would be there to join him.

The car fell silent as everyone waited for the brief two minutes to pass before their bodies dozed off to sleep.

Martin leaned his head against the window and gazed at the year 2019—his year, his current life. He wondered if he'd ever see it again and said a quick prayer to whoever wanted to listen to his helpless soul.

Little did any of them know, the Road Runners were striking

a deal with Chris in Alaska that would flip the organization forever.

Martin woke up last, the others already standing outside of the car and admiring their new surroundings. The open field was now a five-level apartment building, possibly abandoned by the look of its deteriorating brick façade, busted out windows, and random ivy running up and down the exterior.

Martin stepped out of the car to join his group. The building they stood in front of was part of a community of similar buildings, all equally destroyed.

"What happened to this place?" Brigham asked.

Gerald sighed as he gazed at the building. "A complete massacre. In 2055, President Poe called for a cleansing of the country, calling for all pure Revolters to extinguish the slime of any one who wasn't one of them. It was a call to action that every Revolter pounced on. You should understand that many Road Runners and non-Revolters all moved far away from the city to places just like this. They built new communities, started their own schooling systems, and even their own political systems with elected leaders. The people lived in peace and remained out of sight from the Revolters, but unfortunately, not out of mind." Web nodded to himself as if he'd heard this story before. "When the Revolters got word that everyone they had pushed out of the city were thriving without them, the leadership grew scared. They felt if a group of people could create a new life so quickly, that they could one day grow into a force big enough to overthrow them."

Gerald paused and looked to the building as if it were supplying him with its history.

"So what happened?" Brigham asked.

"Genocide," Gerald said, rubbing his face. "A cold-blooded

slaughter of innocent lives."

They all gawked at Gerald, unsure if they wanted to know more details. He continued anyway.

"We didn't know it was coming—we didn't exactly watch the Revolters' news channels. They wanted us to live separately from them, so that's what we did. We minded our business, and assumed they would mind their own. April 15, 2055 was the day. Thousands of these monsters piled into their trucks with their automatic guns and boxes of ammunition. They started downtown, shooting anyone who wasn't a Revolter, setting buildings on fire, running kids over with their trucks."

"Wait," Martin cut in. "Were you there?"

Martin noticed the story didn't sound like a historical re-counting, but rather a personal one.

Gerald nodded and rubbed the scar on his face. "That's where this came from. I was living outside of Chicago at the time—after living in the city my whole life before being forced out. So I don't know exactly what happened here at this Denver location, but I'm sure it wasn't too different from what happened in my experience. It was around four in the afternoon when word started to spread about what was happening downtown. We watched in shock as the city we loved was destroyed. We didn't realize at the time that it was going on all around the country, we thought it was just in Chicago. Have any of you actually seen a loved one get killed?"

Martin nodded, thinking back to the night he had watched Lela carry their dead daughter to the trunk, causing a shudder to run up his back. Everyone else shook their heads.

"I've seen the aftermath of a loved one's murder, but not the actual event," Web said.

"I watched my best friend get beat up by three men, doused

in gasoline, and set on fire," Gerald continued. "On live television. It was horrific watching these grown men laugh at what they had done. Right when we thought the worst of it was over, they got back in their trucks and drove out of the city. Helicopters followed the scene as it led to the outskirts where most of us lived. The only news stations that had the cameras were the Revolters' channels, so we watched and listened as they cheered on what they called a 'cleansing' of the country."

"How many survived?" Brigham asked.

Gerald shook his head and shrugged. "We don't know. After these attacks, many fled the country or went into hiding. Some went undercover as Revolters just to stay alive. There are 80 million people unaccounted for since these attacks, and we suspect 60-70 million of those were killed."

Gerald paused and let the astronomical number hang in the air.

"That's almost a fifth of the county's 2019 population," Web added.

"2019, yes," Gerald said. "But by 2055, there was already an exodus of about 100 million people that happened after Poe's third election. So at the time, the murders account for roughly thirty percent of the population."

"Jesus Christ," Brigham said, a hand covering his mouth.

"Jesus had nothing to do with it."

"How did you survive?"

"Pure luck. Right place at the right time—or the wrong time, I suppose. I was at work when all of this started. That's where I was watching the news when I saw the trucks leaving the city. They blew out my office's windows, and I caught a chunk of glass in my face. I didn't have time to worry and raced home to my family, only to find they had already beat me there."

A tear glistened as it streamed down his dark face, following the trail of the scar.

"When I got home, everyone was dead. We lived on a quiet block of one-story houses, big backyards. When I turned into the neighborhood I knew there was no chance. Every house I drove by was shredded by bullets. Bodies were in front lawns, blood was pouring from the driveways into the street like a river. I saw one of the trucks speed off when I reached my driveway. All of my windows were shattered and there were probably a thousand bullet holes in my house."

"You don't need to continue this story," Martin said, eyes filled with tears. They all knew what came next.

"I do. I don't talk about it enough. When I went inside, I found my wife and two sons in the kitchen. My wife had her arms over them, but it didn't matter. There were just too many bullets for her to have stopped it. My boys were eight and ten."

Gerald paused, his lips quivering, arms trembling, and buried his face into his hands.

Martin stepped to him and embraced the man nearly twice his size. "I lost a child, too," he said, sobbing. "I know how hard this is."

His words felt empty when they left his mouth, but he didn't know what else to say. He knew from firsthand experience that there wasn't actually anything one *could* say to a grieving parent. The pain never leaves, and every passing day comes with a growing numbness that eventually turns your soul into stone.

They had clearly forgotten what they came to do, standing outside the tattered building that surely had its own, similar story to tell. Martin looked up its five levels and thought about all of the families that had once lived in it. Families that came home after long days at school and work, ready to relax and enjoy each other's company for the evening. Families that had already survived hell, but still held on to a thread of hope for a better world.

It was clear why Gerald was here. There is nothing more frightening than a person who has lost everything. Martin was glad to be by his side for what was sure to be meaningful work. Hearing Gerald's story showed Martin that this mission went beyond his selfish need for a medical cure. He belonged to an organization that strove to save itself from a looming apocalypse, an extinction of their very existence. Because if they didn't, the world as they knew would further dwindle into a dystopia. A world that Martin was now in, with nothing to hold on to but the past.

10

Chapter 10

Chris didn't sleep all night—not that he needed to. He spent another two hours in his office after the mysterious Road Runner had left, watching his screen and hoping by some long shot that the man would come back. He wanted to make the deal immediately, having an epiphany that he shouldn't waste any more time. What would his counterparts around the world think if he had hesitated on the opportunity to have Strike in their possession? That was something they had drooled about for years. Opportunity literally came knocking on the door, and Chris told it to come back later.

Duane had left him alone, as he did require sleep to function as a mortal being. "We can discuss this in the morning," he had said in regards to devising a plan for when to release the twenty-five prisoners to guarantee Strike's exact location.

It was morning now, and Chris was ready. He'd still have to wait two days to get Strike, and that was two days too many. It had been decades since he last had a morning routine of eating breakfast and getting ready for the day ahead, so he wasn't sure when might be a good time to page Duane to continue their discussion. Not that he needed approval from anyone; Chris respected Duane's perspective on every matter that arose. He was a wise man with an ability to spot the vulnerabilities in any decision, a gift Chris never took for granted.

When the clock struck seven, Chris pushed the intercom button and called for Duane. He drummed his fingers on his desk for the next five minutes as he waited, thinking about the prospect of Strike sitting in this very office across from him, forced to spill the Road Runners' secrets or suffer a most painful torture.

A steady rumble of footsteps came from the hallway, and Duane finally barged into the room, dressed and wide-eyed. "You were up all night, weren't you?" he asked Chris after a quick glance around the office.

"Why sleep if it's not necessary?"

"You know, you could probably lure more people into our group if you offered them the ability to stay fully functioning without sleep. I know I'd kill for an extra eight hours a day."

"The world doesn't need people out and about any more than they already are. I love the silence at night. That's not what we're here to discuss anyway, stop distracting."

Duane nodded and gestured for Chris to continue. "So what did you come up with?"

"I want to release those prisoners today. Right now. Tell me why I shouldn't."

Duane sat down in the chair across from Chris's desk with his face scrunched. "You know, I've thought this over and I can't come up with any logic for one time being better than another. This entire thing is riding on a mutual trust that has no backbone, so the playbook is out the window."

"Do you think they're bluffing?"

"It's possible, but not likely. Even if we released half of the prisoners and they backed out of their end of the deal, what good would that do them?"

"We'd kill the rest to send a message."

"And I'm sure they know that. It sounds like there's turmoil within the Road Runners, or at the very least, someone pushing their own agenda."

"I find it interesting that this happened *after* our friend Martin decided to join them with his special gift. Maybe they can't agree on how to use him?"

"That seems most likely. Here they are thinking they've struck the key to the war, but they don't know what exactly to do with him. That's the kind of situation that can cause friction in an instant."

"Now, do we think Strike will even talk? None of these other bastards do."

"Well, we don't torture them aside from making them live in a three foot space. With Strike, we'll break out the big guns. She'll talk. No amount of loyalty can withstand the pain we'll bring onto her. It might take time, but she'll crack."

"I'd hate to release these people for nothing."

"It's a risk, but we have to trust ourselves in getting Strike to talk. If she really wants to die as a martyr with all of their secrets intact, then good on her. But we won't actually kill her if that's what she's hoping for. We'll show her death, but not let her meet it."

Duane chuckled at this, looking to the ceiling with a crazed look of a man who didn't get much sleep.

"Well, it sounds like the decision is made," Chris said. "Let's release twenty-five prisoners right now. Can you head down to arrange it?"

"I can't. That approval has to come from you directly. You made that rule."

"Ahh, yes. Okay then, you start preparing to drop the barricade. I want every soldier in this house armed and ready when it drops. We still have enough to cover every side of the house. When it drops, we'll give the prisoners thirty seconds to get out of the house, then I want it back up immediately."

"Perfect, I'll get on it."

Chris nodded and stood from his desk, shuffling across the office to his private elevator. He whistled while he waited, and entered the elevator car with a wide grin as he watched Duane slide in behind his desk. A sliver of doubt still tugged at his mind. *There has to be something bigger at play.*

Chris had taken a quick peek into the future last night, but saw nothing of substance. Most times the future didn't reveal itself, especially when a decision was up in the air much like his. He now had to live in the moment and trust his instincts that rarely led him wrong.

The elevator stopped on the basement floor, opening to its usual darkness and dank smell of solidarity. The room had always remained fairly quiet, only erupting into chaos whenever Chris decided to show his face.

The basement was designed so the outer perimeter was left in complete darkness, leaving guards the ability to roam the area without being seen. The center of the floor, where the Road Runners were held hostage, was illuminated by the soft glow of overhead lighting, done to force the prisoners' eyes to adjust to the dim light. Should they ever escape, stepping outside would blind them as a result. Chris had forgotten about this detail until he stepped foot out of the elevator. The visiting Road Runner had made it clear they didn't want any of their people damaged upon their return.

The perimeter lighting was turned on, something that had become the norm after the prisoners and guards had grown tolerable of each other. The guards had no need to hide from the prisoners, not that they ever needed to since the Road Runners were chained to the ground, but it helped maintain the peace at first. Once the Road Runners realized they were never going to be released, they accepted their fate and tried to make the best of the situation by befriending the guards and sharing stories with those closest in proximity.

Chris couldn't deny that the Road Runners had a knack for making the best of any situation. They marched forward—emotionally—as the days, weeks, and months all eventually formed into one big, hellish blur.

He cut the perimeter lights with a flick of the switch, not wanting to be seen on this brief visit, and worked his way around the walls to where the guards always sat. Some murmurs spread throughout the room, but there was nowhere near the fuss that would have risen had the prisoners seen Chris.

"Is that you, boss?" a wary voice called out to Chris.

"Yes. Sorry if I scared you. Can we have a word in private?"

"Certainly."

In the darkness, Chris listened as the guard pushed open a door, hinges creaking before thudding against the inside of a small office. Chris followed the sound of the guard's footsteps and closed the door behind him, causing an automatic light to flicker on above. This light was slightly brighter than the one that shone above the prisoners, but still dim compared to what Chris was used to in his personal office.

"Everything okay, boss?" the guard asked, his droopy face

making no attempt to hide the exhaustion. His name tag read *Wheeler*, and the young man had a strong jaw and wavy brown hair, but also fear that Chris could smell oozing from his pores.

Chris knew many of the guards were having a tough time after the massacre of their teammates outside the mansion. Some suffered from survivor's guilt, others from a growing paranoia that they were next. Chris understood their minds had already been fucked beyond repair thanks to him, so their overreactions were understandable.

"Everything is just dandy," Chris said. "We've just come into a situation where I need to release twenty-five of these fine Road Runners as soon as possible."

The guard's face scrunched as the words processed.

"Twenty-five? Who?"

"It doesn't matter. If everything goes according to plan, they'll all be released in the next few days."

The guard looked around the room as if someone was going to jump out and tell him it was a prank.

"Am I still going to have a job?"

"Of course," Chris chuckled. "It won't be down here, but we'll have lots to do. Don't even worry about such a thing."

"What do I tell the prisoners? They'll have questions—especially the ones not leaving today."

"Tell them they're being moved to another location, and leave it at that. Tell them that's all you know."

"That *is* all I know."

"Easy enough, then. How long do you think it'll take to have them rounded up and ready to go upstairs?"

The guard checked his watch. "Half an hour."

"Works for me. Myself or Duane will meet you upstairs in half an hour to fill in the Road Runners on what they need to do.

I'll send down some help for you to get everyone together."

"Thank you, boss."

Chris clapped a hand on Wheeler's shoulder and winked at him. He loved when he saw his rigorous brainwashing in action. The guard asked no questions that didn't pertain to his job, and responded respectfully to Chris by calling him "boss." When it felt like the world was crumbling all around, it was refreshing to know he still had thousands of soldiers and Revolters below him, all working toward one common goal of making the world a better place.

"Thank you, young man. I appreciate everything you do for us." Chris patted him one more time, the guard now grinning and wide-eyed from the compliment.

He turned and pushed the door open, the light immediately turning off as they stepped out to the perimeter and watched the prisoners sitting or lying on the floor, oblivious that they were about to have their lives altered once again.

And so is mine, Chris thought, a smirk smacked on his face. He strolled down the dark hallway to return to the elevator, knowing that the next forty-eight hours would bring change he'd never imagined possible. As soon as he stepped in the elevator, all of the lights in the basement blasted on, causing moans and screams from the prisoners as their eyes made the adjustment to normal lighting.

"I need twenty-five of you to stand up right now and put your hands behind your back," the guard shouted. "We're going for a little walk upstairs."

11

Chapter 11

"Ladies and gentlemen," Chris said to the group of twenty-five Road Runners standing in the mansion's entryway. "Today, you'll be released. Don't ask why—it's none of your business. In five minutes I'll unlock this door and you're free to go. Your people are somewhat expecting your release, so they may or may not be around to assist you. From here you'll want to head north, which is straight out this door. There's nothing south or on the back side of the mansion, so don't bother."

The group of Road Runners looked around at each other, not sure if they should believe the Revolters' main leader.

Chris smiled to himself. "I hope there are no hard feelings. We did what we had to in the name of war." A sudden tension rose to the surface after he said this, but still no one said anything. They probably wanted to rip his head right from his shoulders, but they all had their hands cuffed behind their backs. "I want you to form a single file line. When the door opens, you'll step outside one-by-one, have your handcuffs removed, and be free to go. Don't try anything cute; we have guards all around this place who won't hesitate to shoot. Any questions?"

Nothing but blank stares.

"Perfect." Chris rotated and started to unlock the numerous bolts and chains that kept the front door sealed. The shell of the barricade remained, but Duane waited upstairs for the official word to drop it. Chris turned back to the small crowd. "We only have five minutes to get you all out of here, so form your line now and move quickly. If you don't make it out, it'll be your own fault."

The Road Runners looked at each other one final time before wiggling around in the crowded space, forming a sloppy line that curved around the room.

Chris nodded to a guard standing on the stairwell that led upstairs. The guard returned the nod and disappeared upward.

Thirty seconds later, a humming sound filled the house, much like a mechanical motor. Darkness had filled the windows, giving the appearance of night time, but daylight slowly seeped through the gaps in the house, filling it with a golden glow that provided a sense of life compared to the dungeon they had all been living in. Some of them winced at the sunlight.

"We've tried readjusting your eyes as best we could, but they're probably not back to normal quite yet. You may need to wander outside with your hands over your eyes. Don't try to be a hero, you can go blind if you take in too much light right away. There is a pretty heavy overcast today, so it shouldn't be too bad."

The humming motor stopped, and Chris felt like a sitting duck with no protection around his house. The Road Runners could have ten thousand of their troops waiting to storm the property, and there would be nothing they could do to stop them. His heart raced at the thought.

"Let's move!" he barked to the Road Runners, all craning their necks for a view of the world they thought they'd never see again.

The two guards who had stood by the front door worked their way outside, the first Road Runner in line following.

"Goodbye. Come again," Chris joked, more to calm himself down.

They filed out as instructed, stepping onto the porch, turning their backs for the guards to uncuff them, and jumping down the steps to freedom. Some broke into sprints, others wandered aimlessly like they had just woken up in Jurassic Park. Only a handful looked back at the mansion, and when they did, they turned and ran like it was an evil force trying to claw them back in.

When the final Road Runner stepped outside, Chris nodded to the guard who had reappeared on the stairs, prompting him to vanish once more into the abyss where Duane waited for the next command. The two outside guards stepped back in and Chris slammed the door shut, cutting off the view of the Road Runners dashing across the open field toward the woods.

"Goodbye, old friends," Chris said with a smirk. "Now we wait."

The humming motor kicked back on, leaving Chris and his guards to watch the brief glimpse of daylight slowly vanish and return the house to its dark mood and dim lighting.

"Thank you, gentlemen," he said, and climbed up the stairs to return to his office.

Duane still sat behind his desk and stood up when Chris stepped into the room.

"I'd say that went pretty smoothly," Chris said with a wide grin. "No complications, no surprises. Just an easy release of

Road Runners back into the wild where they can try to spread their nonsense."

Duane laughed as Chris sat down, turning his attention to the monitor. Almost all of the Road Runners had already vanished from sight, minus a couple who were taking their sweet time crossing the open field. They had taken his word, as not one of them ventured to the back of the house. In a different scenario, he would've led them to their deaths, but there was a price to pay for obtaining someone as valuable as Commander Strike.

"I was thinking more about what happens next," Duane said, crossing his hands on his lap. "This could be a Trojan horse type of play they're making."

"How do you figure?"

"Well, they now have twenty-five Road Runners who know their way around the basement. They're offering their leader to us on a silver platter. What if their plan is to turn around and use those prisoners to attack us at the exact moment we capture Strike?"

Chris scratched his head and leaned back in his chair. "Do you really think that's what they're up to?"

"No, but I'm thinking of every possibility, and this one seemed realistic."

The two men sat in silence, sizing up the possibility of an ambush.

"Why now?" Chris asked. "We've had their prisoners for almost a year. Why wait until they've failed an attack on me and after the barricade has gone up?"

Duane shrugged. "There are hundreds of reasons we can talk ourselves out of the possibility, but that doesn't make the reasons for it any less important. They see you as the key to this war. Even if they can't kill you, if they *have* you, the war can't go on. We don't have a chain of command like they do, and they know that. The Revolution would have no leadership in North America if you vanished."

Chris nodded, stroking his face with a nervous hand. "Well then, I guess we should plan for the best and prepare for the worst. When we go to get Strike, I want every soldier in this house with us, armed and ready for any surprises."

Duane nodded. "What about the house? We can't leave it abandoned."

"We have before when we all go out on a journey together."

"That was before this. What happens if we return to a burned down house. We've certainly burned down plenty of theirs."

"Fine. Then you stay here and put the barricade back up after we leave. Don't talk with anyone who tries to come by."

"I can do that."

"Good. Now we just have to wait for our friend to come back with the information we need. Now's a good time to fill in our soldiers on what to expect in the next few days. Stress to them that this a highly secret operation we're taking on, and to not mutter a word about it, even to each other. Doing so will result in immediate death."

"I'll handle it."

"Thank you. Now, I want to know more before we capture Strike. What *do* we know about their chain of command? Who could be calling the shots?"

"I know Strike's number two is a younger guy named Julian. He's been by her side since she came into power. Then there's an older man, Bill. He's been a Road Runner forever."

"Ahh yes, I remember Bill and Julian. Looking back, I can't say I'm surprised they joined those fools. It's always the ones who ask the most questions that end up leaving me. Just like

Briar. I swear the guy was going to have a panic attack if I didn't answer his thousands of questions."

"Sounds like we should revamp our recruiting process, then."

"That's for another time. Tell me what you know about Bill and Julian."

"I spoke with our team in Europe, and they let me in on a little secret."

Chris's eyebrows raised to the top of his head.

"It appears that Road Runner leadership in Europe, Asia, and Africa is not at all pleased with Strike. They're all making plans for after her term ends."

"Fascinating. Do you think this deal is coming from across the ocean, then?"

"It's very likely, and that's why I'm not buying the theory of an ambush. I think the Road Runners don't want Strike anymore and see her as trade bait. They may be known for their loyalty, but that shouldn't discount their ability as strategists. They really do put the greater good of their organization over any individual."

"Do you know what this means?" Chris asked, standing on excited legs. "This means—and I know it's a long shot—that we can maybe convince Strike into joining us."

Duane shook head in a jerky motion. "She would never."

"Oh, she might. If she finds out that her own people turned her over to us. Don't underestimate the tug of revenge in someone who's been betrayed. I've seen it play out numerous times. Why do you think so many people leave us for the Road Runners? They feel a sense of betrayal, even though I let them know the terms of our deal well before anything bad happens in their life."

"Why would we want her if her own people don't?"

"If she commits to us, we'll have access to all of their secrets. Where the hideouts are, what their plans are, whatever we want to know, we'll have an answer to. We may need to reconsider our plans of torturing her, and instead plan to court her. Make her feel welcome. Sooner or later, she'll have that dreaded realization that the Road Runners were nothing but a huge lie. And we'll be here, ready with open arms."

"How was she when she first met you?"

"I'm actually not the one who gave her the Juice. She's originally from Europe and joined from there."

"We should try to find out her backstory. If we're going to court her, it's best to know what's been driving her."

"We can inquire, but don't get your hopes up. Our European friends don't distribute the Juice the same way we do here. We try to tempt people who have suffered in their past, and they like to hand it out like it's a charitable cause. They use it for fun and historical research. I'd guess half of Europe has access."

"How do they get away with it? Keeping it a secret?"

"It's not a big deal to them. They don't treat it as this mystic gift like we do here. It's almost like it's a right, not a privilege."

Duane stared blankly at Chris, shaking his head after a moment of silence passed.

"Good for them, I suppose," Duane said. "I guess we'll have to wait and find out for ourselves how she really is behind closed doors."

Chris nodded and turned his attention back to the computer monitor, watching the now open field, abandoned by all of the released Road Runners, knowing his world would change within the next two days.

12

Chapter 12

After sharing sob stories, they entered the abandoned building with heavy hearts. Even inside, deep in its halls, bullet holes peppered the walls, along with random splatters of dried blood. Martin half-expected the odor of dead bodies, but the place had been cleaned out of any human remains. Gerald mentioned how, in Chicago, the Revolters had stacked all the corpses in an open field and set them on fire, claiming mass cremation as the best option. The handfuls that had survived watched their friends and family burn like logs on television. Gone were the Road Runner networks, leaving only channels run by the Revolters, who praised the attacks and the cremations as a huge success for cleansing the soul of America.

Martin tried to not think of this horrific imagery as he walked through the apartment building, but could still hear the helpless screams crying out from the walls.

There was no power to the building, or to the neighborhood, for that matter. Gerald led them down the main hallway, having only the soft glow of daylight that broke through the shattered windows at the ends of the hall. Doors lined the hallway, former entryways into family life and innocence. Cracks zigzagged down the walls, weaving between the craters formed by bullets. The musty smell of abandonment filled their lungs as they reached the back of the hallway where the fire exit stood across from a closed door that concealed a stairwell.

"This way," Gerald called, his boots clicking on the tiled floor, echoing throughout the building. Martin's paranoia kept him looking over his shoulder, positive they were being too loud and would be found by a group of passing Revolters with nothing better to do. But they never came, and they never would. Their work had already been done here, and Gerald assured them that the Revolters mainly stayed in their upscale neighborhoods in or around downtown. The war was won, as far as they were concerned, and they no longer believed any group of surviving people to be a threat. Yet, when a Road Runner did appear, they simply shot them dead without question.

Gerald swung open the stairwell door, and led them into a dark pit where they had to rely on the sounds of his obnoxious boots to lead the way. When the door shut behind Brigham, who was at the back of the line, the stairway fell into pitch-blackness. Martin waved his hand in front of his face and couldn't see a damn thing. It reminded him of following Lela through the fog that fateful night when she decided to dump Izzy's body into the lake.

Fucking bitch.

They all clopped down the stairs until bottlenecking and bumping into each other as Gerald stopped to knock on what sounded like a steel door. Someone let out a nervous laugh after they had all fallen into each other like dominoes.

Martin's paranoia vanished. No Revolter would go out of

their way to step into the darkness and climb all the way down these stairs. It was a perfect hideout for the Road Runners, something he realized they excelled in creating.

"What's going on?" Brigham whispered from the back.

"He's coming," Gerald said. "Just give him a minute."

A few seconds later they heard the rattle of chains and the clunking of bolts as someone on the other side unlocked the door, swinging it open to stinging lights that filled a basement the size of two football fields.

A young pale man with long, wavy brown hair to his shoulders greeted them with a smile. "Welcome, gentlemen," he said in a nasally voice. "Come on in."

Gerald stepped in first, shaking the man's hand and admiring the walls that stretched into the distance, every inch of them covered with guns of all sizes. Webster stepped in next, followed by Martin and Brigham.

"Holy shit," Brigham said. "How many guns are in this place?"

Not only were the walls completely smothered with firearms, there were dozens of tables spread across the room displaying more guns, bombs, swords, and knives. It looked like a trade show for all things weaponry.

"We have over 10,000 firearms, ranging from muskets to fully automatics, and even bazookas. More than 3,000 explosives, and 2,000 blades." The man explained this proudly with his hands on his hips.

"Gentlemen, meet Ralph," Gerald said. "The craziest son of a bitch I've ever known."

Ralph threw his head back, revealing a bulging Adam's apple on his skinny throat, and cackled to the ceiling. "He only says that because I sleep in this room."

"You could sleep in any room in this building, but you choose the one that could blow up the entire state," Gerald joked back, the comic relief spreading its gracious arms around the men.

"If it's gonna blow up the state, what does it matter where I sleep?"

Gerald burst into laughter, a welcoming sight from the behemoth.

"In all seriousness," Ralph said. "I'm here for you guys. Anything you need, I have it and can tell you exactly where it is."

"We'll be making a plan first. Do you still have some office space we can use, or did you fill that room with guns, too?"

"Funny. No, it's still a conference room, and it's all yours. I haven't had too many visitors lately, so make yourselves at home."

"Let's meet in the conference room in five minutes," Gerald said to the group. "It's that door along the wall." He pointed to the only other visible door across the room.

Gerald walked off, into the rows of weapons, picking up various swords and explosives to examine. The three of them weren't sure if they were supposed to follow suit, or if they were even allowed to touch anything. Ralph stood in front them, his grin wide.

"You guys, this entire room belongs to all of us. I just maintain it. You can go touch anything you want, and take anything you want—all you have to do is tell me for inventory purposes."

"Thanks, Ralph," Web said, and immediately dashed into the aisles. Brigham broke toward the walls, touching every gun within his reach as he skipped down the hall like a child in the toy aisle.

"How long have you been here?" Martin asked Ralph. He'd take any weapon that Gerald deemed necessary, but he didn't care about looking at all of the stock to make his own decision.

"I've been here for four years now," Ralph replied. "I love what I do and the people I get to meet from around the world and all throughout time."

"Do you never travel to other times, then?"

"I do on occasion, mainly on trips to get new weapons—they're much cheaper and more accessible in the past."

"Aren't there less laws now surrounding guns compared to the past?"

"If you're rich. If not, it's almost impossible to get your hands on a gun without going through the black market. Can't have poor people defending themselves against their murderous government." Ralph shook his head, his face scrunching as if he just bit into a sour grape.

"Is this your real time?" Martin asked.

"It is. I was born in 2034 and have lived all 30 years of my life here."

"You never thought about going back in time and not aging? Why live in a world like this?"

"I've thought about it. But, why live through any amount of time knowing it still ends like this? Even if I traveled back 500 years, it all leads back to this point in time. I'd rather just live my life and die when I'm supposed to. And it feels more refreshing doing my work in this era—it's more purposeful because I'm still fighting the good fight. I'm with the good guys, even if they bomb us in the middle of the night."

Martin scratched his head, unsure what to do with the life story Ralph threw his way, and decided to keep him talking—he had grown an immediate interest in the "history" of the future.

"So why do you have the Juice?"

"The Revolters damn near handed that stuff out after they took control. Once they wiped out the towns, they tried to sway any middle-class people the opportunity for a better life. They called it 'giving the gift of time.' Basically, they thought anyone who survived the attacks and still lived in the poor areas deserved a chance at a better life, as long as they weren't any type of minority."

"How generous of them. Did you lose any family?"

"Not through death," Ralph said, shaking his head. "See, I was part of the rich circle, a trust fund kid who never had to work a day in his life. But I wasn't your typical rich snob. I wanted to do good with the money. I spent my time researching various charitable organizations that I could donate both my time and money to, making sure it wasn't the sort of bullshit where seventy percent of your donation goes to some sleazy CEO. I had a good thing going with a dozen different organizations, but I didn't keep up with politics. If I had, I would've known that our fearless leader Poe had been slashing non-profit organizations for years already, squeezing them out of existence with different tax laws that made it impossible for them to stay in operation. By the time I knew what was going on, it was too late."

Ralph paused, head still shaking, as he retrieved a flask from his back pocket. Martin's eyes bulged at the sight.

"Relax," Ralph said. "This is a normal flask, with booze. A habit I took up recently; it really settles the nerves."

Martin knew that feeling, but put up a hand when Ralph offered some.

"I brought up the issue to my parents," Ralph continued.

"Asking what they thought, if they agreed with me on how inhumane all of this was. What was the harm in letting non-profits run their businesses in peace? They weren't out taking potential money away from businesses run by the government. But my parents had become so brainwashed by this New Age Revolution shit—something else I had apparently been too busy to notice. They and my sister supported every word that came out of the White House, and had become racist, anti-humanity pigs. So I did what any sensible person would've done and moved out in the middle of the night, after taking $100,000 out of my dad's safe, of course."

Ralph chuckled at himself, his eyes distant as he surely replayed that night in his head.

"And that's how you ended up here as a Road Runner?"

"Oh, there was resistance. They thought I was an undercover spy for the Revolters at first. I understood why, so I had to go through all sorts of tests to prove that I was more aligned with the Road Runners' values than the Revolters. They eventually let me in, and that's when I decided I wanted to keep helping where I could. These days, this is the only real way to help, short of risking my own life out in the public." Ralph tossed his hands in the air and pivoted around to admire the room of weapons. "I've had a lot of fun traveling back in time and gathering this collection. I've had enough face time with the past, that I don't think I could actually live there. I've grown conditioned to be paranoid and always looking over my shoulder, even though I know no one dangerous will come here. I suppose it's just part of growing up in this time. I wouldn't last in any other era being this way."

"That's an incredible story, Ralph. I don't know what to say. Thank you, I suppose."

"No, don't thank me. I want to thank *you*. You guys are the ones who come here ready to fight. I don't have half the courage as you do. Shit, I need to sleep with a rifle at my side to make sure I don't have any bad dreams. You guys are the real heroes, and I don't even know your backstories. You have a meeting to get to, though, so it'll have to wait for another time."

Ralph nodded across the room where Gerald and the others had gathered outside the conference room.

"Yes, thanks. I'd love to continue this conversation."

"I'll hold you to it." Ralph slapped Martin on the back before he rushed across the room.

Ralph had shown him that the world was as dangerous as advertised, but also, reassuringly, that there were still good people in these dark times. Even if they had to hide in the shadows, they were there, working to move forward and never giving up hope.

13

Chapter 13

Gerald paced around the conference room, shoving chairs aside with his hips, clearing the way for him to write on the dry-erase board that ran the length of the front wall. A long table faced the front where Martin, Brigham, and Web all sat and watched.

"I've been thinking about a plan," Gerald said, twisting the cap off of a marker and drawing a blue circle. "This is Denver. We're about thirty minutes away. I'm thinking we move to the edge of town and get a spot wherever we can find. There should be some hotels for cheap, and we can create a base there. Is that close enough to the city for you, Web?"

Web nodded, his hands folded and relaxed on the table. "I can try to hack the hospitals' security systems so we can look around their cameras," he said, pulling out a laptop from his bag and typing furiously as Gerald spoke. "I can break into anything."

Gerald smirked and nodded. "In that case, it'll be a waiting game until we get some more information on the insides of these buildings. Martin, we can use this downtime to have you explore downtown and get a sense for what's going on.

Commander Strike believes Sonya has escaped to this era, so we might as well poke around and see what we can learn. I'm sure Web will have some insight on an escape route, but you might as well get familiar with the area—learn the hidden alleys and back doors, things like that."

Martin still felt out of place, essentially being thrown into the situation as a sort of spy. He had no experience doing such things aside from the James Bond movies he had seen. And there was no fancy car or beautiful woman to help him along the way.

"Alright, I can do that," he said, hoping he wouldn't be found out and shot dead like a rabid dog.

"And what can I do?" Brigham asked. "I know I'm just here for the medicine, but there's gotta be something I help with."

"I'd suggest you hang out with Web and pitch in where he might need help. If you're not comfortable with combat, then I'd advise you stay inside when we arrive downtown. You'll put yourself in danger if you don't have experience in fighting these people."

And I have experience? Martin wondered. *I didn't ask to be a part of this war, just to get my mom's medicine.*

It felt like he had left home months ago, even though they had been in 2064 for an entire hour. He imagined his mom at home, worrying about him, waiting to find out if he'd make it back.

I'll be back, and I'm pouring this damn Juice down the toilet so I never have to come back. I'll be long gone before the world goes to shit.

"I can help Web," Brigham said.

"Martin and I will go out and get a feel for the current situation. Like I mentioned, I'm from this era, but from

Chicago. Things could be slightly different in Denver, but I wouldn't count on it. Either way, we'll find out for sure."

"Gerald," Martin said abruptly. "Do you think we might die?"

The room fell silent as everyone turned to Gerald, their fearless leader who seemed to have all the answers.

"It's definitely a better possibility than most missions," he replied, choosing words carefully. "But that's why we're going to put so much preparation into this. If we just went downtown and barged into the hospital without a plan, we'd be dead within minutes. Every decision we make will be carefully thought out, our plans regarding the medicine will be detailed to the exact second. We'll always know where each other is and how to get in contact."

Martin nodded, along with Brigham. Web continued typing away on his laptop, likely trying to hack the world's greatest computer servers for fun.

"Because of these plans, we need to get moving. It'll be best for us to arrive in the middle of the day and check in to a place. Everyone will be at work, and there's no need for us to get tangled with other Road Runners right now. The less people who know who we are, the better. We can't have people talking about the group of four men who showed up with their bags and guns. Word gets around fast, and once it's out, it'll eventually reach the Revolters."

"So we're going downtown already?" Web asked, not looking up from his screen.

"Yes, we'll plan to leave here in an hour, after you guys pick the weapons you want. I think the machine guns are pretty fun."

Web didn't acknowledge the response and remained entranced by his computer screen, glowing a blue haze across his face.

"Any questions?" Gerald asked, and when no one replied, "Let's get to it."

They exited the conference room and returned to the warehouse of weapons, none of them sure where to even begin their search.

* * *

Ralph had more than weapons. He provided them a busted old van to travel in, instead of the cramped sports car from 2019. "You'll blend right in," he said proudly. "Just wait till you see it. You'll be Gerald the soccer mom and his three kids." He cackled at himself, grabbing his belly as if he just told the funniest joke in history. They offered polite chuckles, except for Web—the researcher seemed to be in another universe at the moment, remaining distant and quiet.

"I understand you'll need a new wardrobe, so I've prepared a suitcase full of new attire." He rolled out a black suitcase and pushed it over to Martin, patting the top of it. "Everything you need. At the bottom is all of the fine attire: suits, shoes, ties, pocket squares, and a box of jewelry. Remember, the flashier your appearance, the more they think you'll belong. On top of that I packed your regular lounging clothes, which should only be worn when you're back at home base with these guys. Even the super-rich people in these times don't believe in relaxing in a pair of sweatpants. They'll stay in dress pants and a button-up right until bedtime."

"Do they sleep under gold sheets?" Martin asked, smirking.

"Some do, yes. Go somewhere like the governor's mansion, and you'll see everything in gold, all the way down to his very toothbrush."

"Obnoxious."

"Indeed, but that's the luxury of funneling all tax money to yourself. Politics has become even more of a cash grab than what I've heard about in your time. Politics is now a wealthy way of life for only the elite of society to participate. Everyone else just tries to mind their own business and pray they don't get killed for no apparent reason."

Every bit of information that both Gerald and Ralph mentioned felt like a new layer being peeled off an onion of fear. They were inching closer to the core, and the thought terrified Martin to his bones. Within the next hour he'd be arriving downtown with his small caravan of Road Runners, an easy target should they be discovered. He had seen downtown Denver grow from the 1980's all the way through 2019. He even had a taste of life in 1919, but none of that prepared him for whatever horror lived on this side of the century. Would the city look the same? Were all the familiar buildings and skyscrapers still standing strong? Did Revolters march around town with automatic firearms looking to shoot anyone who appeared as a threat? He tried to imagine such a world, but couldn't, refusing to accept that life could've taken such a dramatic twist during the course of history.

His flask throbbed like a hot cast iron in his back pocket, begging him to return to his normal life in 2019. It was a much different experience traveling forward compared to backward. Going back in time, he knew what would happen for the most part. There were no major surprises kept out of the history books, and life in general seemed more relaxed.

Jumping into the future sparked a constant tension that hung over every moment. An obvious sense of the unknowing tickled the back of his thoughts, creating fear and doubt. How was he supposed to return to 2019—even with the cure to Alzheimer's in hand—and pretend that everything was okay? How was he supposed to attempt to return to a normal life, knowing what lied ahead less than twenty years ahead when President Poe ran for office? It reminded Martin of a classic scene in many suspense movies where the protagonist found themselves strapped to a conveyor belt, inching closer to a pool of boiling water. The future was the water, time the conveyor belt, and Martin was strapped down, praying someone would come rescue him.

Will he make it before turning into a boiled lobster? Tune in tomorrow—same Bat-time, same Bat-channel!

"Briar!" Gerald shouted from across the warehouse. "It's time."

He locked eyes momentarily with Ralph and felt an odd sense of comfort. "I suppose I'll need to take your recommendation on a gun; I need to get going."

Ralph grinned and led Martin down the aisle.

14

Chapter 14

It hadn't even been twelve hours, so Chris jumped out of his seat when he saw a figure appear on the monitors. It was 9 p.m., hours after he had released half of the prisoners back into the wild. He resisted every temptation to jump forward a day in time to see what happened, but as he had learned in his decades of time travel, it was sometimes best to let time pass.

If good things come to those wait, then I'm about to receive the ultimate present.

And as long as the Road Runner wasn't bluffing, he would. He'd kept faith that his enemies were as true to their word as he was, and watching the figure approach from the distant woods caused a rapid heartbeat he hadn't felt in years.

His hands fumbled across his desk, batting papers and loose articles out of the way in search of the intercom control. "Duane, please come to my office. This is an emergency."

Chris couldn't think of a time where he had ever mentioned an emergency publicly over the intercom. For convenience, the intercom reached every inch of the mansion, including the basement. He imagined the remaining prisoners panicking like caged dogs on their way to the pound. Perhaps it was his heart's desire, but he swore he heard their shouts from two levels below.

Within a minute, Duane knocked and entered the office, unbothered as usual.

"What's going on?" Duane asked.

"Our friend is coming back."

"Already? Are you sure it's him?" Duane pulled his sleeve down to check his watch. "It's only been eleven hours."

"Perhaps they were giving us broad timelines as well. But I don't know who else would be walking from the woods in the middle of the night."

Duane hurried around the desk to look at the monitor, his face stretched into a studious gaze. "It's one person again, gotta be him."

"I *know* it's him, Duane, that's why I called you up here."

They watched in silence as the small figure on the screen once again grew larger with each approaching step. The distance between the mansion and the woods was much longer than Chris had remembered, as it took this man nearly three minutes to reach the front porch.

Duane had already opened the software that allowed two-way conversation with the outside world.

"Good evening," Chris said, unable to hide the grin on his face as he slid the headset on. One of two things were about to happen, both making him drool at the thought. The man was either back to disclose the plan for capturing Strike, or he was here to try and negotiate a new deal and back out of the old one, in which case he'd be killed within two minutes. No one backed out of a deal with Chris Speidel and lived to tell the tale.

"Hello, Chris," the familiar voice responded, and the man waved to the cameras he couldn't see.

"I see you're back so soon. Did you get your people back in the shape you wanted?"

"We did, yes."

The Road Runner said nothing further and stood in silence, staring at the steel barricade without any outward sign of emotion. He was again bundled up from head to toe, leaving them unable to make out a single detail aside from the man's height.

It's a fucking negotiation tactic, Chris realized. Refusing to speak first was one of the oldest tricks in the book, putting the pressure on whoever decided to utter the first words.

Chris muted his microphone and turned to Duane who had sat down across the desk. "I need you to round up everyone we have and make them wait at the front door. I think this guy is going to try and talk his way out of this, and we will not accept that."

Duane nodded and disappeared as effortlessly as he had arrived. Chris preferred having Duane at his side in this sort of situation, but he had to think ahead. This scum Road Runner was not going to walk away without giving Chris the promised information.

The man remained silent, each passing second growing more awkward, before Chris decided he had to say something. "Is there something I can help you with today?"

The question was vague enough to suggest the Road Runner had no negotiating power.

The man turned, the fuzz on his jacket blowing in the wind, and stared directly into the camera from behind his ski goggles.

"I'm ready to discuss the terms of our deal," he said in

monotone. Chris had no way of knowing, but assumed this Road Runner was on the verge of shitting his pants. This could have all been some far-reaching goal for him, not expecting Chris to actually turn over the prisoners. But here they were, face to face, and he now had to turn in their one and only leader. "I'd like to come inside to talk—I don't want to say anything out here in the open."

Chris leaned back and thought. It was still possible this was all a big ploy to try and get into the mansion. There was no one visible in the distance, but that didn't mean they weren't nearby waiting for the barricade to drop.

"I've come here in peace," the Road Runner said, as if he could read Chris's thoughts. "No weapons, no backup. Just here on my own to work this out." He raised his hands in the air as if this proved all of his words as true.

"Give me a minute," Chris said, his arms crossed and head shaking. As much as he believed the Road Runner, it was still a Road Runner. One of the same lower species he'd been trying to exterminate for years like the filthy rats they were. "Wait right there, don't move."

Chris removed the headset and leaned over his intercom microphone. "Duane, please cancel what you're doing and return to the office immediately."

He planned to lower the barricade and let the Road Runner inside to discuss the next steps, but he didn't want to just drop their steel shield and leave everyone vulnerable without a warning.

Duane entered a minute later, calm and cool. "Why did you make me stop?"

"Our friend outside would like to come in to discuss the details. Says he doesn't want to say all of this outside where he can be heard. I'm going to let him in."

"Don't do it, Chris."

"I have no choice. He's not going to talk to us unless he comes inside. And we need Strike."

"You didn't even know you needed Strike until a couple days ago."

"Are you kidding me? Just because an active effort to capture her was never discussed doesn't mean we don't need her. This is a gift from God."

"No, it's a gift from the Road Runners, which is exactly why you should be suspicious of him acting so desperate to come inside."

Chris sighed and folded his hands on his desk. "Here's what's going to happen. I'm going to drop the barricade, and you're going to send two of our soldiers outside to greet our friend. Have them check him for any weapons and bring him inside to this office. No tours of the house, just straight here. Then I want three of our soldiers here in the room, guns cocked and aimed at Mr. Road Runner in case he tries to make any moves. Are we clear?"

"Yes, sir."

"Great. Head downstairs and gather the soldiers needed. I'm going to disarm the barricade in two minutes."

Duane left and Chris placed the headset back over his head and looked at the monitor where the Road Runner had indeed not moved. "Okay, sorry about that, just working out some logistics before we let you in."

"Understood."

"It'll be a couple minutes before we disarm the house, so hang tight. My team will meet you outside to pat you down before coming in."

"Fair enough."

The Road Runner said nothing further and stared blankly at the concealed mansion in front of him, small clouds of his breath slipping out through the ski mask stretched over his face.

Chris took off the headset and drummed his fingers on the desk, anticipating the upcoming encounter. He'd never had a Road Runner come to the upper floor of the mansion, and certainly had never sat down to have a civil discussion with one. They were never worthy of so much. He thought back to the dozens he had personally killed, and the millions murdered under his watch throughout time, causing a smirk he couldn't quite keep away.

What would happen if I flipped the script on this guy and shot him dead in my office? There's no better Road Runner than a dead Road Runner, right?

As delicious as it sounded, Chris would have to resist. If anything happened while the man was in his office, he'd end up dead anyway. Because if this wasn't some cheap setup, then the future became a lot brighter for his team and their goals.

He opened the software and punched in the code to drop the barricade. The familiar hum carried throughout the house as the steel shields lowered. The Road Runner didn't flinch.

When the humming stopped, Chris watched the monitor as the front door swung open and two of his soldiers stepped into the cold night, approaching the Road Runner with their guns drawn. The man returned his hands to the air and rotated to give his back to the Revolters.

One soldier kept his rifle fixed on the Road Runner while the other stepped up and began patting down his legs, working his way up to the neck. He nodded to the other soldier, and turned the Road Runner to lead him inside.

Chris could have changed the camera view to follow them through the entryway and up the stairs, but didn't bother. He'd be in his office within a minute anyway. A handful of soldiers stepped outside, rifles cocked and aimed into the distance, anticipating anything that might come from the woods. Duane must have given this order, clearly forgetting about the last time they had soldiers outside like sitting ducks.

The rumble of multiple footsteps coming up the stairs sent small vibrations into Chris's office, churning his stomach at the thought of an upcoming meeting with his enemy. He closed the software on his computer and pulled open a drawer to make sure his loaded revolver was still there, waiting to protect him from any attack.

The stomping grew louder and stopped outside the office door before a rapid knock banged on it.

"Come in," Chris shouted, hands trembling with excitement.

The door swung open with Duane leading the way, the masked Road Runner behind him, followed by three Revolters, each with a rifle pointed at the man's back.

"Hello, Chris," the Road Runner said, muffled through his mask.

"Please, have a seat." Chris gestured to the open seat where Duane normally sat during their sessions together. "Shall we begin?"

The man nodded. "Let's do it."

15

Chapter 15

The four men loaded into the van after wishing Ralph farewell. Ralph assured them he'd be in the same place should they need to come back for anything, although he hoped they wouldn't need to. They filled the trunk with six firearms, ten smoke bombs, one grenade, and a half dozen cases of ammunition, all at Gerald's instruction.

Gerald whistled once they reached the freeway toward downtown, leaving Martin to wonder how he could be so chipper. It was a few minutes past noon as they coasted down the empty road, and Martin couldn't recall the last time I-70 was free of any traffic.

"I want you guys to know you don't need to live in fear," Gerald said. "Stay alert, be aware of your surroundings, but no one will bother you unless you bother them. It's not *as* bad as you think."

"You said they gun down Road Runners for fun," Brigham snapped. "How am I supposed to *not* live in fear?"

Gerald chuckled a morbid sound. "We're covered. That's why I had us change to long sleeves and baggy pants. The only way anyone will see the glow from your skin is if they get right in your face. And the only reason they'll get in your face is if you bother them. Besides, where we're going there won't be many Revolters, if any. They don't exactly hang out in the slums looking for people to shoot. They stay in their area and protect their turf from outsiders."

"So it's like segregation is back?" Martin asked.

"One hundred years after it was abolished, yes, it's back. People have always been ignorant to the fact that history actually does repeat itself, and it's only become worse now that the Revolters have taken control of the education system and erased any details from the history lessons that paints what they're doing as a negative thing."

"What's the rest of the world like?" Martin asked. "Or is this just happening in America?"

"Well, I'm sure Brigham can tell you about Europe," Gerald replied. "They haven't been fully infiltrated yet, but they're on shaky ground."

"We're fighting," Brigham added nonchalantly.

"But as for Asia, Africa, and South America, they've all been taken over by the Revolters and are going through the same things we are here. Their plan is to rule the world in unison, which would be the end of civilization as we know it."

Martin shook his head. "What about Australia? You forgot them."

"Ah, the Aussies. Yeah, that's the one place they're having an incredibly difficult time taking control of. The Road Runners have a strong presence there, but I'd say ninety percent of the population has zero interest in picking a side between the two of us. They view us all as outsiders and want us to get the hell off their enormous island. They really are our last hope, and even though they reject the Road Runners, they're helping our cause by being as equally turned off by the Revolters. It's actually quite funny to watch the Revolters' leaders try to offer people the Juice down there. They usually return a blank stare and tell them to *fuck off, mate.*"

They all laughed at this, picturing someone like Chris being told to fuck off by a pissed off Australian.

"Won't they eventually just start executing people?" Martin asked. "Like if it comes down to them being the final country to take over, can't they just force their will at that point?"

"They could, but it wouldn't be wise. They'd be going up against two groups instead of one: the Road Runners *and* the Aussies. The people down there are already suspicious of any outsiders, and they have no issue unifying to protect their country. See, they actually read history books and take the lessons seriously. They would never allow something to happen to their people the way it did when the Europeans came to the Americas to rape and kill all the natives. The Revolters thrive on dividing and conquering populations of people, but the Aussies have proven resistant against such a threat."

The open fields gave way to city buildings, and Martin saw the skyscrapers of downtown in the distance, through a dark smog that hung over the city.

"We're about five minutes out," Gerald announced, shifting the mood immediately to the seriousness of the task at hand. Martin understood why Gerald was thought so highly of. He had a knack for calming the mood, making them forget where they were or why they were there.

They're all here because of me, Martin reminded himself, no longer sure if that was entirely true. Would they still have come on this mission without Martin? All across the spectrum of time, Revolters and Road Runners alike were working toward their lofty goals of ruling the world and protecting the world, respectively. Would the Road Runners really have granted a newcomer their own mission out of a simple gesture of appreciation for risking his life?

With the expanded knowledge he had gained about the Road Runners and their worldwide mission, it seemed less likely. He presumed this mission was already planned, and they took advantage of the situation to both please Martin and also add another foot soldier.

Regardless of whatever the truth might be, they trusted him enough to go into the future, something their very own leader refused to do. The group was there for both a common goal, but also their own individual reasons. If a choice came down to saving one of these men's lives or grabbing his mom's medicine, Martin wasn't entirely sure what he'd do. On the flip side, could he trust these men to save his life should a situation arise?

There were too many unknowns as they pulled into the city, but Martin pushed them aside and focused on one step at a time. And right now was all about exploring the city and knowing the best way to stay alive in it.

The van exited to I-25 southbound from I-70, the city now towering in front of them. The skyscrapers looked the same as Martin had known them from 2019, and there were even a handful more added to the skyline that overlapped the blue Rocky Mountains in the backdrop. A thick, gray haze clouded their vision.

"What's with the smog?" Martin asked. Being the only person in the vehicle who was a Denver native, he realized his responsibility to compare the city's 2064 version to the

2019 one he had left behind.

"Poe's biggest donors were from the coal industry. Once the Revolters had full control over Congress, they passed all sorts of tax breaks for companies who remained powered by coal. Such ridiculous incentives that clean energy has damn near disappeared."

"No one fought it?"

"Of course they tried. But any sort of environmental protection group run through the government had been terminated. And all the Earth-loving hippies were obviously seen as anti-Revolution and were executed. The government actually hires fake scientists to explain why coal is better for the world—and these morons believe every word of it."

They turned again off the interstate, this time taking the exit ramp for Park Avenue, and Martin's eyes bulged at the sight of a somewhat familiar building in front of them.

"Is that Coors Field?" Martin asked.

"Is that what it used to be called?" Gerald replied. "Today it's called Denver Energy Ballpark, named by the state's largest coal company, and owners of the team."

Gerald rolled his eyes as they pulled up to a stop light in front of the stadium. Martin looked out his window at the building that had undergone a transformation. Gone was its brick exterior and purple neon lighting, replaced with gold-tinted glass that shielded the view inside the stadium, a similar effect as Mandalay Bay in Las Vegas.

"Let me get this straight," Martin said. "While the rest of the country is going to shit, baseball stadiums got an upgrade?"

"All sports got an upgrade," Gerald said. "Two things happened: with the Revolters came a bunch of new billionaires, and President Poe openly admitted that sports were important to keep around so that the poor and middle class can remain distracted from what's actually going on in the government. Since the Revolters came from all eras of time to join the big takeover, these billionaires were essentially playing with fake money, as far as they were concerned. They bid against each other for ownership of all these sports franchises, and since they're playing with fake money, they simply paid athletes more while dropping the prices of the cheap seats for the general public to get in. As a group, they bought into the idea of controlling the poor and middle classes, and it worked."

"Of course it worked. All those people had a new opportunity to go catch a game; something they probably never thought possible."

"You got it. And inside you can register to vote, but only if you plan on voting for the Revolution. Poe praised himself for making it possible. He called it his gift to those less fortunate. It gets bad when Poe starts talking about himself in the third person. 'Thank President Poe. Enjoy all of the games, his treat!' he'd say. So fucked up, but people eat it up every season."

They drove away from the ballpark, and Martin thought it looked more like a palace than a baseball stadium. *I wonder what the inside looks like.*

As the luxurious, golden ballpark faded into the distance behind them, it became suddenly clear where they were. The skyscrapers stood tall and mighty a few blocks away, but the other buildings—the restaurants, stores, and small apartment complexes—were all decorated with graffiti and deteriorating from the inside out. Most of the buildings were constructed from brick, as they had always been, but now bricks had fallen out of place and were never repaired. Windows were shattered behind the iron bars that kept the thieves out. And the biggest surprise of all was the amount of homeless people crowding the sidewalks.

"Why do all of the homeless seem so organized?" Martin asked after they drove down a block where sleeping bags and tents filled the entire sidewalks on both sides of the street.

"They're restricted to camp out on certain blocks. Some of the businesses down here can pay the government extra tax money to ensure the homeless won't park themselves in front of their stores."

"How do they enforce that?"

"Quite simple. The business owner calls the police if they find a homeless person outside their store. The police department confirms that the business has paid its annual fee for this special privilege. Then they come out and shoot the homeless person, and take the body off to who knows where."

"Jesus Christ," Brigham uttered, having remained silent during the drive. Web gazed out the window, but they had grown expectant of his reticence.

"We can continue the history lesson another time," Gerald interrupted. "Because we're here, gentlemen."

He pulled the van to the side of the road and parked in front of a three-level building, a crooked, faded sign calling it *The Last Stop Hotel & Suites*. It appeared no different than the other buildings they had passed, only this one had a welcoming patch of two-foot tall grass, and black, dreary trees. Atop the building, a crow cawed into the quiet afternoon.

"Say hello to your home in 2064," Gerald said, killing the engine.

Martin pressed his face against the window to soak in his surroundings. The buildings were practically stacked on top of each other, separated only by narrow alleyways where groups of people huddle around each other, shooting dice on the ground with dollar bills in short piles.

Just remember why you're here, Martin reminded himself. *It's not that bad. When you get the medicine, all of this will be forgotten.*

He leaned back, knowing none of this would ever be forgotten. The images from his brief time in 2064 would already be burned into his memory forever, serving as a constant reminder of what waited for him later on in life.

16

Chapter 16

Commander Strike awoke in a dark hotel room. Sleeping in the Denver office had grown exhausting, as she never actually received a full night of sleep. The pull out beds had springs that dug into her back all night, and the temperature always seemed to be just off, either too hot or too cold, never perfect.

She had wished the team farewell before leaving, letting them know she was heading back to Alaska to plot the next steps of the war with Julian. While she could've slept on the plane ride home, all she really wanted was a moment alone. She had wandered down the street from the office and found a small hotel called the Jet Hotel. She could've stayed for free at the Oxford, but walking into any place filled with Road Runners always drew their attention and swarmed her in a mob of excited people.

At the Jet Hotel, she walked in the front door like any normal person looking for a room, minus the trailing security team who followed, blending in as if they didn't know her. When she checked in to her room, she immediately collapsed onto the fluffy bed, splaying her limbs in every direction and enjoying the room's perfect temperature. It had been at least ten days since she had a day off, and she'd plan on spending it in bed, watching trash TV, and ordering room service for all meals of the day.

Even on the brink of passing out from fatigue, she wondered how the crew was faring in 2064. Mainly she wondered about Martin. Something about him drove her a bit wild. He had a confidence that he didn't realize, yet a soothing presence equally oblivious to him.

She wondered what drove Martin Briar. After losing his daughter so many years ago and going back in time to helplessly witness it, *something* had to keep him moving forward. She'd seen similar scenarios play out where people had killed themselves or let their life spiral out of control with drugs, alcohol, and gambling. But not Martin Briar.

She didn't just think about him, but *worried* about him. She was in 2019, and he was in the dangerous year of 2064, 200 years after the Civil War had ended, yet seemed to be starting again. The Road Runners had statisticians who ran numbers throughout the spectrum of time. She pulled a report and found that anyone who traveled beyond the year 2050 had a six percent chance of being killed if they spent an entire day in any following year. Those numbers jumped up to ten percent and eighteen percent on days two and three, respectively.

She shared this data with Gerald, insisting they get in and out as quickly as possible. He projected a week's time to complete the mission, which carried a forty-five percent chance of death.

"They can run their numbers all they want," Gerald told her. "But they can't factor for me. Those odds don't mean shit to me. The crew will be safe as long as they listen and stay by my side."

Strike sighed in her silent room, thinking back to this brief conversation and only feeling temporarily relieved by Gerald. She wanted Martin back, not only to ensure his safety, but to ask him if he'd like to join her inner circle in leading the Road Runners. She had Julian and Bill to bring him up to speed, and believed he'd be the perfect fit with those two. Working alongside her would guarantee he'd never have to leave on a dangerous mission again, unless he really wanted to.

Thinking of them reminded her that she'd need to have a talk with both men. As a departing Commander next year, she was to endorse an individual to succeed her. Endorsed candidates had won the election ninety-five percent of the time throughout the Road Runners' history, and while Bill had plenty of seniority and wisdom, she believed Julian had the mettle and toughness to lead the organization into the next wave of the future.

Bill had always been laidback, so she hoped this scenario would be no different. He'd make a fantastic leader during a time of peace, but they simply weren't at that point yet. For her, she considered who would have the greatest odds of capturing Chris, and that was a no-brainer to choose Julian. He had the ambition, passion, and a wealth of fresh ideas. Deep down she knew she wouldn't be the one to get Chris, but had no issue imagining Julian pulling off the task.

Julian can end the war, and Bill can lead them into peace afterward, she thought, and would plan her pitch to them on exactly this.

A shallow knock came from the door, causing Strike to jump in the bed. The room was pitch-black except for the soft glow of the clock on the nightstand that read 6:42. She had breakfast scheduled for delivery at 7:30, and couldn't imagine they'd be this early with the food. Perhaps they thought she asked for her delivery at 6:30. Or it could have been one of her guards, but they never disrupted her, especially during sleep.

They'd either knock again, or leave, realizing their mistake. Strike rolled onto her back and stared into the darkness. The thick curtains had been drawn shut to keep any sunlight out. She turned to the door, where a sliver of light from the hallway seeped through the bottom gap. The light divided by the shadows of two feet as the person who knocked remained on the other side.

A second knock echoed throughout the room.

"Who is it?" she called.

"Room service. Breakfast delivery."

Dammit, she thought, dreading that she now had to get out of bed a whole 45 minutes earlier than planned. She had the room till noon and planned to eat herself into an early morning nap.

Strike rolled to the edge of the bed and swung her legs over where they landed into a pair of white slippers. A robe lay on the ground which she pulled over her naked body. "I'm coming!"

She shuffled across the room, tasting the sourness of her morning breath, and knowing her hair was a frazzled mess. The unpleasant sight of her opening the door was their fault for being so early. She flicked on the light switch in the entryway, splashing a soft glow across the room. A quick check through the door's peephole showed a young man dressed in a suit, a tray of breakfast held in his arms.

Strike pulled open the door to receive a warm smile from the man. "Good morning, Ms. Strike, we have your breakfast ready."

"Thank you, but I had asked for it at 7:30."

The man's face scrunched as he checked the receipt on the tray. "I show that as your regular request, but that you called in to request it earlier."

"I never called in. I've been asleep almost the entire time I've been here. It must have been a call for a different room."

The man peered at the paper, his arms trembling from the weight of the tray.

"Please, you can put the food down on the dresser. You don't need to hold it this whole time," Strike said. The young man entered the room and slid the tray on top of the nearest dresser.

"Of course, thank you. It just doesn't make sense. It was a handwritten note passed over to me about the change of time. I don't know who did it."

"I did," a voice called from the open door, and they both swiveled around to see Chris standing there with a wide grin.

"Who are you?" the man asked.

"Just an old friend of Ms. Strike," Chris replied calmly, his grin not fading.

The man looked from Chris to Strike. Strike had a stern expression smacked on her face.

"Ma'am, are you okay?" he asked. "Or should I stay?"

"You can stay," Chris cut in, lunging across the room and pulling a pocket knife from his coat.

The poor kid never saw it coming. Chris jammed the knife into his gut, getting a faint grunt sound as the hotel employee collapsed to his knees, eyes staring blankly at the crazy old man.

Strike balled her hands into fists, fighting off the urge to leap across the room and tackle Chris. He had a weapon, leaving her no option but to stand by and watch, her pistol tucked away in her suitcase.

Where the hell is my team? she wondered. It was completely unacceptable for Chris Speidel to even be in the same building as her, let alone standing at her room's door.

"So we're killing innocent civilians now?" she snapped.

Chris tipped the man on his back, his skull hitting the carpeted floor with a hollow *thock!*

"I'll kill whoever gets in my way," Chris said, turning his maniacal expression to her. "Especially with such a grand opportunity like this."

"What are you talking about?"

Beneath her confident tone, Strike shook with terror. This was her own mistake, insisting to stay in the hotel. *Where are they?!* Surely one of the guards had to have seen Chris slip into the building. Strike focused on her heart rate as it tried to leap out of her throat. She was alone in a private room with Chris Speidel where he could kill her and disappear without a trace. The weight of the entire war now hung on to her ability to talk her way out of this predicament.

"I'm talking about an end to this war," Chris said.

"I see, so you're here for a peace offering."

Chris giggled like a child. "Peace? I think too much blood has been shed for this to all end with peace. I always imagined the ending as more of an explosion. An ending of all endings. A big *boom*." He held his hands open and apart to mimic an explosion.

Chris returned the knife to his pocket after wiping the blood clean with his fingers, which he slurped off like barbecue sauce after attacking a rack of ribs. The sight sent instant chills down Strike's back.

"You see, Ms. Strike, I came here with two options. I can either kill you and watch your people flounder for leadership.

Or, my preferred option, I take you with me, and we watch together as your people scramble. We can laugh at it like a good comedy movie."

"We have systems in place," Strike cut in. "This exact scenario has already been planned for. We have a chain of command that falls into place, and everyone moves up one position."

"How precious. That's a good sentiment, and I'm sure it'll resonate with the general population of your people, but what about your leadership? Your Lead Runners, as I believe they're called?"

"How do you know that term?" A tsunami started to form in her gut. Chris already knew too much.

"That's a fair question, but have you considered the other glaring one you've yet to ask? Aren't you curious as to *why* I'm here? *How* I got here?"

"Your people have been following me. It's no secret. And this is my own fault for insisting on a non-Road Runner hotel."

"I see. Thought you'd have a romantic getaway, eh? Well, I hate to be the bearer of bad news, but we have not been tailing you."

Chris paused, and his grin somehow widened even more, revealing his yellow-tinted teeth.

"I don't know what you're getting at."

"Strike, my dear, your own people turned you in. *Your* people told us where you'd be and how to get to you. *Your* people told us where your security team was, so I killed them all before coming to your room. We made a deal where I release the prisoners I've kept for so long, and they hand you over. I thought the offer was too good to be true, but here we are."

Strike studied Chris, unsure if she should believe him or not.

He kept his childish grin, and that's what made her think it all true. He clearly enjoyed getting a reaction, and not a fake one. That was his purpose wasn't it, to feed off the raw emotion from those around him?

Her mind immediately jumped in circles, wondering who in the hell on her team would stoop this low. Her face softened with the sudden realization that she had no way out of this situation.

"I know, my dear – this must be sickening for you to hear. I never thought such a loyal group of people could carry out such huge betrayal."

"I don't believe you." Doubt clung to her every word.

"Let's cut the shit. You're coming with me and it's time to decide how. I can force you, or you can cooperate, and I just might spare you further down the road. So what will it be?"

Strike wanted nothing more than to grab her pistol in the closet and empty it into this old piece of shit's skull, but it wouldn't accomplish a thing. He'd just stand there, giggling through it like someone was tickling him with a feather.

She wondered what the nerds at the office would say of her chances of death right now. Her only chance of living now relied on Chris's mercy, and she had to do anything to increase those chances.

"Before I go with you, I want some sort of proof. I still don't believe someone on my team would do this."

"Certainly," Chris said as he rummaged in his pockets, pulling out a folded up piece of paper. He stepped toward her and held it out for her to grab.

She unfolded it and flattened it to read the scribbled handwriting.

"Holy shit," she gasped. The writing was the next 24 hours

of her schedule neatly listed in bullet points, down to the minute. Her flight back to Alaska was the next thing shown, where they'd expect her in another five hours.

"The holiest of shits, I'd say," Chris added.

"This can't be."

"Let's go, my dear. We have work to get done."

Chris stepped to her and took the paper out of her trembling grip, sliding an arm around her shoulder.

This is actually happening, she thought, mind spinning. The deathly sensation of Chris's arm around made her want to vomit. He smelled like a funeral parlor, and his arm felt like a block of ice over her shoulders.

"Who did this?" she demanded, squirming to get out of his grip.

Only a handful of people had access to her complete schedule: Bill, Julian, and her security detail who trailed her every minute of the day. The security team consisted of a rotation of ten different members who typically traveled with her and stayed by her side when she left one of the offices. Except today when she demanded they stay in a hotel room down the hallway.

"I wish I could tell you," Chris said into her ear, the odor of death oozing from his pores. "It was a man, but he remained anonymous, insisting to never be known. And since he came to me with such a generous offer, I felt compelled to oblige to his request."

If it was a man, that only eliminated the two women on her security team, leaving eight others plus Bill and Julian. But why? Who would gain from having her kidnapped by the Revolters? Julian would step into her role as Commander, with Bill moving up one spot closer. But she couldn't imagine either of them orchestrating this, especially with her term up within a year.

It had to be someone on the security team. Just because Road Runners were sworn to loyalty, it didn't make them immune to the temptations of an offer. Who knows what Chris put on the table in exchange for her schedule, but it had better been worth it, because if she ever found her way out of this mess she wouldn't rest until the traitor was brought to justice.

Her fear and anxiety quietly slipped away and gave way to rage. Her fists had been balled, and she now felt her fingernails puncturing the inside of her palms.

"Let's get out of here, shall we?" Chris said with his smirk. "We've got so much work to do and so little time."

He pulled her in closer, daring her to make a move she would only regret.

"Let's get this over with," she said.

Chris nodded, and led them out of the room.

17

Chapter 17

The hotel suite reminded Martin of his old place in Larkwood. It had every feel of the bachelor pad that he had grown to love. The chipped walls had larger holes covered with tape and a half-hearted paint job. The blinds, crooked in the window sill, let the sunlight seep in through a slanted angle. The stench of cheap cleaning chemicals filled their noses when they entered the vacant space.

Web studied the space with his lips pursed and brow furrowed, and touched the furniture and countertops with such caution that he must have thought a diseased creature would jump up and kiss him.

"Don't fall in love with the place, gentlemen," Gerald said. "We're here to sleep and work—won't exactly be hanging out to watch football on Sundays. Web, you're going to have the master bedroom since you'll be doing the most work inside. Set up the room however you see fit. There are two other bedrooms, so who wants to sleep on the living room couch?"

Brigham and Martin locked eyes for a brief moment. "I'll do it," Brigham said. "My wife used to threaten me to sleep on the couch, but little did she know I liked it; my own private space where no one could steal the sheets."

Gerald snickered. "Suit yourself. Martin, I'll take the north facing bedroom since it has the best view of the front of the building."

"Sounds good."

The men split separate ways to examine their new living spaces. Bedroom doors creaked open as Brigham flopped down on the raggedy couch, kicking his shoes off and grinning the way only a free man could.

Martin entered his room to find a bed pushed into the corner next to a closet. A lone wooden desk sat below the window and faced the city. Forty years earlier the view would've been stunning, but with the gloom and smog, it was borderline depressing to see what had happened to Denver.

The walls were thin, as he heard Brigham whistling to himself and Gerald humming a tune. Martin pulled open the desk drawers to find nothing but some blank sheets of paper with pens and pencils. The closet also had no trace of life except for the empty hangers. He wondered if this building had been slaughtered like the one they had first visited to see Ralph, and decided he didn't really want to know, seeing as he had to sleep in this room.

"Gentlemen!" Gerald shouted loud enough to make Martin jump. "Living room right now."

Martin stepped out of the bedroom and met everyone around the couch where Brigham now sat up with his smile gone.

"We have a problem," Gerald continued once they all arrived. "I just got an email from headquarters. It appears Commander Strike has been kidnapped by Chris."

Web gasped, and Brigham shook his head in disgust.

"We don't know any of the details, other than she had checked into a hotel in Denver the night before her return flight to Alaska, and when she never showed up to the plane, the team started their search. She only had one bag of things she had packed, but it was still in the hotel room."

"How do we know it was Chris?" Martin asked.

"That bastard left a note. 'I have your girl,' was all it said, signed in his name.

"Jesus Christ," Brigham said, a sour look stuck on his face. "What does this mean for us?"

"At the moment, nothing. They're scrambling to figure out what to do next and deciding if they need to implement the chain of command that's written in our bylaws. They first want to see if there's even a chance of finding her before making that decision."

"You don't suppose she ran off?" Brigham asked. "Did they not check her tracker?"

"I'm sure they did, but they're not sharing all of the details."

"That means it's an inside job. They are transparent with everything. If they're hiding something, that means they don't want it to fall on the wrong ears."

"Let's settle down. This is how rumors start. They may have the details and just didn't tell me. It was more of a notice in case we happen to hear anything here in 2064."

"Right, because they would run off to this shithole," Brigham said, shaking his head. "No offense."

"None taken," Gerald snapped. "This does make our work a bit harder, more in the sense of our timeline. We'll need to hurry instead of taking our time. Just because we have a system in place doesn't mean this won't have an effect. There could be a ripple all the way to this year."

"What does that mean?" Martin asked.

"It means we need to get to work right now so we can help with whatever the Road Runners need. Let's get our thoughts in order and meet back here in fifteen minutes to start a plan."

"Fifteen minutes? I don't think you understand what I do," Web added, a tinge of anger in his voice. "I need at least an entire day to gather research on the area."

"I know that. I said to *start* a plan, not an entire strategy ready to go. I know this will all take time. I'd rather get started now instead of wasting a day doing nothing." Web stormed off to his bedroom and slammed the door like a moody teenager. Brigham giggled as Gerald sighed and crossed his arms. "Anyone else have any issues they'd like to discuss?"

Brigham stared to the ceiling and Martin shook his head.

"Great then. Martin, if you don't mind I'd like to meet in your room and go through that suitcase Ralph gave you. Knowing what's in there should help us plan what you'll be doing."

"Okay, let's go."

Martin pivoted and led the way to his bedroom. He had pushed the suitcase into the corner, and tossed it on the bed to examine its contents.

Gerald shuffled into the room and closed the door. "How are you doing?" He dropped his authoritative exterior, softening his voice and facial features as he watched Martin.

"I'm fine. Why do you ask?"

"I know this is your first mission with us, and it's one hell of a difficult one. I'm just making sure you're not having any regrets."

"No regrets. I just want this medicine. I *need* this medicine."

Gerald nodded. "I know. We're gonna try to get it as quickly as possible. What do you think of our team?"

"I don't know, everyone seems nice enough. I like Brigham, he keeps the mood light. Web stays to himself, so it's hard to get a good read on him."

Gerald chuckled. "Brigham is a character, that's for sure. He's scared shitless, that's why he's always saying things. He's keeping the mood light for himself, not us. And Web is a wizard, you'll see. He's honestly the key to everything. He'll get us into the hospital, or wherever we need."

And what do you think of me? Martin wondered. *That I'm in over my head? Are you wondering why you got stuck babysitting some newbie on a fool's mission?*

"So let's see inside this bag," Martin said, pushing his thoughts aside.

"Yes."

Martin stepped forward and unzipped the suitcase to reveal a stuffed bag of clothes.

Gerald reached in, pulling items out and examining them. It was mostly shirts and pants, but a few accessories like earrings, chains, and rings were found in a separate pouch. Martin studied the clothes that looked no different than polo shirts and jeans. Each article of clothing had a letter P sewn into it, small like a dime, but visible nonetheless.

"What's the P for on all of these?" Martin asked.

"Our fearless leader. Poe Enterprises is the name of his company, and they make a little bit of everything. It's easy when you're in charge of setting the regulations. Poe gives company stock to every single member of Congress—after he abolished all the rules against it, of course—that way he can ensure every decision made will have his company in mind."

"How did he manage that law?"

"Again, it's easy when your party is aligned in all three

branches. Even the Supreme Court allowed it. He probably paid everyone off to get the votes. It's one of those things where no one says, and no one asks. If anyone dares to question Poe, they might as well sign their own death certificate."

"So these clothes are supposed to make me look like a supporter?"

"That's the idea. His brands are so heavily advertised—for free—that it's all anyone really buys. He damn near has a monopoly on every industry, and in the ones he doesn't, he only allows his friends to operate their businesses. He has no competition."

"So the law against monopolies has been erased, too?"

"The law? Try the entire SEC. There's only one group overlooking everything in the country, and it's the Revolters."

Martin stood in silence, looking to the clothes scattered across the bed. "You think they have Strike alive?"

"They do. I'm also in a hurry to join you guys back in 2019. I'll be volunteering for the mission to rescue her, and you should, too."

"I think I should see how this one goes first, don't you think?"

"Nonsense. I'll barge into any room for a chance to save Commander Strike, and I like my odds in most situations. But for you, it should be all about helping the Road Runners move forward. We can't truly move forward without our leader."

Martin remembered what he had heard about a major decision waiting after Strike's term had ended. How could Gerald not know? Or was he too brainwashed by the Road Runners to see clearly? Gerald would take a bullet for Strike, while Martin just wanted out of this situation. If only he could've left Izzy in the past, he'd never have met Sonya, his mother would've never come down with Alzheimer's, and he'd be happily blackout drunk in his apartment, dreading the day at the post office ahead.

It had been a while since he reminisced on his life before meeting Chris, and never thought he'd actually long for a return to the fuzzy days of his horrendous routine.

"This is all bigger than us. Remember that, Martin." Gerald spoke as he looked at the clothes piled on the bed. "You should head into town in the morning and get familiar with the area. You'll want a backstory, just in case. I think a good job to say you have is as an attorney. There are thousands of those now, and they all make ridiculous money. There are some suit jackets in the bag, throw one on. Do you know anything about lawyers?"

"Sure. I've gone through a divorce."

"Perfect, play off that. Say you're a divorce lawyer. That's even better because no one wants to go into those details, unlike a criminal attorney."

"What exactly am I looking for around town?"

"Since we know where the medicine is kept, I'd say to get familiar with the area around the hospitals. Learn any side doors, hidden streets, anything that can help in case we have to escape in a hurry."

"Question. Why aren't we planning on taking our Juice with us and drinking it as soon as we have the medicine in hand?"

"Brigham and Web will be here, and we can't leave without them."

"Can't we call them when we have it and take our drinks together? It just seems like an unnecessary risk to try and escape after stealing."

"Calling would be the risk. Privacy laws have been abolished, meaning the government listens to all phone calls that take place, read every e-mail and text message that are sent, and likely bug houses wherever they might have a suspicion. We have to pretend there is no way of communicating with each other once we leave this apartment."

Martin thought back to his brief trip to 1919 with Sonya where they also had no means of communication. Maybe if they had, he wouldn't have been sucked in as a Road Runner.

"In fact," Gerald continued. "If you brought your phone, I urge you to leave it here. There's no point in taking the risk of temptation. They might even be trying to track you. Unlikely they think you're in this year, but you never know."

Martin shook his head, the future becoming grimmer with every detail that was further revealed. At this point, he simply wanted to get the mission over with and return home, and that's what he told Gerald before changing into his new clothes and preparing to explore the city as an undercover Revolter.

18

Chapter 18

Julian pushed open Commander Strike's office door, letting it creak as it revealed the dark and abandoned space. Everything remained exactly as Strike had left it. Her desk was clear of any clutter, a lone framed picture of Strike's former family smiling as they posed at a local park. The filing cabinet on the back wall was covered with mementos from around the world and history. She had collected coins, which were spread across the surface, mixed in with handcrafted wooden and glass figurines.

Julian stepped in, flicking on the light switch, and planting himself on the couch that faced the desk where his boss always sat and vented to him. Being the second-in-command was as awful as it sounded. While he technically had the power to make sweeping decisions, he couldn't do so without the Commander's approval. Everything was run through the Commander, for better or worse.

He leaned back on the couch, falling into its soft embrace, and soaked in the office ambiance. A picture hung on the wall of the seven Commanders, standing strong together with stern expressions. Julian remembered this picture because he took it on a spur-of-the-moment trip where the leaders decided to meet to establish goals for the near and distant future, most of which surrounded the capturing of Chris.

It was the only picture of its kind, the past leaders of the Road Runners never having taken a photo together despite the dozens of times they met. Strike insisted on the picture, and after seeing it printed, the organization decided it should hang in every Commander's office around the world, and updated whenever someone new was elected into the position.

It was getting late, 9 p.m. to be exact, but Julian wouldn't sleep, his mind flooded with excitement and angst. It wasn't the way he imagined it, but he was now in charge of the North American Road Runners thanks to the laws for an existing Commander unable to fill their role.

Julian was sworn in earlier in the day, taking the oath to protect and serve the Road Runners will all of his might, willpower, and mental fortitude. He thought these all meant the same thing, but said "I do" just the same.

From that moment on, he was free to assume his new role as Commander. The guilt, however, had kept him out of Strike's office at first. He could've spent the next week dwelling on the guilt, but that served or protected no one. As leader, decisions needed to be made quickly and with purpose. *The world must go on,* he thought, echoing a thought from his late grandfather.

Julian rose from the couch and crossed the office to the desk—*his* desk—now taking in the view from the other side. As he sat down, the cold leather chair welcomed him, screeching as he adjusted in the seat. He slung his arms on the armrests and enjoyed the private moment where he realized the weight of the world that had been gently placed on his shoulders.

Commander Strike had always told him about the pressures that came with the position. One decision could mean life or death, and while deploying Road Runners for dangerous missions was agreed upon as a necessity, it never made it easy to authorize, knowing the odds of survival in certain situations.

Even though she didn't make the greatest of leaders for their organization, she did serve as a great mentor for Julian—he couldn't deny that. Maybe she was the right leader at the wrong time, similar to Bill, who would make a fine Commander during a time of peace. She liked to beat around the bush when it came to the aforementioned sending of troops into danger.

Julian had to capitalize on the situation. A window would soon be opened, and he saw no reason to not take advantage of the chance to end this war once and for all.

"It's going to happen under my watch. Even if I have to do it myself." Julian spoke to the empty office in a calm voice, grinning as his legs bounced wildly beneath the desk. He closed his eyes and imagined the explosions, green and magnificent, glowing victorious in the silent Alaska air.

He pulled out his cell phone and sent a text message to Bill, asking him to bring Julian's laptop from his office and meet him immediately. Bill had become the new lieutenant commander after Strike's kidnapping, yet Julian hadn't heard from him beyond the day the news had broken.

Bill let him know he'd be there shortly, and Julian slouched back into the chair, enjoying the comforts of his new office space. Down the hallway, the security team was split into two, one half trying to find a way to get Strike back, and the other planning their security detail for Julian as the new Commander.

Bill knocked on the door and let himself in.

"Good evening, Julian."

"Good evening. How have you been? I feel like I haven't seen you in days."

"I've been fine. Working around the clock to try and get Strike back. It's not looking good."

No shit it's not looking good, Julian thought. *She's with Chris. It'll be impossible.*

"I'm sure we'll come up with something; we always do," Julian said.

"I don't think that applies to this situation. This is new to all of us. People are wondering why you're not making more of an effort to get her back."

"Christ, I've only been in charge for a day. I haven't even made a public speech yet to the organization. Besides, I've been toying around with another idea, and that's why I called you here."

"Alright, what's going on?"

Bill approached the desk and sat down across from Julian, sliding his laptop across the polished wood.

"Right now, Strike is in the air with Chris. We've been following Strike's tracking device. The connection has been lost, but that only means they're too high in elevation. He's either taking her back to his mansion, or his store in Nevada. The store has no protection compared to the mansion, so we believe they'll be landing here in Alaska in the next few hours."

Julian sat forward and smirked, his hands clasped on top of the desk. The light reflected off his slicked hair as he stared into Bill's soul.

"What are you getting at?" Bill finally asked.

"I know we have bombs. Lots of them."

"Those are strictly for use in a time of crisis, only to be deployed as a final resort."

"Is our leader being kidnapped *not* a time of crisis? Have we *not* tried shooting Chris multiple times in the head, only to see him live? I think we reached our final resort after he rose from the ground and laughed his way back into the mansion."

"Dropping bombs never ends well. There are too many innocent people who can die."

Julian sighed. Bill was very much cut from the same cloth as Strike. Neither of them had the balls to drop a bomb, all because of a false sense of morality.

"All I'm saying—and it should be considered— is that we take the chance since Chris is outside of his mansion. We can blow him up in the sky, or wait till he's on his way home."

"You want to bomb him with Strike by his side?"

"It's not that I *want* to, but we *need* to. Strike would die happy knowing she was sacrificed to kill Chris. Besides, if we don't have a way of getting her back, then she's only going to spend the rest of her life in his prison. Why make her suffer through that? What do you think?"

Bill stood up, his face curled into a snarl. "I think you've already gone power-hungry on your second day. You need to think about what you're saying and come up with a better idea—one that doesn't involve killing *our* Commander." He turned to storm out of the room.

"Wait," Julian said with a hand raised. He stood to meet Bill's eye level. "I didn't ask for this. This isn't how I ever imagined I'd come into this position. I was going to run a fair campaign in the next election cycle. But none of that matters. She's not coming back, and the sooner we can accept that as an organization, the sooner we can get back to ending this war. That's why I'm up all night plotting away, and I thought you'd like to come along for the ride."

"You know if Strike lives this will never cease. Whether it's you or some future Commander, the people will expect an idea for getting her back."

"I know that, but I have my sights set on bigger things. We can end this war today if I can just get some support on these bombs."

Funny enough, the number two in charge had to give the final approval for deploying the bombs after authorization from the Commander. Julian technically had more influence on the decision as Strike's number two, compared to now as the Commander. *Goddamn checks and balances.*

But maybe he was closer now. Strike would never have authorized a bombing, even on the tragic day after Chris was shot and rose from the dead minutes later. Sure, the barricade went up and likely made the bombs useless, but why not give it a try? Or at least have a discussion? The worst case scenario was them stuck in the same exact position.

"A bomb will never be dropped under my leadership," she had told him when he first brought it up.

Now that the closed-mindedness was out of the way, Julian only had to convince Bill to approve the bombs. Bill was just as peaceful as Strike, but he had an open mind.

"Sit down, Bill. I want to discuss this."

Bill sighed, crossed his arms, and dragged himself back to the seat across Julian's desk. In the past, Bill could've stormed out of the room without a word, but Julian was now the Commander, leaving him no choice but to do as requested.

"Thank you," Julian said sharply. "Let's get the first matter out of the way. We don't need any tension. You and I are still friends and will continue to work together like we always have. I'm not here to boss you around, just to get shit done."

Bill clasped his hands on his lap, one leg bouncing as he stared at Julian with heavy, exhausted eyes. "I don't want this power to go to your head. I'll be here to support you every step of the way, but please don't overstep any boundaries."

"With all due respect, Bill, there are no more boundaries. I'm the Commander."

"Yes, we know that. But it doesn't give you the right to become a dictator. Don't lose your values."

Julian had met Bill when he was first recruited by the Road Runners. Bill saved Julian, more than he'd ever know, after the complete collapse of his life. Julian was a prodigy in his life before the Road Runners, leaving no wonder as to why he was sought out after he received the Juice from Chris.

Julian had risen as a shining star throughout high school, finishing as valedictorian and leading his football team to their second consecutive state championship as their quarterback. Scholarship offers flooded his mailbox, both athletic and academic. Deciding to enroll at Harvard ended up as the decision that shaped the rest of his life.

He didn't continue with football at the collegiate level, wanting to focus on economics in his schooling. But he remained in shape, and even got talked into running the Boston Marathon in 2013. Always up for a physical challenge, Julian trained every single night to get into top shape for the famous marathon.

Like everything else in his life up to that point, the training came naturally. He reached a point where he ran 15 miles every day after class. At nineteen years old, Julian had quickly found himself in the best shape of his life. He ate chicken and vegetables every single day for the four weeks leading up to the marathon, leaving nothing to chance. He passed on parties, drinking booze with his roommate, and made sure to get eight hours of sleep each night.

Everything led up to a successful day on April 15, 2013. He started with the 10:40 a.m. slate of runners, taking the morning to relax, stretch, and mentally prepare for the grueling task ahead. Always an analytical person, he projected four hours for him to complete the race, not bad for a first timer, but well off the mark of the winners who typically clocked in under two and a half hours.

He didn't join the race to win. There were plenty of runners who dedicated their lives to a chance at victory. Julian popped in his earphones and listened to the four hour playlist of songs he had created to carry him through the race. He maintained a steady pace that he had found to work, and focused on his breathing, letting the cool air fill his lungs as he timed his inhales every five seconds.

The race passed in a blur, and as he approached the finish line with a few minutes to spare before 3 p.m., everything changed forever.

The finish line waited over 100 yards away. Julian had taken out his earphones to hear the roaring crowd cheering on everyone who finished the race. People lined the sidewalks, jumping and waving at the hundreds of strangers who ran by on the street.

An explosion boomed from the left sidewalk, gray smoke immediately rising and filling the air, clouding the view of the upcoming finish line. The ground shook, causing Julian and many others to lose their footing and fall with their hands splayed out. His first thought was that an earthquake had just struck.

By the time he got back to his feet, a second explosion

rang out, this one much closer as the thunderous force sent everyone flying through the air. Julian's ears reverberated as he threw his arms over his head to shield it from what felt like dozens of hailstones showering over him. He had fallen back to the ground.

He looked up to see blood speckled across his legs, as if he had just received 100 small paper cuts across his flesh. About thirty feet away was a sight that would never leave his memory. A man lay on his back, arms splayed to his sides as he cried and shouted to the skies. Both of his legs were gone, cut from the knee down where blood oozed like a river onto the asphalt.

"Somebody help me! It fucking burns!" the man had shouted, his shrieking voice lost in the commotion of hundreds of other people shouting and stampeding to safety.

Julian shook his head free of the shards of glass, crawling toward the man, but not moving. Each movement he made sent a jolt of pain down his back, all but paralyzing him. After five attempts to push off the ground, he gave up and rolled onto his back, looking to the smoke-filled sky and praying this wasn't how his life ended.

Life didn't end that day, but a new beginning waited on the horizon. Julian walked away with no serious injuries, merely a couple of broken ribs and bruising throughout his whole body. While this all seemed innocent on paper—and nothing compared to the man who lost his legs and the countless others who never made it home for supper—the recovery led Julian down a dark path of painkillers and an opioid addiction that would haunt the next three months of his life.

Until he met Chris Speidel.

19

Chapter 19

"Let me tell you why you should give the green light to the bombs," Julian said, sitting up stiffly. He had his cell phone on the desk, a software running in the background to record this conversation, needing at least one soundbite he could work with. "For starters, we've been sitting on these bombs for how many years? Are we ever going to use them?"

"They're intended to use in defense; not to proactively drop."

"I know that, and I understand why. Dropping a bomb can easily get regular people in the middle of this mess. But, Bill, we're in the middle of nowhere, the fucking North Pole. These aren't nuclear bombs, so it's not like we have to worry about any widespread harm to civilians. We can drop hundreds of these bombs and no one will even know."

"So you want to drop them on the mansion?"

"Precisely."

"You know it's barricaded with thick steel. Dropping a bomb would be a waste and do nothing but escalate this war."

"Or it can *end* this war. We're going to have a small window of opportunity when those barricades go down. The rest of our people are going to be released at some point in the next couple of days."

"How do you know this?" Bill asked, staring at his young counterpart with suspicious eyes.

"We have an insider, and that's all you need to know. I think we need to act quickly because no one knows how long this barricade will stay up once its closed again."

"He'll have Commander Strike in there. We need to get her out of there before any bomb is dropped. I won't approve it otherwise."

"I think we can make that work. So you will approve the dropping of a bomb on Chris's mansion?"

Bill sighed and crossed his arms. "Yes I will—"

Got it! Julian wanted to jump out of his chair for obtaining the recording he needed, but kept cool while Bill finished speaking.

"—but only under that one condition. If you can actually pull it off, then what can stop me from saying no?"

"Thanks, Bill. I knew we'd be able to come to an agreement. Shall we toast to our future as the leaders of the Road Runners?"

"Perhaps tomorrow. I don't remember the last time I've slept, and it's time for me to take a day off."

"I'll see you tomorrow, then. Go get some rest."

Bill nodded and bowed out of the office in a hurry, leaving Julian alone to stew in rage.

They both knew there was no chance of getting Strike out of that mansion. Julian had to bite his lip over the past few months as he watched Bill desperately try to win Strike's affection. Bill had the unconditional and blind loyalty of a puppy toward Strike, so it was no surprise for him to make such an outrageous offer.

Julian was also a step ahead, knowing Bill had cornered him with his proposal. If Strike actually escaped the mansion, she would immediately return to power and could override any decision implemented by Julian. And she would never approve of a missile strike on the mansion, even if it was confirmed empty of any Road Runners.

They deserve each other, Julian thought, trying to think of a way out of this virtual handcuffing of his plan.

He had the conversation recorded and could edit it to force the approval. To get to that stage, however, Bill needed to be completely out of the picture.

Julian leaned back and reflected on the difficult decision that now stood between him and his destiny as the Commander who killed Chris.

You can't stop this, Bill. There are too many moving parts, and this train has already left the station. Get off the tracks or else.

Julian tried to shake his head clear of evil thoughts, but they wouldn't leave. No, he didn't necessarily want to see Strike dead, but he also didn't want to see her alive. The Road Runners were in better hands now, under his guidance, and the population would see that soon enough.

"I just need to drop this bomb and end this war. Then they'll make statues of me and crown me as the best Commander ever." He looked at the office walls, dozens of portraits of past Commanders staring back at him with smug expressions, and years of failure hiding behind their eyes. "I can be the one. Someone has to be."

The pictures were in chronological order, leading up to Commander Strike, her portrait slightly larger than the rest to signify her current reign. In her picture, she had pursed lips, a cocked eyebrow, and long blond hair slung behind her shoulders. Her blue eyes pierced Julian, daring him to complete this side project he had been working on behind her back. She had to have known. Even though she was afraid to take chances, there was no denying her intelligence. She rose to power because of her mind and ability to communicate with people, traits that Julian needed to work on to add to his arsenal of talents as a strategist in the war against the Revolters.

Julian smiled and pulled open the desk drawer to retrieve a silver revolver. He spun the cylinder to ensure no bullets were loaded, cocked the hammer, and pointed it at Strike's portrait with a widening grin.

"We can't go on with you. I'm sorry. I know you didn't get us into this mess, but you'll never get us out of it. *I* have to do it."

He squeezed the trigger, a faint click leaving the revolver that trembled in his hand. Strike's portrait continued to stare at him, showing her disappointment with his sudden rise to corruption. Julian giggled, knowing tomorrow her portrait would be changed to a smaller version to make room for his own face. Tomorrow was the public ceremony where a big speech was expected, outlining his vision for the rest of the term. Julian had the unique opportunity to serve longer than the standard two-year term. Since he was succeeding Strike in her absence, he was technically finishing out her term, which had another year left. After that he could run for the following election and be solidified for another two years in power.

If he could get the bomb dropped within the next three months, his popularity would soar and easily carry him through the next election, leaving him to guide the Road Runners not only through the end of the war, but also the transition into peace that followed.

"I have to do it," he said again to Strike's portrait before loading the revolver and standing from the desk. "And there's not a damn thing you can do to stop me."

He cackled one final time before departing the office and turning down the hallway to Bill's office. The main floor had a handful of Road Runners scattered about at their desks, monitoring the screens, searching for a way to break Strike free. The majority were already sound asleep, snoring on the pull out beds underneath their desks.

The leadership team sometimes slept in their offices, but always tried to make it home at the end of the day. Bill's office waited three doors down, and if he was in there, Julian would try to talk him into going home. And if he wasn't there, Julian would head straight to his house for a nightcap.

He reached the door and rapped on it with a shaky fist. He'd never considered himself a nervous person, but with history looming on the other side of tomorrow, a pressure had bubbled up within himself that made it impossible to sit still.

No answer, so he knocked one more time for good measure. Julian checked behind to see if any of the other Road Runners were paying him any attention and was pleased to find they weren't.

He tried the door knob, and let himself into Bill's empty office. The computer screen splashed blue light across the office's back wall as the only source of light. The couch had not been turned into a bed and all the lights were turned off.

He went home.

Julian hadn't expected this to be so easy, knowing anything with Bill was always an uphill battle. The sight of the abandoned office created a fresh wave of nerves that fluttered from his toes to his throbbing temples. The revolver pulsed in his waistband like it had a life of its own.

Go to his house. The stars are aligned for all of your dreams to come true. Don't mess this up.

Julian nodded, stepping back into the hallway and gently closing the door to avoid any attention. Those who worked were too involved in their screens to see what was going on right in front of them. *Keep looking for Strike,* he thought. *You'll never get her out of that mansion.*

Julian retreated down the hall back to his new office. In case any wandering eyes had noticed him, he needed to put some time between his visit to Bill's office and his departure from the building to avoid any suspicion.

"Fifteen minutes," he said after closing his office door and pacing around the room. "Fifteen minutes and I'll go to Bill's house. Ask him if I can come in and talk a little more. He can't send me away; I'm the Commander."

No matter how many times he said it aloud, the ring of his new title never grew old, making him grin every time.

Stop stroking yourself and prepare for this meeting. You can't take that gun.

Julian stopped mid-step at this realization. If he planned to get away with murder, he had to think smarter than shooting Bill with a revolver that only a handful of people had access to, let alone knew about.

"Fuck," he barked. His plans were about to get messy, but his mind had already been made. He shuffled to the desk and frantically pulled open all of the drawers until he found a pair of gloves that belonged to Strike. He pulled them over his hands, stretching them to their limits as the stitching in the seams made cracking sounds.

"There," he said, examining his gloved hands under the lights. The technology in the future could identify a fingerprint within a matter of minutes, and if a highly ranked official of the Road Runners were to show up murdered, they would certainly send all evidence to the future to try and solve the case. "I think we're about set here, Commander Strike," he said to her portrait, patting it with the black gloves.

Julian closed all the desk drawers and arranged the papers on the desk in a neat pile, not wanting to leave a trace behind of his flustered presence. He tapped Strike's picture as he left the office, sure to turn off the lights and close the door silently before slipping out of the building into the night.

20

Chapter 20

Martin tugged at his crotch for the hundredth time as he sat in the passenger seat, Gerald driving him from the apartment to downtown Denver. Ralph had assured them the outfits in the suitcase were authentic for the times, but Martin wasn't sure if it was a prank or if men's testicles had shrunk in the last 40 years.

He wore faded jeans that leeched to his legs, waist, and groin, to go with a silky, shiny purple shirt that would surely glow under the city's bright lights at night. As if everything needed to be tighter, a belt fastened around his hips that matched his polished black shoes. Leather gloves covered his hands while a gray scarf wrapped around his neck to conceal his glowing skin.

I feel like an idiot, he thought.

Martin had rarely dressed up throughout his prior life, but understood the correct times and places to do so: weddings, funerals, rare nights out to fancy restaurants he couldn't afford. But for a casual stroll through the city, this seemed a bit over the top.

With the slums of their neighborhood far behind them, the van slowed as it approached the towering skyscrapers. Martin looked up at the handful of new buildings he didn't recognize, his stare working down to an electric fence standing twenty feet tall and wrapping around the perimeter of the city. The street narrowed to one lane that entered the city through a checkpoint of armed guards.

"What's this about?" Martin asked, no longer shocked by the things he saw.

"That is a 12,000 volt fence that will fry anyone who tries to go through on their own. You can no longer stroll into the big cities around the country. You have to go through the checkpoint and be cleared by the guards."

"What are they checking for?"

"Only that you look like you belong, or if you have official business in the city. I won't be able to get in because I'm black. Ralph is working on a city card for me but will need another day, so I'm planning on joining you tomorrow, at least in terms of getting in. We still can't be seen together or they'll take us both in for questioning."

"How does the city card get you in?"

"It's like a work visa. Says I have business in the city, likely as a cleaner, cook, or server at some fancy restaurant. Today, I'm gonna drop you off and you can go through the pedestrian entrance. You certainly look the part so you shouldn't run into any issues. Just walk through and start exploring. You'll see interactive maps throughout town, and you can also call a car to take you wherever you need."

"How long am I supposed to stay in there?"

Gerald swerved the van to the shoulder and turned on his emergency lights. "Meet right back here at nine. That gives you roughly five hours to get reacquainted with the city. Get a feel for what life is like and where things are. Tomorrow we'll focus more on a plan; hopefully Web will have something we can build off. Now get on out there, and enjoy. Remember, you're rich and belong – don't act any other way."

Martin nodded and patted Gerald on the shoulder before getting out of the van. The line of traffic went on for another quarter mile, but only a dozen or so people stood in line at the pedestrian entrance. He puffed out his chest, raised his shoulders, and walked to the line as if he had done it a hundred times before, jeans riding up his ass.

I belong here, he reminded himself as he approached the electric wall, a faint burning smell radiating from its warmth. By the time Martin reached the line, everyone in front of him had already made their way inside the city, leaving him to pass through the security checkpoint alone. Security towers stood over the entrance and were spaced as far as he could see, roughly 300 yards apart. They looked no different than prison towers, with floodlights and pacing, armed guards.

It was apparently a major issue regarding who was allowed into the city. *Why have guards if there's already an electric fence?* Martin wondered.

The guard at the checkpoint, dressed in full camouflage and toting an M4 carbine assault rifle, watched Martin approach, his eyes concealed behind thick sunglasses.

"Good afternoon," Martin said, unsure if he was supposed to stop or walk through like he belonged. He chose the latter with a shaky confidence, and was relieved when the guard gave him a quick nod.

That's it? No ID? No questions? I could be anyone.

Gerald had dropped him off on the east side of downtown,

where the state capitol stood in its usual location. Only something looked different as Martin passed through a small pedestrian tunnel and crossed to the other side of the fence. While it once had a golden dome, the capitol building was now made entirely of gold, blinding and difficult to look at as the setting sun glared off the exterior.

"Who the hell thought that was a good idea?" he muttered under his breath. The city entrance was nestled behind the rear of the capitol, and Martin strode down Colfax Avenue toward the front of the building and closer to the heart of downtown.

The sidewalks weren't crowded like he was used to for the middle of a workday, and there wasn't a single homeless person in sight. Civic Center Park, the space across from the capitol, was usually filled with the homeless, but only a few businessmen in suits sat on the park benches, talking on their cell phones.

Digital screens and billboards covered the exterior of many buildings, the capitol included, giving the city a feel similar to Times Square in New York with the constantly fluctuating advertisements for movies, sports, and clothing.

Martin continued along the sidewalk, reaching the front of the capitol from the lawn's furthest corner, and turned to look at the golden building. The American and state of Colorado flags both flapped in the breeze from a towering pole centered at the front entrance. A banner hung above the entrance's tall, golden pillars read: *KEEP COLORADO PURE.*

A group of students clearly on a field trip scattered across the lawn, some snapping pictures on their phones, others typing on handheld tablets as an instructor barked information about the building.

"In 2039, President Poe allocated a special budget to every

state to decorate their capitol buildings with as much gold as possible, as part of his Purity Now initiative. As a state, our redecoration was completed in early 2041; at the same time, the Wall of Perfection was installed and activated to ensure that only those of pure American heritage are allowed into the city."

Martin shook his head after listening to the tour guide, feeling instantly out of place. Gerald had mentioned minorities weren't allowed without a special type of identification, and Martin now realized that the "purity" spoken of meant nothing more than white skin and a bank account full of money. Only luxury vehicles lined the metered parking along the roads, every car shiny and polished as if they had just pulled off the dealership lot.

Martin continued away from the capitol, crossing Colfax and approaching the old *Denver Post* building that had been overtaken by a new media outlet called *Revolutionary News Group*. The moving billboard on the structure flashed the words: *YOUR ONLY SOURCE FOR THE TRUTH!*

More people strolled down the sidewalks, mostly men in expensive suits, flashy watches, and polished briefcases dangling at their sides. Martin didn't see any women, but thought nothing of it at the time. Traffic hummed in the background, until a familiar tune blared out of speakers that seemed to be set up on every street corner. A trumpet blasted the opening notes of the Star-Spangled Banner as all of the video screens showed waving American flags.

Everyone who had been walking and minding their business stopped where they were and placed their right hand over their heart. Martin followed suit, not wanting to stick out as the only person not honoring the national anthem.

A woman's voice sang the words, high-pitched and perfect, as if it had been remastered in a music studio. She held the final note for a solid ten seconds as the trumpets faded and a male voiceover spoke to changing images on the screens.

"America," the baritone voice said. "We've come a long way from a once ugly history." The video flashed through images of Martin Luther King Jr., an American flag on fire in the street, and former athletes kneeling. "We've come a long way from the days of hatred when people thought it was okay to disrespect our country."

The screens changed to show a ghastly looking man, black hair slicked to the side, face powdered with too much makeup. He had a crooked smile in the image as he held a skinny thumb up.

"Thanks to the Revolution, we've been blessed with brilliant leaders like President Poe, who have kept America pure, and cleansed our blessed country of the hatred that almost took over God's land."

The still images gave way to video footage of this same man, who Martin presumed to be President Poe. In the video, he wore a black suit with a red tie, an American flag pin on one lapel, and a crucifix on the other. "You won't find a better Christian than me to lead our country back to pureness. Trust me." Poe spoke in a stern voice with a slight rasp underneath his words. "Trust in me is trust in a safe America. Never again will we have to fear our enemies, both domestic and international."

Martin watched the video that reminded him of a campaign commercial with the cheesy images and sound bites, and a wide-grinning President Poe giving a thumbs-up to the camera. The video cut to a live shot of President Poe standing at a podium in front of the White House. His lips pursed together as he winked to the camera before speaking.

"Good evening, citizens of America. Our daily briefing today will be short. As for yesterday's stats, nine people tried to sneak into our country illegally. All nine were shot dead."

The small crowds that had gathered on the sidewalks cheered and howled in excitement, pumping their fists into the air.

"Seventeen Road Runners were captured and sent immediately to the execution chamber for a most torturous end to their lives."

The mention of Road Runners sent an immediate chill down Martin's back, and he looked around suspiciously to ensure no one had an eye on him. The crowd again ruptured in applause at the mention of dead Road Runners.

"Lastly, the country of France is considering war with us. They think we can't take care of ourselves. Their president called me a power-hungry fool." The crowd booed. "Do you know what I did when he called me that? I hung up on that croissant-loving son-of-a-bitch, and increased our budget for more nuclear bombs. Nobody threatens war on God's country and gets away with it." President Poe stared directly into the camera, into the soul of America. "So if you still want to declare war on America, be ready for your country to turn into a hot pile of French fries!"

The crowd jumped and screamed. "Tell 'em, Poe," a man nearby shouted. "Nobody fucks with America!"

Poe hesitated, as if he knew the masses in the streets were cheering. "I want to thank you fine citizens, as I do every day, for giving me this chance to lead our country. Nobody loves America more than me. You can try, but I simply have more love to give. If I have to get in a cage and fight President French Fry, then that's exactly what I'll do, and you know I'll give him a good ol' American ass whooping."

More howling and fist pumping.

"Let this serve as a reminder that if anyone ever badmouths America, you have the right to take matters into your own hands. I can't be everywhere at once, so I have to rely on you, fine citizens, to keep our country pure. Now, I want you all to enjoy your evening, eat a nice dinner, and get a good night's sleep. Tomorrow is a new day with new opportunities to keep America pure. Our work is never done, but that's why we stay in business. I'll see you all tomorrow. God bless you, and God bless the United States of America."

The crowds gave one more round of applause before promptly returning to their days.

Martin continued down the sidewalk—more leery and constantly looking over his shoulder—as he approached 16th Street Mall. He studied everyone he passed by, half expecting them to pull out a gun and shoot him simply because he was a Road Runner. But no one so much as looked in his direction.

The world as he knew it was gone, replaced by a totalitarian society where everyone likely lived in fear of one thing or another. Martin felt it walking down the street, the screams of the past radiating from the very concrete he walked on. An invisible hand was present above each and every person, providing both a sense of safety and a threatening tension to remain a loyal citizen. Or else.

For the first time he could ever recall, Martin felt terrified for his life.

I need to get this medicine and leave.

21

Chapter 21

Julian crouched behind a bush along the sidewalk, his heart drumming in his ears. eHe'd been to Bill's house a half dozen times before for dinner, typically with Commander Strike joining them. A black iron fence surrounded the property, enclosing a manicured front lawn split by an S-curve walkway to the front door. He stepped out from the bush, studying the house concealed by darkness. Inside Bill was lying peacefully in bed, dreaming about rescuing Strike and becoming an instant hero in the world of Road Runners. Julian still had no idea what to do once inside. *Do I try to break in and kill him in his sleep? Should I knock on the front door and have him let me in? I can always blackmail him with his recorded voice.* Julian shook his head, knowing Bill wouldn't fall for such a trap.

Even in the cold Alaska night, his palms turned slick with a nervous sweat underneath his gloves. He chose the latter option for entering the home, and checked over his shoulders for the hundredth time to ensure no wandering eyes were on him. It was almost midnight in the quiet, family neighborhood, leaving no one to mind him.

The front door seemed to scoot back with every step Julian took up the walkway, never seeming within reach until he actually pushed the doorbell with a shaky finger. The urge to vomit suddenly crept into his throat as he took a step back and waited for the door to open.

Nothing happened after a minute of waiting, prompting Julian to ring the doorbell a second time. *Wake up, old man.*

The waiting curbed his nerves to a dull, distant tremble, but they immediately returned when the sound of the door's lock rattled in front of him. The door swung open to more darkness, the tip of a long rifle extending out to Julian's face.

"God dammit, Bill!" he shouted. "Put that thing down, are you crazy?"

"Julian?" Bill's voice asked from inside. The rifle vanished and was replaced by a groggy-eyed Bill, gray hair splayed in every direction like someone had just run a rubber balloon over his head. "Are *you* crazy? Why are you ringing my doorbell in the middle of the night? You know how paranoid I am."

"I know, I'm sorry. I should've called first, but my head has been so flustered these last couple days. Can I come in?"

Bill sighed and turned on the inside light, revealing the living room behind him. "Come in," he mumbled, clearly wanting nothing more than returning to the deep sleep he had been so rudely awakened from.

"Thank you. I'm sorry for intruding on your night like this, but I know if we don't talk, I might never sleep again."

"Have a seat on the couch."

Julian stepped into the living room. Bill was a simple man with no wall decor or anything that showed signs of life. His living room consisted of the lone couch that faced the mounted flat screen TV on the wall. A loaded bookshelf collected dust in the back corner as the only other item in the living room. The house could've been staged for real estate showings as Bill kept it clean and spotless of any clutter.

"Can I get you a drink?" Bill asked, clearing his throat of his deep sleep.

"I'm okay, thank you."

"Well then, what can I do for you that couldn't wait until the morning?" Bill spoke with as much resentment as he could muster, but Julian was too nervous to notice.

"I feel like we're not seeing eye to eye right now, and I want to make sure we're on the same page. We have to be if we're expected to lead the Road Runners, and that's the part I feel you're not understanding."

"What part?"

"Leading. I may be the Commander now, but that means you're my lieutenant. I'm just as concerned about getting Strike back as you, but it's also now our responsibility to lead the Road Runners. We can't just leave our millions of members to run on autopilot, especially in a time like this."

"You haven't shown any effort to get Strike back. Someone needs to."

"Bill, we have entire teams dedicated to rescuing her. Eyes are on Chris's house around the clock, and meetings are constantly taking place to devise a plan to get her out of there. And she hasn't even arrived there yet. *You* need to trust what we have in place and help me lead the Road Runners through whatever comes next."

Bill nodded, his eyes gradually clearing of the fog from his snooze. "I see your point, but I feel like I owe it to Strike. After everything she's done for me, I'd feel guilty if I kicked back and waited for someone else to rescue her. I have to be involved."

"I know she saved you, and you certainly do owe her your life, but Bill, you can influence a lot from your new position of power. You can *lead* these groups working on her rescue and implement whatever strategy you want. You have my full blessing."

If I can get him to commit to the bomb right now, I won't need to get rid of him, Julian thought, a confident smirk spreading over his face.

"I know that, but it still seems wrong to not be the one out there physically doing something. I can't make myself sit still while all of this is going on."

"You can have it both ways. You can implement the strategy from the top, and join the troops out in the field. You'll be like a modern-day George Washington."

Bill chuckled a hoarse sound that could only come from a man in his seventies. "That's a generous offer, Julian, but I know what this is all about. You want me to approve that bomb and are offering me—*bribing* me—into doing it."

Julian's smile snapped into pursed lips, a flash of rage bursting through his head. "Bill, I'm not bribing you. I'm making you an offer where we can both get what we want."

"Except what you want puts Commander Strike at an incredibly high risk. There are too many unknowns."

Julian fought the urge to shout, and kept his most professional face and composure. "Unknowns like what? This has been researched through and through."

"We can't drop a bomb on the mansion if Commander Strike is inside. That's essentially assassinating our own leader."

I'm your goddamn leader, Julian thought, hot anger tickling every nerve in his body. He thought Bill had smirked at him after the snide comment, but couldn't confirm if it was real or in his head. "She'll be in the basement," he replied in his calmest voice.

"We don't know that for sure. It's not like she's some regular Road Runner being held hostage; she's our leader, and Chris knows that. For all we know, she'll be held in a cage in his office. Besides, there has never been a study done at the mansion to know what effects a bomb would have. What if it blows up the basement with it?"

This was always a hot topic for the team who studied the mansion and spent many hours trying to find a way inside without putting lives at risk. The fact that they couldn't get close enough to the mansion without the risk of a bullet in the head spoke volumes to how effective their investigation had gone. The discussion of a bomb had come up before, after it was learned that fifty Road Runners were trapped within the house, and it wasn't until Martin had shared his knowledge of the basement's existence that the topic was revisited. The bombs the Road Runners had in storage would surely destroy the mansion, but their impact to the ground beneath it remained in doubt. Commander Strike refused to take the risk of dropping the bombs if it had a chance of killing the fifty hostages. Multiple simulations were run and bombs were dropped on replica structures to gauge an explosion's impact, but they simply lacked the knowledge of what the inside of the mansion was made of. Each material they tested returned various results, leaving them back at square one.

"The basement won't blow up. Besides, what's the alternative plan to get her out of that house? Are you going to knock on the steel barricade and ask nicely? He's never going to hand her over."

"We'll negotiate. And thank you for bringing up the barricade. Add that to the list of reasons we can't drop a bomb. What if the steel deflects it and it bounces back to us? Then what?"

"It's a *bomb*, Bill. It explodes on impact. I'm beginning to think there's nothing I can say to convince you."

"No shit. That's why I left the office tonight. Not only was I tired, I knew you'd be pressing this matter until four in the morning. And here we are. I'm not approving a bomb, Julian, so I suggest you move on to a different plan or meet the terms we discussed earlier."

"This is why you'll never be Commander." Julian spoke in a relaxed voice, no longer enraged by Bill's stubbornness, but rather clear-headed as he knew what had to be done next.

"Don't get all high and mighty. This new power has gone straight to your head. I used to think you were just young and arrogant, but now you're nothing but an asshole. It's a good thing we only have two-year terms, or you'd run us into the ground like Chris did with the Revolters."

"I'm sorry you feel that way, Bill. I *am* the Commander now, and I'm aware of my new role, that's all. I think leaders are misunderstood because they have to make the decisions that no one else will. We have to sleep at night with the weight of the world pressing down on us like an invisible slab of concrete on our chest. When's the last time you couldn't fall asleep because of a decision you had to make?"

"Every single night," Bill snapped. "Unlike you, I stay up every night worried about our leader and what our future looks like because of her kidnapping."

Julian stood from the couch. "I need to use your restroom."

The sudden change in subject caught Bill off guard as his jaw hung temporarily open. He clearly had more to say and was ready to explode, but Julian asking to leave the room made his mouth snap shut and left a dazed confusion splattered across his face.

"Be my guest," Bill said, defeated. He slouched into the nearby recliner and fidgeted with nervous fingers.

Julian stepped into the dark hallway, turning to Bill before disappearing. "Oh, and I do worry about Strike and our future, but I have a job to do now because of this mess. I wish you'd hurry up and realize that you do too, and help me make sure our future stays on track."

He left the living room without another word, grinning because he knew he just dropped a bomb of guilt on his old friend and mentor. It really was a shame how matters had to end for Bill, but the old man refused to give any support for the most obvious next phase of rescuing Strike *and* ending Chris.

Julian entered the bathroom and flicked on the light switch, closing and locking the door behind him. The mixture of nerves and anger caused a slight quiver in his hands, but he rummaged through the drawers and cabinets with intense concentration. There had to be something he could use to end Bill, and he didn't care how messy it ended up being. Razor blades were nowhere obvious, so Julian scoured through the mountain of toiletries piled on the sink counter.

Jesus Christ, he thought when he couldn't find anything sharper than a toothbrush. He paced around the bathroom, racking his brain for a new option. He could try to sneak into the kitchen, but that left him exposed as he didn't fully know his way around the house in the dark. Bill might also hear him heading the wrong way and come to investigate before he could find a knife.

He sat on the closed toilet and planted his face into his palms.

Trying the kitchen might be his best chance, so he stood and ran through the mental map of the house, imagining how many steps it was to the kitchen through the dark hallway.

Does the floor creak? He couldn't recall, but these older hardwood floors likely had some noisy spots when stepped on.

He stepped to the door, and with his gloved hand on the knob, turned around one more time to make sure he didn't miss anything. His eyes scanned the room and settled back on the toilet.

"That's it," he whispered. "Easy."

Julian returned to the toilet, flushed it, pulled off the heavy porcelain lid from the tank, and reworked the chain that connected to the rubber flapper at the bottom so that it tightened to the point of not closing, forcing the water to run constantly. He had placed the tank lid on the sink countertop, and opened the door to shout down the hallway.

"Bill! We might have a small problem in here."

Julian returned to the toilet to give the appearance that he was studying inside the tank, even jiggling the handle for good measure.

"What's the matter?" Bill asked from behind.

Julian turned, fake worry as his expression. "I don't know. I took a leak and flushed, but the water won't stop running. I don't know too much about toilets."

"Let me take a look," Bill said confidently and approached as Julian stepped aside, toward the sink. He leaned over the tank, his gray hair exposed as a wide-open target.

The excitement bubbled up within Julian, who couldn't recall a time where he had ever felt so nervous and giddy in unison. Bill started whistling as he examined the toilet, and Julian knew he had a handful of seconds to take advantage of the old man with his back turned.

He tiptoed to his left, grabbing the tank lid as gently as possible, the inevitable sound of its clunky porcelain washed out by the toilet's running water. He held the lid vertically from the middle, hands fixed as if he were reading a thick, hardcover book, and raised it above his head, adrenaline drowning his veins, heart bulging into his throat.

"It looks like the chain got tangled and isn't letting it close," Bill said into the tank, oblivious to the world behind him.

"Is that so?" Julian replied, damn near laughing as he spoke.

You're doing this for the betterment of the Road Runners, not because you're a monster, he reminded himself, as if murder could be actually be justified.

His eyes throbbed as he tightened his grip and swung the lid down with all of his body's force behind it. The porcelain met Bill's skull with a *THUNK!* sound, sending the old man's face briefly into the tank before his body collapsed to the floor in a heavy thud, knees hitting the ground before falling flat on his back to stare lifelessly at the ceiling.

Julian had struck him as square as a baseball bat connecting on a crisp home run swing, and he hoped the one hit was all it took. If the porcelain didn't break, then surely the skull had. Julian grinned at the sight of blood pooling behind Bill's head, and squatted for a closer look.

Bill's blue eyes remained open as his jaw hung, and Julian saw what he believed was a look of relief on his face. If you added up all the time Bill had spent traveling through time, he had likely been living for over 500 years. Perhaps Julian did him a favor by finally letting him get a deep sleep. Perhaps that was just the expression a dead person made after a surprise end to their life.

Julian closed Bill's eyes with his gloved hand and propped up his jaw to make him look somewhat peaceful. The blood continued to expand into an imperfect circle around Bill's head.

If he's not dead yet, he will be soon. That's too much blood to lose from your head, Julian thought, smirking.

"Sorry, old friend," he said to the body, standing back up. "This really was my last resort. You forced my hand, but I had to do what's right for the Road Runners. Now we can end this war, and I'll even dedicate it in your honor. Rest easy."

Julian turned and left the bathroom, the toilet's water still running, as it would until someone showed up to find the mess. He wanted to go back to the office and start preparing for the bombs, but had to wait. An investigation would soon be underway to solve Bill's death, and cameras at the office would show what time Julian had left and returned. He would already have questions to answer for leaving the office before the timeframe of Bill's death.

He left the house as quietly as he had arrived, whistling the same tune Bill had while examining the toilet, knowing a new fate waited ahead to change the course of this godawful war once and for all.

22

Chapter 22

Martin continued exploring the city, unable to shake what he had just witnessed from the live broadcast of President Poe. In his brief speech, Poe revealed his true colors and made it clear how the country had progressed to where it was today. If he had time, Martin would try to visit the library—if such thing still existed—and read up on this new president.

For now, though, he did as Gerald had instructed and explored downtown, avoiding eye contact with everyone he walked by, keeping his head down to blend in with the rest of society. Even the classy businessmen, dressed in their fine suits, had cheered and whistled at the nonsensical video that halted the middle of the day.

The buzz from the daily presidential address had died down and people continued their day as normal, businessmen on their cell phones, briefcases swinging in their grip as they skittered down the sidewalks. There wasn't a single homeless person on 16th Street Mall, an anomaly as far as Martin was concerned. The sidewalks were clean and even had a fresh smell oozing from the cracks, instead of the usual stench of piss and body odor he was accustomed to.

Martin spent the next hour walking up and down the mall, making mental notes of all the new stores and restaurants, none of which would provide any help on their mission. The hospital was another ten-minute walk south of downtown from his starting point at the capitol, and he planned to stroll by there after the sun went down. Knowing how all of the population felt about Road Runners, he decided it best to hide until the sun went down and move in the darkness.

He stepped into the next bar he approached, a two-level building with chatter pouring from the rooftop and music booming inside. The bar was called Viewpoint Pub, and inside looked no different from any bar Martin had ever been: neon lights in the windows, televisions showing sports, groups of coworkers taking rounds of shots together, and men hitting on women.

Women! He had passed a couple during his walk, but there were at least five within the bar, not counting the trio who pranced around in tight white shirts and shorts, balancing trays of drinks.

Martin worked his way through the bar, squeezing through rows of tables until he found a table for two in the back corner. He plopped down and immediately lifted the menu in front of his face, his eyes peering over the top to see if anyone was watching him.

A waitress skinny as a twig greeted Martin, her black ponytail swaying behind her head as she grinned pearly teeth. "Good evening, sir, my name is Cecilia. Is there something I can get started for you?"

Martin hesitated lowering his menu, but decided the room was dim enough and this young lady was not likely a headhunter for the Revolters. "I'll take a glass of scotch and a burger."

"Certainly, I'll bring those right out." Cecilia flashed one more smile before turning away, a nearby table of five men in suits watching her every step, howling like horny dogs after she disappeared into the back.

From the corner Martin could see the entire bar. He leaned back in his seat, trying to appear relaxed and blend in. So far no one had paid him any attention and he intended to keep it that way.

There were a couple others sitting alone, but they seemed content on their cell phones, something Martin wished he had to kill some time. Instead, he gazed at the nearest TV and watched football analysts discuss the week's upcoming games.

Over the next ten minutes, the bar filled with downtown workers escaping the office for the day. Cecilia brought him his drink and burger simultaneously, leaving him to eat as the noise level rose to the typical, blurred chaos common in bars and restaurants.

"Excuse me, sir," a man in a suit said, approaching Martin's table. "Can we borrow this chair?" The man placed a hand on the chair across from Martin.

"It's all yours." Martin's hand immediately fell to his waistband where his instincts thought a gun should have been, but remembered Gerald insisted he not carry one in the city.

"Thank you, have a good day," the man said with a quick smile before returning to a nearby table with the chair in hand.

Martin scarfed his burger while savoring every sip of the scotch, an incredibly smooth blend with a smoky flavor and subtle taste of the barrel. It was comforting to know that scotch improved even more in the future.

He ordered another round, having at least another 90 minutes before the sun would start setting. His life had turned into a never-ending cycle of chaos once he stepped into 1919 with Sonya, and he couldn't remember the last time he sat in a bar drinking scotch by himself, a pastime he enjoyed more than life. The alcohol left its tingling sensation from his throat all the way down to his stomach in a pit of delightful warmth. Martin's fingertips and lips turned numb halfway through the second drink, and that's when he knew he had the perfect buzz.

The man in the suit returned with the chair twenty minutes later as his group of friends all stood up to leave. "Are you having a good evening, sir?" he asked.

Martin had avoided eye contact during their first encounter, but looked at the man this time. He had wavy brown hair, green eyes, and a strong jaw bone. He was built much like Martin's new chiseled physique, but was at least 20 years younger.

"I am, thank you," Martin responded curtly, not wanting to leave the door open for a long conversation.

The man sat in the chair, planted his elbows on the table, and leaned within a foot of Martin's face as if he wanted to kiss him. "You're not from here, are you?" he whispered loud enough to be heard over the music that clashed with the chatter in symphony.

Martin immediately locked eyes with the man, his pulse jumping at least 30 extra beats.

"I was born and raised in Denver," he replied casually, focused on keeping his voice steady and confident.

"That's not what I mean, and you know it. Tell me what year you're from." The man returned his own confidence as he peered in Martin, demanding the truth.

"Are you feeling okay, young man?" Martin asked. "It's

2064, in case you've forgotten."

"What year were you born?"

Martin opened his lips to respond, but let his jaw hang. The young bastard caught him red-handed. Martin had never bothered to calculate what his year of birth should have been to go along with his lie.

"I knew it," the man said, unfazed. "Who sent you? Are you here on official Road Runner business?"

"What's a Road Runner?" Martin had no choice but to resort to the childish tactic of playing dumb. *Very* dumb, in this case.

"Cut the shit. We've heard rumors that there would be a few Road Runners around town this week." The young man inched even closer, the stench of booze seeping from his lips as he whispered in a practically inaudible voice. "I'm a Road Runner. You can trust me."

Martin wanted to believe the kid, but had no idea who to trust. Could the Revolters have been following him all along, inching him on like a donkey chasing a carrot? He looked down his arms, ensuring they had been properly covered up to hide his glowing skin.

"How did you know?" Martin asked, defeated and unable to look the man in the eyes.

"We can tell," the man replied. "A few of us have been undercover long enough to know when someone looks out of place."

"Can the Revolters tell?"

The man looked around the bar to be sure no one was looking at them suspiciously. "Not in a place like this. Maybe in a government building or somewhere with heavy security, but just around town, you'll blend in fine. I followed you from outside, asked my group of coworkers if they wanted to stop in here for a quick drink once I saw you come in. The moment I saw your reaction for the National Anthem, I knew you weren't from here. It's an honest mistake for anyone not from this time—Revolter or Road Runner— but the way you kept looking over your shoulder told me all I needed. So where are you from, and who are you here with?"

Martin had learned after mingling with plenty of Road Runners that when asked where you're from actually meant *when* you are from.

"I'm from 2019, sent here by Commander Strike with a group of three others. Who are you here with?"

The man nodded. "Straight from the Commander, huh? Impressive. I'm not here with anyone. I was born in 2040, right in the middle of this shit turning for the worse. My family stayed in hiding to survive, and raised me to be a Road Runner at heart, but a Revolter by all outer appearances. There's a lot of us like this, raised to survive. None of us have ever been to the fancy Road Runner headquarters. The only time we leave the city is to board a plane and fly to another wealthy city across the country."

"So you haven't seen your family since you left them?"

"That's right," the man nodded, staring distantly into the table. "It's impossible for us to know what's going on with the organization, all we have as resources are whatever the Revolters want to give us—which is never news about the Road Runners, unless one is getting murdered."

"Do the Road Runners even know about you guys?"

"They know we exist, but I don't think they realize how many of us there are. I wouldn't say we could overthrow the local government, but we would put up a fight. The Revolters are too consumed with themselves to ever know what's actually going on."

"What's your name?" Martin asked, the question itching since the man sat down and started accusing him of being a Road Runner.

"I'm so sorry, it's an instinct to not give my name. I'm Marcus."

"Pleasure to meet you, I'm Martin."

Martin didn't know what protocol was in 2064 and waited to see if Marcus stuck out a hand to shake, which he never did.

"I really should be going, though, Martin," Marcus said, standing from the table. "I've had a long day, but wanted to make sure I said hi. It's not every day we get to meet someone from the outside."

"It was a pleasure," Martin replied. "I hope to see you around again."

"Don't count on it. We have strict rules about mingling with anyone in public. I really shouldn't have come over here today, but to hell with rules, right? You take care of yourself, Martin, and stay strong."

Marcus turned and vanished through the bar with a rapid grace.

Martin watched as the young man weaved through the final tables, then his heart froze when his eyes caught something he thought they'd never see again.

Sitting alone at a table near the front door, facing Martin's direction, was Sonya.

23

Chapter 23

The room was illuminated by nothing more than a lone lamp tucked away in the far corner. The damp, murky smell of a basement filled Strike's nose as she woke up, all four limbs handcuffed to the chair in which she sat. She tugged with her legs to find they only had two inches of range. She flexed her arms and yanked, a piercing pain shooting up from her right forearm to her neck.

A white bandage was wrapped around her forearm, a small dot of blood appearing in the middle like the Japan flag. She stared at it, longing to touch it, but unable to soothe the pain that throbbed beneath. The pain came from where her tracking device had been, and she knew they had removed it.

"Good morning, Ms. Strike," Chris's voice called out, calm and steady. "We thought you were never going to wake up."

Strike felt the crazy old man behind her, and made a conscious effort to stay calm. Part of being elected to office was taking an intense training course on staying calm in the most strenuous of circumstances, including torture, which she suspected might be around the corner. She focused on maintaining her heart rate and breathing, taking long, calculated breaths and exhaling steadily.

"I will say this, Ms. Strike," Chris continued. "Your people love you. You should see the hell they're raising to find you. We dropped your tracking device in the middle of a field in Idaho, and a search crew arrived there within ten minutes. It was quite entertaining watching them flock like birds to a tiny piece of bread."

Strike kept her focus on her breathing while Chris spewed his nonsense.

"I've been dreaming about this day for a long time. The Commander of the Road Runners is in my house. I never knew which Commander it would be—you guys rotate out so quickly—but I knew sooner or later this time would come."

His footsteps whispered across the ground, approaching Strike until he stood in front of her, crouched down with his evil grin in front of her face. She'd never been this close to a Revolter.

"One of two things is going to happen today," Chris continued. "You're either going to surrender and allow the Revolution to claim its righteous victory, or we're going to force you to tell us all of your dirty secrets about the Road Runners. I suspect there's zero chance of you surrendering, so I'll let you know that option number two is not going to be very fun for you." Chris held his grin, stale breath seeping from his lips. "It's only a matter of time before your people come knocking on my front door demanding you back. Anyone who steps foot on my property will be shot dead, so I suggest you talk fast. And if you do decide to give us all of the information, you'll be free to go, but I can't say how well you'll be able to move."

Two men chuckled somewhere in the background.

"So what will it be, Commander?"

"I'll never surrender to you," she replied quickly and confidently, her faith waning. How the hell was she supposed to stay calm and talk her way out of *this*? She was strapped to a chair with no way out, and who knows what kind of torture on the way.

Focus away from the pain. Torturers never want to kill you; they need your information. Trust that you can buy the time necessary to be rescued.

She had never been one to rely on others, but had no choice. She prayed that Bill and Julian hadn't given up hope yet and would come busting through the door to save the day.

"Let's begin, shall we?" Chris said, nodding to someone in the corner. A bright light flashed like a strobe, reminding Strike of going through haunted houses as a teenager during Halloween season. Strobe lights were known to heighten fear, but since she knew this, she managed to block out the constant flashing.

"Tell me, Commander, where is your main headquarters?"

Strike had a tough decision to make. She could either feed him answers of things he should already know, to show cooperation, or she could play difficult and let the torture begin.

"You know where our headquarters are."

"I just want to know you'll work with me, Ms. Strike. Please tell me where your headquarters are." Chris spoke calmly.

"Down the street."

"Underneath that little shack? That's your *main* headquarters?" Chris threw his head back and laughed. "Why not your lavish New York office? Or Miami? Those places look like fun."

"Our headquarters is wherever makes sense, and right now it's keeping an eye on you here." Strike spoke with disgust dripping from every word.

"How nice of you people. Tell me, Ms. Strike, who's in charge or your little group while you're . . . occupied?"

Strike shrugged her shoulders immediately. "How would I know? I've been here with you."

"Please. Don't act like you don't have a system in place in case the Commander goes missing. You people have systems for everything."

"I'm sure there is, but I don't know the system for this; it's never been used before."

"Tell me right now who's in charge in your absence," Chris snapped like a scolding parent.

Stay strong, Strike reminded herself, and shrugged again.

Chris grinned and turned his face toward the corner, nodding to someone hiding in the darkness. Footsteps approached as Chris reached out to grab a pair of pliers. "Thank you," he said to the figure that was nothing but a dark blob from Strike's view.

"Pliers," Chris said, admiring the tool. "A universal tool of sorts. I can break toes, remove fingernails, even play dentist and take out some teeth." He stroked the pliers with a steady thumb as his grin grew wider. "So tell me, Ms. Strike, who's in charge of the Road Runners?"

It was a simple question, but telling him could put the entire organization in grave danger. Should Julian go missing, Bill would take control, but there was no one beyond Bill in the line of succession. Chris could play this game with the Road Runners until there was no one left to lead them.

"I told you I don't know."

"Very well, Commander," Chris said, reaching toward Strike's left hand with the pliers open. "Let's start at the pinky and work our way up."

The cool metal clasped around her pinky finger, right on her middle knuckle. Chris wiggled the pliers to make sure he had a good grip, and then twisted the finger backwards toward her wrist.

Strike clenched her jaw shut as the tendons stretched and popped, sparking an explosive pain that erupted all the way up to her shoulder. Tears welled in her eyes, but she managed to show no emotion aside from a subtle grunt through clenched teeth, choking down the urge to gag.

"Tell me who is in charge," Chris said calmly, moving the pliers to her ring finger.

She didn't respond, and Chris repeated the action. This time she couldn't help but shriek as her arm turned completely numb. She looked to her hand to see two fingers going the wrong direction while the others remained in place.

"Now, Ms. Strike, I already told you someone from your group handed you over. They came right up to my front door and told me what city you were in, what hotel you were staying at, and how to get around your guards."

"I don't believe you," Strike uttered, her head dizzy. She thought she could withstand more broken fingers if it came to it, as her entire hand was numb with adrenaline.

"I didn't believe it, either, but that's what happened. How else could I have gotten you here?"

"You're full of shit."

"It was a younger man. He kept a disguise so I can't tell you at all what he looked like. I don't suppose it's a young man who is now leading the Road Runners? Surely a Road Runner would never do such a thing just to get into a position of power." Chris howled with laughter.

"We wouldn't ever do that."

"Funny, that's what he said, too. But he also said you're too much of a stickler for the rules, that it holds you back from being a good leader. This young man questioned all of your decisions and came to the conclusion that he had to have you removed from office to further the Road Runner agenda. Now, I'm not as dumb as I look, but even I know the Road Runners' agenda is to kill me. That said, it's in your best interest to tell me who is in charge over there, because there are strict orders in place for your death should I get killed."

Strike paused, the pain in her fingers and arm constant, seemingly permanent. "I thought you can't die. You sound worried, Chris . . . is everything okay?" She managed a grin through the pain.

Chris responded with a stern face before nodding to his assistant in the darkness. The footsteps shuffled around as Chris reached out for a box with wires flowing from it. He quietly untangled the wires and pressed the adhesive ends of them onto Strike's flesh, scattering them across her arms, chest, and head.

"I'm done with the games, Ms. Strike," he said. "In my hands is a control panel that decides how many volts of electricity I want to send through your body. Let's give it a test run, shall we?"

She tried jerking her body out of it, but it was a waste of energy as her wiggle room remained within a couple inches.

Chris turned a dial, causing the machine to hum as he raised it in the air like a teasing child. His thumb settled over a red button the size of a half-dollar coin. He smiled like a lunatic, and then pushed the button.

Strike jolted, her every limb thrusting into the restraints for a quick second as the stinging shock hit her all at once. The sensation reminded her of the time she had stuck a finger in the outlet as a child, the emotional shock more dominant than the physical one sparked by electricity. It was a morbid feeling to get electrocuted, as a quick realization forms around the fragility of life.

"That was the lowest setting," Chris said grimly. "Shall I crank it up a notch?"

"You're a chickenshit," Strike replied, her mental stability wavering. She could handle most pain, like the broken fingers, but when electricity flowed, it left her body a seizing mess.

"Just tell me who is leading the Road Runners. Is this even worth your suffering? You know I'll find out who it is eventually. Why not just make this easy on both of us?"

"Go fuck yourself," she snapped, proud she could still muster the energy to push back against his demands.

"Okay, very well." Chris turned the dial again and held down the button.

The higher voltage created a burning sensation as Strike's body tensed from head to toe. It immediately felt like she was flexing every single muscle in unison as her head jerked backwards, thudding against the chair. Chris might have only held the button down for three seconds, but she would never know for sure, as it felt like an entire ten minutes.

Chris cackled when he released the button, even grabbing his stomach to hold in his guts from spilling out. "Oh, Commander, this is more fun than I thought." He walked circles in place, having virtually no slack from the wires connected to his console, and started conversing with himself. "Can I know who's leading the Road Runners? No? Okay!"

He pushed the button, waving the console in the air like a baton and dancing in front of Strike as he shrieked with laughter. Whoever hid in the shadows joined the chorus as electricity pulsed through Strike's body, leaving her stiff and motionless in the chair.

24

Chapter 24

The sunlight didn't seep through the windows as it normally did in the mornings. The sky remained gray, clouds pregnant with enough rain to downpour well into the afternoon. Julian still sprouted out of bed at eight o'clock, knowing a long and emotional day awaited.

He had arrived home shortly before one in the morning and popped a couple of sleeping pills, as he knew he wouldn't be able to drift away on his own. He felt guilty, but also accomplished and proud. The Road Runners were now free from their ultra-conservative ways and could proceed with a dramatic move to end the war.

"It's a great day to become an international hero," he said to his mirror as he prepared for the day. Everything would change after the realization of Bill's death. Currently, all of the security detail that followed the Commander was still focused on Strike, working around the clock to find a way to break her free from the mansion. They had offered their services to protect Julian right away, but he insisted that they resolve the Strike matter before making any changes. Once they discovered Bill had been murdered, Julian would no longer have a say in the matter, as the security team would have no choice but to follow and protect him.

It didn't matter to him at this point. He had Bill's recorded voice authorizing the bombs, and no Bill to deny it. It would take a few hours for the decision to be agreed upon by the Council, but he fully expected to see fireworks before dinner.

Julian lived in the city of Barrow, a quick five-minute drive to their secret entrance in the middle of nowhere. When he arrived, he jumped out of the car and rushed to the elevator. He entered the office and no one paid him any attention, an immediate good sign that the terrible news had yet to break about Bill, but concerning that his tracking device had not set off an alarm when he died.

He did die, right? Julian asked himself, remembering Bill had definitely stopped breathing. But what if he started breathing again after he left? That would be catastrophic if Bill somehow survived and remembered who had clocked him over the head with a slab of porcelain. Julian would immediately be put on trial and risk ex-communication from the organization.

He proceeded to his new office and entered to find a security team rummaging through the desk drawers. "What the hell's going on?"

A large man of at least six-and-a-half feet tall, with tattooed arms as big as his legs, crossed the office to meet Julian.

"Commander, I'm Garrett Anderson, the head of Protection in Europe," he said in a crisp British accent. "Your team called me in overnight. There's been a crisis, and they are still working on Commander Strike."

"Crisis? What kind of crisis?"

"I'm afraid Bill has been murdered."

Garrett paused. Julian had to make a conscious effort to react as a normal person would, so he moved a hand to his open mouth in shock.

"I was just talking with Bill last night, right in this office. Why wasn't I notified immediately?"

Garrett raised an open hand, fingers the size of bananas. "I'm afraid you're a suspect, since we believe you were the last person to see him alive. That's why we're in here, checking for any clues that might point to his death."

"Oh, I didn't realize I was the last person to see him—I thought he stayed here for a bit after he left my office."

"We have the video footage of him leaving your office, going to his office to grab his things, and then leaving. May I ask what you were speaking about with him?"

"We were discussing strategy, both on how to proceed with the war and in the rescue efforts for Strike."

"Did he seem worried at all?"

No," Julian said, rubbing his head as if in thought. "He seemed like himself—business as usual."

Garrett jotted notes down on his handheld pad.

"May I ask how he died?" Julian questioned, forcing what he believed to be concern in his voice.

"He was struck on the head with a toilet tank cover. The cover was off and the toilet water was running. We believe he had his head in the tank to try and fix it when someone struck him from behind."

Julian let his jaw drop again and moved a quick hand to cover it, acting speechless.

"Any thoughts on who might have done it?" Garrett asked, an eyebrow cocked at Julian.

Julian shook his head slowly and thoughtfully.

"I can't imagine it being anyone we know. Have you looked into the Revolters? They could very well be plotting revenge for the men we killed on Chris's property."

"We're looking into all possibilities. We're going to take his body into the future, study it in the labs there to see if we can find anything. In the meantime, Commander, I suggest you remain vague when explaining this situation to the public. It can create a widespread fear that is unwarranted. Our team is in complete control of the investigation, so there's nothing to worry about."

"Got it."

"And please keep your phone on you. We may have follow-up questions about your conversation with Bill."

"Of course."

Julian's heart thumped so hard he thought it might burst out of his ears. He shook Garrett's hand, worried the monstrous man would feel the adrenaline throbbing in his fingertips.

"Give us about ten more minutes to clear out of your office, then you'll be able to get back to work," Garrett said.

"Not a problem—take your time."

Minutes after the security team left the office, Julian returned to his desk and sat with his face buried in his hands. He closed and locked the door, not desiring any distractions as he prepared for the next phase in his rapidly advancing plan.

Garrett had raised a good point that he hadn't yet considered. A message would need to be delivered to the public. Those in the Alaska headquarters already saw the security team raid the office with no explanation. Did they even know Bill was dead? Surely rumors were already spreading across the world.

The office was equipped with a podium that pulled out of the closet in case the Commander needed to deliver an impromptu message to the nation, and this situation certainly called for it.

He crossed the room to the corner closet and pulled open the door that revealed the podium, among a couple of file cabinets and old campaign posters from Strike's last election that read *Don't Strike out, vote for me!* He wheeled the podium out and positioned it in front of the wall of the past Commanders. The Road Runners had no flag to call their own, believing a physical symbol could risk their cover in the general public, so the American and state of Alaska flags hung high on the walls above the portraits, creating a formal backdrop for the upcoming speech.

Julian pulled open the door to the rest of the office. "Danielle, can you come here when you have a moment, please?"

Danielle was the office manager and had the answers to anything in the building, including how to turn on the cameras to go live for a speech.

"Good morning, Commander," she said, strolling into the office on her short, pudgy legs. She was known for wearing excessive amounts of perfume and today was no exception as she entered with a fruity breeze that would linger for several minutes. Danielle offered a youthful smile as she brushed back her short brown hair. "Is there something I can help you with?"

"Yes. I need to broadcast live to the nation. I already set up the podium, but have no idea how to turn on the camera."

"Easy enough. Are you ready now?"

"How do I look?" Julian asked, having dressed casual in jeans and a button-up.

"Relaxed and confident," Danielle replied, reaching out to brush lint off his shoulders. "How long of a speech will you be giving? Should I get you a glass of water?"

"Shouldn't be more than five minutes; no need to worry about it. Thank you."

"Whenever you're ready, get behind the podium and I'll make sure the camera is centered before we broadcast."

Julian nodded and proceeded to the podium, grabbing the sides in a stern grip and looking straight ahead where a camera protruded from the wall behind his desk. Only a handful of people knew that a Commander's office also doubled as an underground bunker. Should there ever be an attack, Julian could seal up his office much like Chris did his house. Everything he needed to run the organization was available within the office, including a month supply of food for two people, should he decide to have someone stay with him.

Danielle pulled a tablet out of the top drawer beneath the camera and ran her fingers across the screen as she whistled. The camera made a robotic creaking sound as it moved up and down before centering on Julian. "That should do it," she said, and crossed the room with the tablet stretched out to Julian. "Push the green button to start the broadcast. It will show you the countdown until you actually come on the screen. After that, the same button will become red. Just push that when you're done."

"Perfect, I think I can handle that. Would you mind staying in here? I think it's weird to give a speech to an empty room."

"Whatever you need, Commander," Danielle said and took a seat behind the desk.

Julian fought off a slight tremor in his hands, knowing he needed to lie to everyone's face to move forward with the plan. He pushed the green button and watched as a fifteen-second countdown appeared.

Preceding a Commander's speech was a quick jingle and

video that showed images of Road Runners hard at work around the world. The broadcast was sent out nationally to all offices, as well as direct to the other Commander offices on the different continents. The countdown struck zero and Julian stared into the camera's soul.

"Good morning, Road Runners. It's with a heavy heart that I must announce our very own Bill Jordan has passed away. He died in his home last night, and our team is working hard to investigate what exactly happened. We will not be slowed down by this tragedy. We will do what we always do, and keep moving forward.

"I was extremely close with Bill. He mentored me soon after I joined the Road Runners, and I know I wouldn't be here today if it weren't for him. Bill worked tirelessly for our organization – for our cause – and many times put us ahead of his own happiness. He had been working on finding a way to rescue Commander Strike, and I suspect he was getting close if the Revolters felt this was the best way to respond. I genuinely believe this attack was carried out by them."

Julian held his stare into the camera, but could see Danielle in his peripheral vision, her brown eyes bulging out of their sockets.

"We've come to a crossroads in our history and have arrived to a tough decision that needs to be made. Bill and I were just discussing the matter last night before he left the office, and we came to an agreement."

Julian paused and sighed to release the tension.

"We are going to deploy our bombs onto Chris's mansion and put an end to this war. It's been a decision many years in the making, and I feel this is the right time to move forward with it."

Julian thought he heard Danielle gasp, but it might have been the group of Road Runners huddled around the TV just outside his office walls. Either way, he knew the message was delivered with the authority he had hoped for. Once the shock wore off, he returned to the camera.

"Road Runners, right now is an extremely dangerous time for us. No matter where you're located, it's imperative you keep an eye out for yourselves and your neighbors. Bill is just the start, so be vigilant, especially in the days following the bombing, as there will most certainly be retaliation from whoever is left of the Revolters. I wish you all the best. Good day."

Julian nodded and pushed the red button on the tablet to cut off the feed.

"How was that?" he asked Danielle, frozen in the desk chair.

"It was fine—I mean, it was great. But is it all true?"

"Is what true? Of course it's all true."

"Bill was killed by the Revolters in his own house?"

"We *believe* it was the Revolters," he lied. "The investigation is still taking place, but who else would do it? Bill was beloved by everyone within the Road Runners."

A tear trickled down Danielle's cheek, leaving a moist streak through her makeup.

"I can't believe it. I know we're in a war, but you never think something like this will actually happen, you know?"

"I know. They've done us enough harm by taking Commander Strike, and now Bill. We have no choice but to make a move."

Danielle nodded as she stood and moved to the door. "There was some worry among us about you taking over. But I think you'll have everyone's support with these bombs." She said this robotically, like a history teacher repeating random facts to a bored classroom.

"Thank you, Danielle."

She left without another word, and Julian returned to his desk, knowing that someone would shortly be in touch to try and talk him out of the dropping the bombs.

25

Chapter 25

Martin rose quietly from his seat, as if she could hear him approaching over the constant roar of the bar. His legs wobbled, a sensation of walking through wet cement. Sonya had her face down towards the menu while Martin approached her like a rare, exotic bird he didn't want to scare away.

He reached her table after what felt like ten minutes, even though it had only taken him ten seconds to move thirty feet. His arms shivered with anticipation as millions of thoughts ruptured his mind.

He was within arm's reach of the table and she still hadn't looked up. Her face appeared relaxed, free of the stress from their last encounter at her house. The thought of her bullets tearing apart his legs made him want to lunge across the table and strangle her. But he also remembered the time they had spent together in 1996, and no matter what anyone said, he knew their connection had been real.

Instead of lunging, Martin pulled out the seat across from Sonya and sat, remaining silent to not startle his bird into flapping away.

"Sonya," he said, watching her head jolt upright at the sound of his voice.

Her eyes grew another inch, head jerking side-to-side like a chicken as she scanned the bar behind him. "Martin," she whispered. "What the *hell* are you doing here?"

Her hands slapped the table as she jumped out of her chair. Martin raised his hands in self-defense, and waved her to sit back down.

"I could ask you the same thing," he said, his hands shaking underneath the table. Martin clenched his jaw shut, afraid his teeth might chatter and show his boiling rage. *Remember,* she *shot* you. She *left* you.

"I . . . I don't know what to say." She sat back down, but her hands remained planted on the tabletop.

"I think you and I need to have a long talk, and you can start by saying everything I don't already know."

"I don't know what you mean. I was just doing my job—you shouldn't be here. It's dangerous."

"Dammit, Sonya, we're way beyond that. I'm here. You're here. Now tell me what the hell happened!" These last words flew out of his lips with a snarl.

"Okay, okay. Relax. You need to tell me first why you're here and who sent you."

Her hands inched closer to her body, but remained on the table. Martin focused his stare to them, plotting his words wisely, as he no longer trusted the woman across the table.

"I'm here to get medicine for my mom. I was told it existed here and asked to come." Sonya nodded as if she knew this. "And no one sent me. Commander Strike gave me permission to come with a group of others, but I would've come either way. Now start talking."

Sonya looked around, her blond hair swinging behind in a ponytail. "We shouldn't talk here in the open. Can we go somewhere else?"

"Wow, so you're a Revolter now, huh? You're surely not one of these undercover Road Runners, since you betrayed me." She finally raised her hands, waving for Martin to shush. "Sorry, but I'm not going anywhere with you. You're crazy if you think I will, after that stunt you pulled at the Oxford."

Sonya gazed into him with her hazel eyes, and Martin thought he saw regret swimming beneath the surface.

"Okay," she said. "That's fine. But we can't talk here in a bar filled with Revolters. If one person hears the wrong part of our conversation, you'll be dead in seconds."

This much was true, and Martin had let his emotions get the best of him as soon as he saw Sonya. He needed to not lose track of where he was or who he was supposed to portray.

"Can we talk outside?" he asked. "Maybe go for a walk?"

Sonya nodded. "Yes, but if we walk by someone, anyone at all, you need to drop the conversation until we're clear. They're always listening in the city."

"Who's listening?"

"The government."

With this dramatic comment, Sonya stood again and pushed in her chair, prompting Martin to do the same.

When they stepped outside, nighttime had started to take its hold as the street lights illuminated the sidewalks, and the city's buildings glowed like candle flames. Golden spotlights danced across the sky, coming from the direction of the capitol.

"Where to?" Sonya asked.

"Is Civic Center Park safe at this time of day?"

"Everywhere is safe. There's no more crime in the city; it's all been pushed to the outside. Where are you staying?"

"None of your business," he snapped, pleasantly surprised by his own sternness.

They walked in awkward silence, a quick two blocks to downtown's biggest park across the street from the capitol steps.

They crossed Colfax to the park, prompting Martin to stop and admire the setting. The park was its usual self, only more attractive. New lighting ran along the pathways that cut across the grass. Additional benches had been added, along with a water fountain that provided a soothing background noise. Couples walked around, hands intertwined, while joggers ran by for their evening run through the park.

"There's not a homeless person in sight," Martin noted, remembering the park as a main hangout for those without a home.

"President Poe signed a law that forced all poor people out of the big cities," Sonya explained. "He claimed that cities were designed for the wealthy, not the suburbs, and as of now the, roles have reversed. Places like Highlands Ranch and Boulder belong to the poor now, and all of the rich reside in the city."

"Protected by guards and an electric fence. Don't tell me you agree with this."

"I don't have much of a choice. This is my home now. Forever."

"Why did you shoot me? Do you have any idea how long it took me to recover?" Martin tried to keep his tone soft, but his disgust leaked out just the same.

"I didn't want you coming after me. I knew if I didn't shoot you, you'd have followed me into the bedroom and grabbed me as soon as I drank my Juice. I couldn't have a single person know where I was going."

"Why here?"

"I'm protected here. I know the Road Runners want to kill me. Hell, I even understand *why* they need to, but I'm not going to just turn myself in. I don't want to die, even though I know it will save the world."

"Did you hear that Strike was kidnapped by Chris?"

"Of course."

"What do you plan on doing here for the rest of your life?"

"I don't know. Just living without fear. It would be a first, and it was peaceful until you showed up. I thought for sure you'd blast my head off."

"I could never kill you. The Road Runners sent me with that poison to your house, but I was never going to use it."

Sonya grinned. "I didn't think you would, but I had to play it safe."

"I need to know the truth, Sonya," Martin cut in, redirecting the conversation back to what he wanted. "I've heard all sorts of things about our relationship being a lie. Is it true?"

Sonya looked to the ground and kicked a rock out of the way. They hadn't moved since arriving to the park, standing on the sidewalk like nothing else in the world existed. "I don't know what you want me to say. I had a job to do. I may have fallen in love with you, but I couldn't give all the way into those feelings. Doing so would only put both of us at risk. I took this job because I'm emotionally scarred. My childhood was absolutely fucked up. Chris killed my mom when I was a kid. Nothing has been right ever since then. Then he injected his blood into me to keep himself immortal. I don't know how it all works, but it was supposed to give me purpose in life. Like he thinks I actually love him for being such a shitty father."

"Does he know you're here?"

"Of course. He set me up with the apartment."

"I don't understand your relationship. He's your father, but you hate him? But he also wants to keep you alive for his own reasons." Martin shook his head again, nothing making sense.

"We had to make a pact, him and I. When I ran away when I was 17, I joined the Road Runners—obviously this drove him crazy. I was trying to figure out life on my own and he'd just show up at the worst times, and he knew there was nothing I could do about it." Sonya shook her head while reminiscing. "Since his life depends on mine, I had to threaten suicide for him to leave me alone. And not just a verbal threat, I had to cut my wrists in front of him to show him I wasn't bluffing. Once he saw the blood he agreed to our pact."

"What's the pact?"

"To live and let live. He can no longer publicly acknowledge me as someone he knows. Even if I'm in the middle of important Road Runner business and he shows up, he has to pretend that everything is normal. Remember that date we went on to the steakhouse in 1996? He does shit like that all the time, showing up unannounced to mess with my head, never saying a word to me."

Martin nodded, remembering the encounter and his panic to ensure Sonya didn't find out that the two had known each other. Apparently, everyone already knew everything, Martin being the only oblivious party. He thought back to all the times Sonya had asked to not see the old man ever again, and the dots started connecting.

"When we returned to 2018 and went to the Wealth of Time store, you went inside with me. Why?"

"I wanted to surprise him the way he always did to me. It was a good idea in my head, but he wasn't fazed; probably knew I was coming." She shook her head in disgust.

"So now you both work for opposite teams, but have a mutual agreement to leave each other alone?"

"Well, we did. I don't know what I'm supposed to do now."

"Let me talk to them for you. I'll tell them you're alive and well and want to stay with the Road Runners."

"Are you shitting me? Want to stay? They sent you to kill me. At my own house! I don't want to stay."

"So you're joining the Revolters?"

"Hell no. I'm just living and waiting to see what happens. As long as my dad is alive, I have to stay in hiding. I'm at just as much risk as him to get killed by the Road Runners."

"So you hide out in the city where Road Runners aren't allowed. It actually makes sense. But did you know there are undercover Road Runners in the city? I got through just fine."

"Of course I know that. That's why I don't mingle with anyone unless I know for certain who they are."

"Is it just dumb luck that I happened to be sitting in the same bar as you?"

"I suppose it is. I go to new places for dinner every time I go out— I don't want to be seen as a regular anywhere. But Martin, you can't tell them about me. If the Road Runners know where I am they will hunt me until I'm dead. Who's in charge right now anyway, with Strike missing?"

"I have no idea. I was only told that Strike was missing, but they might already be onto you. Strike told us to keep an eye out for you before we came on this trip."

"It's logical to assume I would hide in this era within the walls. They know I can blend in with the Revolters if needed."

"So what am I supposed to do? Just go home and pretend

like nothing happened?"

Sonya nodded. "Yes. But I know you won't actually do that, so I can sweeten the deal for you."

Martin's eyebrows raised in curiosity. "What do you mean?"

"I can get you that medicine."

"Are you shitting me? You've had access to the medicine this whole time?"

Sonya raised her hands for Martin to relax. "Look, I was just doing my job. I know it was a dirty thing to do, not telling you."

"You can say that again," Martin snapped, rage instantly flaring through his body. Not only had she laid the perfect trap for him in 1996, she had access to the most valuable medicine in the world, at least to Martin.

They paused as a couple of joggers passed them by on the park's trail.

"I'm sorry, Martin," she finally said. "Let me help you get the medicine. It's the least I can do."

"You can answer one question for me, actually," he responded dismissively. "Why did you drag me along for 6 months in 1996? Why did you come back with me to 2018, only to plan another trip into the past where you eventually led me into the trap? It seems like you had plenty of easy opportunities to turn me over."

"The Road Runners don't just recruit anyone," she said, her nervous stare returning to the ground while she spoke. "It's a long vetting process that often times can take an entire year."

"And what is it you're looking for during all that time?"

"Certain traits. I was actually on a special mission from Strike to find a worthy successor to her Commandership. She had trust issues with Julian, and wanted to see other options."

"Me as Commander? That's absurd." Martin shook his head,

grinning at the thought of him leading the Road Runners in any capacity.

"It's not. You don't give yourself enough credit."

"I've never had any leadership qualities. Not in this sense."

"Really? Then why are you here? Where's the rest of the group you came with?"

Martin paused, thinking of a good response, but coming up short.

"Martin, you have the traits of a high-ranking Road Runner. You take initiative, are organized and extremely determined, and for the most part seem to be fearless. These are the things I had to judge as part of my job, getting to know you behind closed doors. When you came out of your coma ready to continue work, I knew you were the real deal. Anyone else would have called it quits at that point; you did not." Sonya let her words hang above Martin like a cloud of truth.

He thought back to their time together in 1996, mentally picking apart each moment and trying to categorize what had been real, and what had been a test. "Was the coma done on purpose?"

"Of course not. We would never cause a potential Road Runner any harm. But it was a unique opportunity for us to see how you'd respond in the most difficult of moments. Look, we can talk all night about this, but nothing will change. We're in 2064, and you're not even allowed to be in this city. Come back tomorrow morning. Let's meet in this same spot and I'll have your mom's medicine."

"What happens after that?" Martin asked, sensing a familiar desire to spend every waking moment by her side.

"You go home and save your mom, and we never see each other again. I'll be moving to another city. Even though I trust you, it's too risky having someone know where I am."

"Sonya, you don't have to do that. I'll leave you in peace."

"I think we both know that's a lie. I know in some other universe, where there's no such thing as Road Runners or Revolters, you and I probably have a life together. But that's not our reality, and it never will be. After tomorrow, we'll say goodbye forever." Sonya leaned in to Martin to kiss his cheek. "I'll see you in the morning. Please don't follow me home."

Martin watched her turn and walk across the street, back where they had come from. Somewhere in the city she lived her life, hiding out one day at a time. He checked his watch to find it was already nine o'clock, and Gerald was waiting for him outside the city walls.

26

Chapter 26

Julian locked himself in his office. Tension and pandemonium brewed outside as teams of Road Runners prepared for the upcoming attacks on Chris's mansion.

"Can he do this?" people murmured, excitement and angst heavy in their voices.

I certainly can, he thought. Only one group could attempt to stop him. The Council, a panel of seven Road Runners appointed by the commandership, served a role similar to the United States Supreme Court. With the Road Runners lacking a type of congress, the Council provided the only checks and balances on the commander, aside from the lieutenant commander.

Anyone within the organization could bring an issue to the Council for review. If interested, a member of the Council had to motion the topic for review, and it needed to be seconded by one other member. Once a motion was approved, The Council gathered in their private chambers to hash out a discussion before putting the matter up for a vote. Every Council member was required to vote, and not a single person could overturn their decision.

Julian had always found this unfair. Why should one group of Road Runners be able to wield all of the power? Not even the commander had any influence over them, so who was really in charge of the organization?

If there were only two Council members who felt strongly against dropping bombs on Chris, then the issue was already being discussed in New York City. All Julian needed was four Council members to side with him and everything would proceed without backlash. For whatever reason, the Road Runner community blindly accepted whatever decision the Council made.

It had only been thirty minutes since he delivered his speech, and his office phone began ringing constantly. The issue appeared more polarizing than killing Sonya, only this one had involvement from the public.

Julian left the phone off the hook, basking in silence as men and women worked in organized chaos to prepare the arsenal of bombs for deployment. He had decided to move forward as if nothing would stop him. Even if the Council ordered him to stop, he would still push forward, pretending to not receive the message. Disobeying the Council put him at risk of life in prison, but if the people could just see what a peaceful world looked like on the other side of the bombs, they'd have no choice but to forgive and forget.

"All leaders will be faced with one decision that defines them," Strike had told him once. "That decision forms how you're viewed by the public. It can turn you into a hero or the enemy of the people—there is no in-between."

He hadn't known why she shared this with him, but figured she was more talking to herself to arrive to a final decision on

Sonya's fate, but he looked back at her words today with a wide grin.

"This is my grand decision," he said to the empty office. "Only my second day on the job, and the people will love me for ending this war."

Forty-five minutes had already passed since Julian authorized their preparation.

The Council was surely up in arms over the issue, hopefully equally split on the matter to burn more time while the rest of the world waited.

A knock rapped on the door, authoritative and rushed.

"Who is it?" Julian called out, not moving from his desk.

"Sir, Councilwoman Murray is on the phone for you. She needs to speak with you." The voice belonged to Danielle, and Julian sat in silence. "Sir?"

He wondered if he sat there long enough if she'd give up and tell Councilwoman Murray to call back later. But the call was too important; they would deliver the message to him one way or another. *No way they came to a decision that quickly.*

"Danielle, can you please give me two minutes?"

"Yes, sir, I will let her know."

Julian whipped out his cell phone and scrolled through his list of contacts until he found the one he needed, pressing on the call button with a shaky thumb.

"This is McGuire," a deep, hoarse voice answered.

"Mr. McGuire, this is Commander Caruso," Julian said.

"Hello, Commander, what can I do for you?"

"It's time to deploy the bombs to our target. I authorize you to do so immediately."

A brief silence filled the airwaves, and Julian sensed McGuire hesitating, debating to take the order or not.

"Mr. McGuire, right now, please."

"Yes, sir."

Julian hung up the cell phone and picked up the desk phone. "Danielle, you can patch through Councilwoman Murray."

"One moment," she replied before the phone cut to a brief silence.

"Commander Caruso," a woman's voice said, stern and disgusted.

"Good morning, Councilwoman, is everything okay?" Julian asked in the most laidback voice he could muster.

"No, Commander, it is not. We need you to cease all of your operations immediately. The Council has voted unanimously against dropping bombs on the Revolters' headquarters."

"Unanimous!" Julian jumped out of his chair, nearly choking on the word. He had expected this phone call after a long debate between the Council members, but a unanimous decision? "Why on Earth was it *unanimous*?"

"Commander, you're a suspect in Bill's murder. We can't have you making any major decisions until your name is cleared. There is support for the bombs in the Council, but this is the right thing for us to do. Once we clear your name, we can resume this discussion."

Julian checked the time to see two minutes had passed since he spoke with McGuire. In their prior conversations, McGuire had mentioned it would take four minutes for the bombs to be deployed upon receiving the order. Julian needed to stall two more minutes.

"Councilwoman, this isn't fair. I have a voice recording from Bill himself giving his approval. The Council has never reversed a decision agreed upon by a Commander *and* his lieutenant. Never."

"That is true, but this is an investigation. The recording will be part of it, and if our team determines the recording is real, we have no choice but to allow the bombs to move forward."

"How would I get a fake recording of Bill agreeing to this? Do you know how crazy you sound right now?"

"I know it's frustrating, and I know it's been an emotional morning for you," Murray responded calmly. "And I know this is probably the most difficult start to a Commandership we've ever had, but I need you to understand these are our laws, and this is how we have to enforce them."

"I understand," Julian said with a darkening grin. "By the way, Councilwoman, I already placed the call to authorize the bombs, the fireworks should begin in about thirty seconds."

Julian hung up the phone, leaned back in his chair, and clicked on the TV hanging on the wall. He flipped up one channel for the camera view showing Chris's mansion. It stood peacefully in the snow, moments away from its steel barriers being destroyed.

A helicopter flew above, rumbling their underground head-quarters, signaling the start of the bombing. The crew in the helicopter studied the wind and relayed the information to the nearby arsenal where the bombs were loaded into futuristic cannons.

Julian dashed to the door to join the rest of the office huddled around the main screen. "It's time, everyone!" he cried. A few whispers spread through the office, but it remained otherwise deathly silent.

Julian leaned against a desk and crossed his arms, already proud at his decision and being the first to authorize the bombs that had been stored for years. He grinned, thinking about Councilwoman Murray on the opposite side of the country, running around in a panic trying to figure out a way to stop this already moving train of destruction. She could thank him later when they recovered Chris's body from the rubble.

Due to the silence, the rupture of four blasting cannons was heard clearly. Julian's heart raced as all eyes turned from the sound above their heads back to the big screen TV. It seemed ten minutes had passed with no action, but it had maybe only been ten seconds in reality.

The first bomb hit squarely on top of the mansion's barricade, exploding into a ball of flames and black smoke. The next three bombs followed within seconds, smoke filling up the entire screen in a blackout of doom. Julian giggled, but no one would ever hear it above the majestic explosions. More bombs struck the mansion in terrifying unison, rumbling the entire world.

One more round, Julian thought, smiling wide like a child walking into Disneyland for the first time.

Twenty seconds later the final bombs dropped, leaving them to wait for the smoke to clear and see the results. Surely the mansion was a pile of rubble. It took three treacherous minutes for the smoke to clear.

The mansion stood in its same place, undisturbed with the exception of black powder marks scattered across the steel barricade like a muddy child's handprints

"Are you shitting me?" someone screamed out from the back. "Not even a dent?"

Julian watched in disbelief, nausea eating away his insides. With nothing to show for this bold stunt, the Council just might vote to remove him as Commander, or worse, send him to prison.

"No!" Julian screamed, barging back into his office and

slamming the door shut behind him. "Goddammit!" he grabbed the phone from his desk and hurled it across the room, bits and pieces exploding in every direction. He debated running away, but had nowhere to go with the tracking device lodged in his arm, a virtual handcuff that kept him in place.

After all of the risks of going to the mansion to negotiate with Chris, turning Strike over to their greatest enemy, murdering Bill, and ignoring orders directly from the Council, the reality sunk in that Julian was fucked. All of these truths would be uncovered during an investigation that would surely be underway by the evening, and he had violated nearly every major rule in the book.

The screens cut out, flickering as if searching for a signal. After a few seconds, the signal strengthened, but showed Chris sitting in an office, the same office Julian had met him.

"Hello, Road Runners," Chris said, grinning into the camera. "I hope you're all having as pleasant of a day as I am. I have Commander Strike here, and she is fine and well. For now."

He paused and took a drink of water he didn't need, only doing so to add dramatics.

"I need whoever ordered these silly bombs to come over here right now. If you do, we can all carry on business as usual. If you don't, I'm afraid I have no choice but to respond to your malicious attacks. And trust me when I tell you this, there will be no more Road Runners by sunrise tomorrow. So, I suggest you turn yourself in and save thousands of lives. You have six hours to arrive before I unleash every weapon you can imagine on your little hideouts. *Ta-ta* for now." Chris winked and blew a kiss to the camera before the screen cut back to the still image of his charred mansion.

Julian sunk into his chair, an invisible fist pressing into his gut as a million thoughts flooded his mind. *The next six hours won't end well for me.*

The Road Runners had no time to grow an allegiance to him, and they would absolutely turn him in to spare their own lives. Stepping foot outside of his office all but guaranteed his death by Chris's hands, probably in a public humiliation for all of the world of Revolters and Road Runners to see. If he stayed in the office, a crew sent from the Council was surely on its way to arrest him. If found guilty of Bill's murder, the penalty for killing a fellow Road Runner was death by firing squad.

He briefly debated making a run for it, but how far would he honestly make it with both Road Runners and Revolters chasing after him? There wasn't a place in the world to hide and feel safe.

Julian looked around the office, the wall of past Commanders gazing into his soul. They would never hang his portrait, even though he was soon to be the shortest-tenured Commander in history. The walls closed in around him, barricading him within his own mental prison. He heard the initial banging on the door from those in the office, surely trying to break in and take him to Chris's house. They punched and kicked the door, shouting mumbled phrases that he'd never hear.

No one was going to dictate how Julian Caruso left this world, so he pulled the pistol out from its drawer and pointed it at the door that would soon burst open, his hand steady on the desk.

The tumultuous knocking and banging ceased and was replaced by the sound of a bigger, quaking thud that rattled the door in its hinges, dust and debris puffing from the edges of the door frame in little clouds.

Here we go, Julian thought as he cocked the pistol.

With the next bang, the door burst open, revealing a desk

they had used as a battering ram. At least twenty Road Runners stood behind it, all peering into Julian's office, shouting in such disarray that it was impossible to know what anyone said.

Six rounds of ammunition had no chance at holding off two dozen pissed-off Road Runners. As the first of them lunged into the room, Julian slipped the pistol into his mouth and squeezed the trigger.

27

Chapter 27

Martin didn't speak much on the ride home with Gerald, his encounter with Sonya gnawing at his conscience like a rabid goat. Gerald filled in Martin with everything he had learned about Commander Strike's disappearance and the ensuing catastrophe with Julian.

"It's complete turmoil for us right now," Gerald said. "We have no leader. The next in the chain of command is the head of security, I think, until we have a special election."

"I can't believe all of this has happened since we left. We haven't even been here a full 24 hours."

"This is poor judgment on Strike's behalf. Julian should have never been her lieutenant commander. He was too young to be in such a position, and already lacked respect from others. Bill would've been the better choice, even if most saw him as too soft; we wouldn't be in this mess right now, that's for sure."

They pulled into their hotel parking lot, a tall lamp post flickering to provide the dimmest of light.

"I need to tell you something," Martin said when Gerald turned the van off. "Something happened downtown today."

"Something is always happening downtown." Gerald chuckled.

"No, not like that. I met some people. Some Road Runners."

The grin on Gerald's face vanished immediately. "How do you know they were Road Runners?"

"They told me."

"Martin, you're lucky to be sitting here. That's a common line for Revolters to use to sniff out the real Road Runners." Gerald bolted upright, raising his voice like a disappointed parent. "If that had been a Revolter, you'd be dead—I warned you about this."

"Well, then it must have really been a Road Runner. It was one man who came over to me in a restaurant and we spoke privately at my table. I didn't think anything of it. He told me he was one of the undercover Road Runners living in this year, and wanted to wish me the best."

"How did he know?"

"No idea. All he said was that he could tell I wasn't from here."

Gerald shook his head. "Doesn't make sense. There were others?"

"Yes, I met one other. Someone who said they can help me get the medicine. In fact, said we can get it tomorrow morning."

"Why does someone inside the city know about the medicine?" Martin sensed that Gerald would stand up if physically possible, but they remained trapped in the vehicle. "They said you were smart, but it sounds like you made nothing but horrible decisions today. Are you trying to end up next to Strike? Or worse?"

Martin recalled being somewhat of a prisoner in Chris's

mansion, and imagined there weren't many things worse. Even death was more attractive than becoming a robotic soldier for Chris.

"It was an old friend, quite a coincidence that I ran into her."

"*Her*? Don't tell me—"

"Yes, it's her. She's hiding inside the city, and just happened to be in the same bar as me tonight."

Gerald sat quietly, his thick fingers rubbing his lips in discomfort. "You know we have to kill her. That's our order."

"Order from who? We don't have to kill her. She made a promise to help me, and she will. I'm not going to be involved in killing her. I'm going to get this medicine that I came for, and go back home. She already knows she's being hunted."

Gerald shook his head. "I don't like the sound of this. She betrayed the Road Runners and now lives in the city. She's clearly in contact with Chris and can't be trusted."

"I can trust her."

"Oh, so you're an expert now? You can tell when she's telling the truth or leading you on for six months of your life?"

"That's low."

"That's the truth."

"She feels guilty. She knows my mom, and doesn't like what Chris did; that's why she offered to help."

"As the leader of this mission, I'm telling you this is a bad idea. It smells like a setup, especially with how valuable you are. I strongly advise you do not move forward this. However, as a human being, I understand you trying to save your mother, and I know you need to take some risks to do so. If you feel you need to do this, then I won't get in your way, but just know you'll be meeting her alone."

"Thank you, Gerald."

Gerald nodded, staring out the windshield into the darkness. "You can still reject her offer and I'll go in with you as planned. We can get this medicine without her."

"I don't doubt that, but she told me she can get it without any trouble. Why put all of us at risk if we don't need to?"

"If you trust her—which you shouldn't—then I can't stop you. I'll look the other way, and if anything bad happens, I'll tell them you went off on your own."

"There is no *them* right now."

Gerald nodded calmly. "Ain't that the truth? Well, best of luck to you. I'll give you a ride in the morning and we'll see what happens."

"Thanks again, I don't know how to ever repay you."

"Just don't get killed, and we'll call it even."

Gerald pushed open the van's door and stepped out into the cool night. A man sat in a lawn chair in the patch of dirt in front of the complex, puffing a cigarette and blowing smoke to the sky. Martin joined Gerald and walked by his side into the hotel.

They strolled down the main hallway, its peeling carpet and chipped walls welcoming them home. The odor of cigarette smoke filled the halls as if it were once a smoking lounge.

Gerald jolted to a stop when they reached their door, his hand swinging up to tell Martin to stay put.

Martin followed Gerald's gaze to the ground, where three droplets of blood splashed on the floor.

"Were those there this whole time?" Gerald whispered, his other hand whipping a pistol out of his waistband.

Martin froze in his tracks and shrugged.

Gerald studied the door, but found nothing out of the ordinary. He lowered his hand and slid it quietly onto the doorknob.

"Stay out here."

Martin reached into his waistband, forgetting that he had left his gun inside the room, advised by Gerald to do so. The insecurity of having no protection besides his fists sent instant panic through his core.

Gerald turned the knob as gently as possible, the sounds of old springs creaking before he thrust open the door and immediately raised his gun in the air. "Jesus Christ!" he shouted as the door banged against the inside wall. "Stay here!"

Martin watched Gerald disappear inside, leaving him paranoid and clueless in the hallway. Not sensing any immediate danger, Martin took a soft step toward the door frame and craned his neck for a view inside.

Web sat on the couch, facing the door, a hole in the middle of his forehead, blood splattered behind him like a bucket of red paint had been thrown on the wall. Web's eyes remained open, glossy as they stared at Martin. His arms splayed by his side as his head hung slightly to the left, held upright by the couch.

"Should I call someone?" Martin asked.

Gerald whipped around, snarling. "I said to stay outside. I need to make sure the suite is clear."

Martin backed away, subconsciously raising his hands in the air. He waited in the hallway, feeling like a sitting duck for any attacker willing to swoop by and take him out. The rest of the hotel was eerily quiet, too quiet considering it was barely nine o'clock. He wondered if their neighbors had also been attacked. But wouldn't the man smoking in front of the building have mentioned something about people barging in with guns?

"Come in, Martin!" Gerald called out.

Martin shuffled back to the door, fighting to keep his eyes off the dead body on their couch, but failing miserably.

Gerald stood in the kitchen, joined by a shivering Brigham.

"I found Brigham hiding in his closet," Gerald said, putting an arm over the traumatized scientist's shoulder. "Are you ready to talk about what happened?"

Martin watched Brigham's hands tremble like he had uncontrollable Parkinson's disorder.

"I'm not ready, but I need to talk about it," Brigham said, his voice matching his hands.

"Take your time, start from the beginning and go slow. We're safe right now."

Martin noticed the choice of the words *right now*, leading him to believe that they weren't necessarily safe moving forward.

"I was in my room," Brigham said. "Wrapping up a couple of things for research and about to lie down. Web was in the living room, working on his laptop. I heard a loud bang and two men yelling at Web. He yelled back, and that's when the gun went off. I panicked and went into my closet, praying they wouldn't open it. I heard their footsteps moving through every room, even mine, but they didn't touch anything from what I could tell."

Brigham's voice teetered off as he broke into heavy sobs, burying his face in open palms. Gerald rubbed his back to try and console him, shaking his head as he studied the ground.

"We need to get Web's body out of here," Gerald said. "If you can help me load him into the van, I'll drive and take him back to 2019." He spoke to Martin, who nodded.

"Are we safe here?" Martin asked.

"Yes. Assuming these were Revolters, they don't ever come back to a place for a second time unless a few months have passed."

"Shouldn't we call the police? Or check on the others in the building?"

"There are no police outside of the city. It's everyone for themselves. If they came in and did this to Web, then it's probably too late to help anyone else. All we can do is clean up, and make sure we complete our mission this week, so we can get out of here."

"How do you want to do this?"

Gerald released Brigham, who had started to slow down with the water works. "Let's wrap his body and lay him in the back seat. I'll drive to Ralph's place and will take Web back to 2019 where they can proceed with getting him back to Europe." He shook his head, unable to hide the disgust plaguing him.

"Don't beat yourself up over this," Martin said. "It's not your fault."

"It's always my fault when someone on my crew dies. Especially when it's someone who has never gone through field training. My only job is to keep them safe, and I failed. You'll understand one day when you have to lead a crew of your own."

Martin felt guilt creep into his thoughts. These men were all here because he wanted medicine for his mother. If not for him, Web would be alive and Brigham wouldn't be traumatized. All of this had happened and he hadn't even seen the medicine yet. Would the Road Runners have sent this group on a mission together if Martin had never asked about medicine? He didn't know for sure, but assumed not. Brigham and Web had volunteered to come along, and now one of them was dead. While Martin didn't believe he'd ever lead a crew on a future mission, he assumed responsibility on this trip.

"Let's do it," Martin said. "I'll help you, and I'll stay

here with Brigham to make sure nothing else happens. And tomorrow I'm getting that medicine so we can leave." He spoke in his most authoritative voice. He had been warned of how dangerous the future was, and now seeing it firsthand, the reality sparked a new urgency. There was no time to waste.

"Grab a couple of sheets from your bedroom closet," Gerald said. "We'll wrap him in that."

Martin retrieved the sheets and returned within a minute. Gerald had made his way to the couch to lay Web on his side, tipping him over like a lifeless stuffed animal. He took a sheet from Martin and draped it over Web's face, stretching it down to cover the entirety of his body.

Gerald worked with the ease of a hotel maid, and Martin wondered if this was something he had done in the past. He lifted the dead body, tucking the loose sheet underneath, starting from the head and working down to the feet, until Web was wrapped in what looked like a cocoon. He repeated the same process with the second sheet, covering the red splotch that had seeped through the first layer.

Gerald stepped back to ensure his work was complete. Just like that, Web had become a mummy on the couch, lifeless under wraps, another casualty of the never-ending war between good and evil.

"May I?" Brigham asked, stepping toward his old colleague. He placed a hand softly on top of the white lump, shaking his head. "We weren't the best of friends, but we worked together on many projects. You were always easy to work with and kept the mood light. You'll be missed. Rest easy."

His words were brief, but meaningful, and he sniffled away more tears as he turned to join Gerald and Martin.

"You ready?" Gerald asked.

"Yes," Martin said, taking the first step toward Web.

"You take him by the legs, I'll take him by his shoulders."

They positioned themselves and hoisted Web upward, the sheets' tight wrapping undisturbed. Martin had never understood the term "dead weight" until this moment. Sure, he had carried Izzy from room to room when she fell asleep on the couch, but that paled in comparison to lifting an actual dead body. If he had never been whipped into shape, poor Web would be splayed across the floor, but Martin's new muscles bulged as they started out the door and down the hallway.

"Brigham, you'll need to come open the van door for us," Gerald said through gritted teeth.

They made their way toward the building's exit, Martin and Gerald thudding down the hall like they were moving a heavy couch. Martin broke a sweat during that short time, the outside air cooling him immediately. The smoker from earlier was gone, leaving just the three of them as they crossed the walkway to the van.

Brigham ran ahead and opened the door to the back seat, looking away from the sight as they lowered Web inside.

Gerald lowered the head in first, pushing it as far in as he could reach. He pulled himself out, leaving Martin to hold the legs like a wheelbarrow, as he rounded the van to open the door on the other side and continue pulling Web in all the way. Martin bent Web's knees to allow both doors to shut without slamming into the corpse.

"You guys head back inside," Gerald instructed. "Order some dinner, try to take your mind off things. I'll be back in about 90 minutes."

Gerald hopped in and sped off like a man on a mission.

"I'm glad you're okay," Martin said to Brigham as they

started back inside.

"Me too. I still can't believe any of this happened."

"I've got some things in place where we can hopefully leave tomorrow morning."

They walked in silence back into the hotel, the tension of their mission feeling like the least important thing as they cleaned the blood splatters off the walls and floor.

28

Chapter 28

Strike woke to the sensation of a stake rammed through her head. She lay on a couch in Chris's office, her eyes shifting in and out of focus as they peered around the empty room.

Would Chris actually leave me unattended? she wondered, knowing damn well he'd never let her escape. Perhaps he was laying a trap.

None of it mattered, as her arms and legs throbbed in excruciating pain. Her muscles had tensed unlike anything before, and she was happy to simply wiggle her toes and know she hadn't been paralyzed. She lay as limp as a sloth on a Sunday afternoon, attempting to lift her head, but unable to, new waves of pain shooting down her spine. She tried moving her legs, but couldn't. He may have not paralyzed her, but Chris made sure she wouldn't move from the couch.

The office looked as if it had been suddenly abandoned. Chris's chair faced the open door, computer monitors glowed, and a fireplace crackled in the distance. Surely they wouldn't have left her alone without the intent of coming right back. Strike was, after all, the most prized possession according to

Chris.

Muffled voices and heavy thuds came from the other side of the wall, in the hallway. It sounded like a group of men chattering, moving something heavy down the hall by the sounds of their slow approaching footsteps.

"Right in here," Chris called out before appearing in the doorway. "Ah, Commander Strike, good morning."

She hated when he called her commander, but there wasn't much she could do about it while being a useless pile of flesh on the couch. She tried pulling herself up through her abdomen, again failing. Even though she wasn't constrained, she was still a prisoner.

Chris entered with a giddy smile and extra hop in his step. Four men followed behind him, grunting as they held a body between them, one holding each limb.

"This way, gentlemen – go ahead and drop him in front of the Commander." Chris clapped his hands and skipped toward Strike.

She watched the men haul the body over. It was dressed in jeans and a flannel shirt, snow frosting the top of black hair. The men lowered the body to the ground directly in front of Strike, and her eyes bulged at the sight of the cold, dead face.

"Ahh, so you do know this person," Chris said. "Your people dropped him in front of the house like a sacrifice. They left a note." Chris reached into his pocket and pulled out a piece of paper, unfolded it, and began reading. "Mr. Speidel, please accept our sincerest apologies. This is the body of the traitor who decided to drop bombs on your mansion. He did this without any approval. We don't want any trouble, just to have Commander Strike returned safely. Thank you."

Chris giggled madly while he folded the note and returned it to his pocket. "So, tell me, Commander. What was his name?"

A tear ran down Strike's cheek, seemingly the only thing moving on her body. "Julian Caruso. He would've taken over when I went missing."

Chris nodded to the men who had stood awkwardly in the corner, and they left the room.

"So I have the pleasure of *two* Commanders in my house at the same time," Chris said to himself. "What a blessed day. You slept through the bombing. I counted over 15 that he dropped on us. It was hard to tell; at one point the house was just constantly shaking and the sounds of explosions were nonstop. I didn't know you peaceful people had access to such bombs."

"We have them, but never planned to use them," Strike said, wanting so desperately to simply sit up.

"Well, it appears Commander Caruso here had different plans. And look at him now." Chris laughed. "So who is in charge now when both Mommy and Daddy aren't home?"

"We hold a special election." Strike lied. Bill would be in charge right now, but she wasn't going to give this lunatic anyone's name. "There should be a new Commander selected within the next two days."

"An election, huh? Think I have a shot?" Chris howled, his laughter echoing around the walls and sending chills through Strike's motionless body. When he settled down, he returned his attention to Strike. "This is unfortunate, though. I was hoping to give whoever dropped the bombs the same welcoming hospitality you received. It's only fair. But he's dead, so that won't be very fun."

Chris paced around Julian's body, studying the corpse like a scientist. "You don't suppose this is our guy, do you,

Commander?"

"What do you mean? He's one of my people."

"Yes, we know that. I mean the man who came over and sold you out. The man was about this size, and his voice sounded younger, much like our friend here."

Strike still didn't believe anyone in the Road Runners would do such a thing. Surely Chris was bluffing, but she studied Julian with suspicious eyes just the same. How else would Chris have been able to get her so easily?

"I guess since he's already dead," Chris continued. "I'll have to move forward with retaliation. His body is a lovely gift—I'll be sure to thank your people—but it's not what I was hoping for. Did you know we have enough bombs to end civilization? And they are all over the world. Talk about a fireworks show you don't wanna miss."

Chris giggled while he shook his head.

"Why would you blow up the world?" Strike asked. "You live here."

"Oh, Commander, I have no plans on blowing up the world. I just like having the option in my back pocket. It's a strong wagering chip, as you might imagine, and most people are smart enough to know I never lie."

"Are you going to tell me what you want? Or just keep talking nonsense?"

"I love your eagerness, Commander, but you really should relax. It's going to be at least two more days before you can lift yourself off that couch. I must say you do look quite comfortable, like a cat taking a day off from its hectic life."

"And what is your retaliation?" She tried to sound unimpressed, but was terrified at learning how many explosives Chris had access to.

"Eye for an eye, Commander. I don't try to one up my enemies, just return the favor. They tried to blow up my house, so I have no choice but to blow up one of yours. Where is your election going to be held?"

"It's not held anywhere. Everyone votes from whatever office they're in."

"I see. Election day might be a fun time to rattle your little underground forts. It would be a shame for the rest of the world to find out about this secret society you've kept hidden for so long."

"What do you want from me?" Her body may have not been able to move, but her voice came out sharp and demanding. "Tell me, dammit!"

"It's not so much what I want from *you*, Commander. See, you and I want the same thing: to end this war. Now that I have you in my possession, that is becoming a reality as we speak. Your pathetic group of warriors are now flailing around like headless chickens. Their leader is gone and their backup leader is dead on my floor. Forgive me for saying this, but you silly Road Runners have never had a day as bad as this, and it makes me beyond tickled."

"You know most wars end with a sort of peace treaty, not destruction."

"Commander, I've *been* to most of the wars throughout history, and destruction is what *leads* to the peace treaty. Trust me. No one is asking for peace until their backs are against the wall. Much like yourself right now." Chris grinned and sat down in a love seat opposite the couch, Julian's corpse between them. "We can work out a deal, but I want to have my fun first. I can't let you walk out of here looking like a hero who negotiated a deal. I have to blow some things up, kill some of your people, and paint the picture that I drove you to surrender."

"You're a twisted piece of shit," she snarled. "All we've ever done is try to keep the world safe from your lunatic ideologies."

Chris threw his head back and chuckled. "Commander, people *love* my ideology. You've seen the future, the whole world loves it. Humans only worry about themselves and not others. I've found a way to stroke those selfish desires and turn the world on its axis. Chaos is the world naturally cleansing itself, resetting us back to our barbaric roots."

"You're wrong. People will always strive to be better and improve. Nobody wants to go backwards."

"I'd say Mr. Caruso here took a step backwards, wouldn't you? I didn't even have the pleasure of killing him myself. I was gonna televise it for all of your people to see what happens when you try to disrupt my life. Perhaps you can fill that role, or maybe we can work out a deal. Maybe both?"

Chris leaned back and stroked his chin, the dials turning in his sick mind. Strike would happily offer both of her legs if it meant getting out of this mansion, but knew even Chris wouldn't accept those terms. He enjoyed mind games more than dead bodies.

"I'll have to get back to you, Commander." Chris pulled up his sleeve and checked his watch. "I'm gonna head to bed, it's about that time. I'll leave you here to catch up with your friend, maybe he'll answer to you why he decided to drop bombs on my beautiful mansion. Have a great night."

Chris stood, winked, and left the office, closing the door behind him.

Strike remained on her side and cried as an earthy odor rose from Julian's dead body, his perished eyes open and gawking at the ceiling. A long night awaited as she would need to decide how to best surrender the war.

29

Chapter 29

Martin woke up the next morning and vomited in the toilet. Gerald had planted the idea of Sonya playing mind games, and he couldn't shake the thought, having woken up in a nervous sweat multiple times throughout the night. His morning meeting with Sonya loomed, and as the hours ticked away each time he woke up, a sense of doom crept into his conscience like a slow moving funnel cloud waiting to demolish a small town.

Sonya had left the Road Runners behind, having no choice, but would she go as far as reuniting and with her estranged, demented father? And actually do him a favor by trying to capture Martin?

He doubted it, but crazier shit had already happened on this brief adventure to the future. Martin owed it to himself to meet with Sonya. At this point, what did he have to lose? He had already braced his mother for the possibility that he might not return. It was a classic high-risk, high-reward scenario, with the reward being a return to 2019 with the cure for Alzheimer's.

Web was dead, so he at least owed it to him to not have his death pass in vain.

After rinsing off under the sink, Martin returned to his room to dress in his Revolter attire of dark jeans and a long sleeve, plaid button-up. His suitcase was filled with plenty of similar outfits to blend in around the city for at least another week.

Today's the day, Martin thought as a knock came from his door. He expected Gerald, and pulled open the door to confirm.

"How did you sleep?" Gerald asked.

"I hardly slept. I just wanna get this medicine and go home."

"If all goes well, hopefully we'll be on our way in the next couple of hours."

"I know." Martin slipped into his shoes and looked in the mirror, wondering if this was the final time he would see himself alive.

"What's bothering you?" Gerald asked, monotone like always.

Martin sighed. "Am I making a mistake, Gerald? Part of me is starting to think that I might not make it back."

"That's always a risk living in this era. Being a Road Runner after the year 2030 is basically a death sentence. But that's beside the point. I take it you thought about what I said about Sonya."

Martin nodded. "I did. I still don't buy it—I don't think she would do that to me after all we've been through. But I still can't make myself rule it out as a possibility. I might show up expecting the medicine and end up back in Alaska with Chris, to never see the light of day again."

"I wish there was more I could do to help, but we can't risk it. If only you could've had her agree to meet you outside of the city, but I doubt she would fall for that."

"It's too late now, so let's head out."

Gerald stepped aside and let Martin pass into the living room.

The blood splatters had been wiped off the wall, but the stains in the couch would never come out, appearing like a deep, black hole in the center cushion, ready to suck another life into it.

"Is Brigham still sleeping?" Martin asked.

"Trying to. I checked on him just now, said he's been staring at the walls all night, going to try and fall asleep now."

"Poor guy must be horrified."

"Yeah, he'll be okay as soon as we get back home."

Thanks for the extra pressure.

Gerald pulled the van keys out of his pocket, and they left the hotel and Brigham behind, oblivious to what the next few hours had in store.

The abandoned roads at seven in the morning surprised Martin as they headed toward downtown. It made sense, though, since everyone who worked downtown already lived there. Those on the outside had no business in town, unless authorized.

Gerald pulled over to the same spot as yesterday to let Martin out. "I'll wait here," he said after not speaking a word during the tense ride over. "One hour, then I'm going back. If it takes you longer than that, I'll be back at noon. That sound good?"

"Yes."

"Good luck." Gerald shook Martin's hand before he headed off to his date with Sonya.

Martin stepped out of the van and never looked back, starting down the long sidewalk toward the checkpoint where a handful of people formed a short line to get through security. He only waited two minutes before stepping through the metal detector and getting the green light to enter the city. He wondered if he had never met Chris, what side of the electric fence he would have ended up living on. Would he have even survived the initial wave of genocide that occurred after the Revolters snaked their way into government?

He shook off the thought as he passed through security and stepped into the bustling city. Even though no one had to commute into the city, there were still thousands who needed to get across town, leaving the roads clogged and jammed like rush hour in Manhattan.

Martin entered through the same location as yesterday, a couple blocks behind the capitol. On the other side of the golden structure would be Sonya, hopefully alone and holding a bottle of medicine. He walked down Colfax, the cars on the street a sitting parking lot that shimmered under the morning sun. Birds soared above, chirping, while Martin fought to keep the weight of his upcoming encounter off his mind.

Within a couple minutes, Civic Center Park appeared, dozens of businessmen crossing it on their way to work, coffee in hand and briefcases at their sides. Martin started straight for the same location where he had left Sonya last night, and believed he saw her sitting on a park bench.

If it was her, then she was alone, easing his mind. Martin had half-expected her to show up with someone else, either to escort the medicine that was apparently a hidden treasure, or to help take him away so Chris could feast on his soul forever.

The walk toward her felt like an eternity, but when he finally reached her, all sense of doom vanished. She sat on the bench, peaceful as she watched a group of butterflies flutter across the park. She was the same girl he had fallen in love with; nothing would ever change that.

"Good morning," he said when he reached the bench, sitting down next to her.

"Hi, Martin," she said, her face lighting up with a wide smile.

She's either excited to see me, or happy knowing this is the last time.

Martin pushed the thoughts aside, knowing how the mind played tricks on itself when paranoia ran wild. "How was your night?"

"It was fine. Yours?"

"It was okay." Martin debated telling her about coming home to a murder, but decided against it. He couldn't afford to let anything derail them from the task at hand.

They sat in awkward silence for a few seconds, neither wanting to speak next while they absentmindedly watched people pass through the park.

"I have the medicine," she finally said.

Martin exhaled, not realizing he had been holding his breath. "Thank you. I don't know how to ever repay you."

"You don't owe me a thing. Just remember our deal."

Martin slouched on the bench, all tension leaving his body. "Can I ask how you got the medicine so easily? They made it sound like an impossible mission for us to get it."

"Let's just say I have connections being Chris's daughter—as much as I hate saying it. I've never used it to my advantage until last night when I went to pick up the medicine. It felt gross dropping his name, but I had no choice. Your mother didn't deserve this."

"Thank you. I'll tell her it was you."

"Please, just forget about me."

"Sonya, you don't have to live the rest of your life in this world. This doesn't need to be your new normal."

"Easy for you to say. I don't have many options if I'm supposed to dodge Road Runners trying to kill me."

"I still don't understand why this became a thing all of a

sudden. Haven't you been a Road Runner for years?"

She nodded. "They didn't always know about my life being linked to Chris's mortality. When it became clear that he can't be killed through any conventional means, they branched out their research to find other ways. And that's how they discovered this."

"How did you find out?"

"They told me. That's the Road Runner way, you know, being transparent with everything. They never made plans to kill me; in fact, they wanted to study me and see what they could learn. Maybe there was a way to kill Chris by removing a part of my body or something, but nothing ever came out of it. Just recently is when these conversations started, but I had friends in high places who warned me."

"Was it Bill?"

She nodded slowly, her hair swaying in a silent breeze. "Bill had become like a father to me during my time with the Road Runners. He was never going to let anything bad happen to me. He tipped me off seconds after the vote was cast to decide my fate, and had an escape plan in place. It was his idea for me to hide out here. He said it was the only logical place where a Road Runner wouldn't be able to get their hands on me. He deserves to be the next Commander if things don't work out with Strike. He may be a bit reserved, but he has such a bright vision for the future."

"I'll be sure to vote for him." Martin couldn't bring himself to tell Sonya that Bill had been murdered; she had been through enough already.

"Whatever ends up happening, just be ready to make a huge decision when you get back."

"What do you mean?"

"This mission you're on is a test. The other Commanders around the world are watching to see if you succeed or not, and how you are when you get back to 2019. I told you, there is consideration for you to run for the Commandership."

"It doesn't make any sense, I just joined not even a week ago."

"And that's exactly what they want: a fresh perspective. There are lots of lifetime Road Runners who will throw their name into the mix, but they want someone with more of an outsider's perspective, and who also has the merit to take on the role. When you return with this medicine, you'll basically be sealing your fate as a future Commander. Once you have the support of other Commanders, it's nearly impossible to lose an election."

"But I don't want to be a Commander. I just want to go back to my normal life."

Sonya sighed, staring straight ahead, but speaking out of the side of her mouth. "Your normal life is gone. You're a Road Runner now, an important one with a special gift. You either stay with the organization, or get hunted by Chris. And he will catch you if you leave the protection the Road Runners provide."

Martin stood up, needing to move around, and rocked on his wobbly legs. *Is she going to give me the medicine? Or keep trying to tell me the future?*

She joined him, reaching into the purse that had been hidden by her side. "I guess this is where we say goodbye."

"It doesn't have to be," Martin pleaded.

"But it is. You're going home and your life is going to change forever. And I'll be staying, living here until I'm an old lady. That's the way it is, and there's nothing you can change about it."

Martin's face flushed, his eyes growing heavy with tears as a lump bubbled his throat.

"Don't cry. I'll never forget you, Martin Briar. You're going to do big things."

"This isn't goodbye," Martin said, his voice shaky while a lone teardrop streamed down his cheek. "If I have any sort of influence with the Road Runners, I'll make sure they drop their mission to kill you, and you can return home safely."

"I'm sure you will, but I'll be staying here. I hope one day, in another life, our paths cross again."

Sonya stepped into his embrace and planted her lips on his. Their kiss lasted a couple seconds, but her flavor would forever remain in Martin's memory. As she pulled away, she slipped a brown paper bag into Martin's hand, closing his fingers around it with her own.

"Go take care of your mother. She needs you. Goodbye."

Sonya stared into Martin's soul with her hazel eyes, and he held on to the moment, storing it for the rest of his life.

"Bye, Sonya."

She walked away, crossing Colfax toward the downtown skyscrapers. Martin's heart insisted she wasn't really leaving forever, but his mind said otherwise. It only took a minute for her to walk out of his life, just as quickly as she had come into it.

30

Chapter 30

Martin dragged himself out of the city, a throbbing sensation radiating from his gut. Every particle of his heart told him to turn around and spend the rest of his life with Sonya. Even his mother would give her blessing if that was what he desired. Passing by all the robotic businessmen convinced him to keep walking. *This is no world to live in.*

Gerald was waiting in the same spot like he said, and perked up behind the wheel upon seeing Martin return so soon. The van idled, and as he approached, Martin heard music for the first time in this futuristic hellhole. The beat was a clash of electronic dance music and hip-hop, notably with no lyrics.

Gerald punched off the radio when Martin opened the door and sat down, the brown bag clutched depressingly in his grip.

"That's it?" Gerald asked, staring at the bag.

Martin nodded and opened the bag for the first time, pulling out a white pill bottle that looked no different from something you'd pick up at the local pharmacy. There was no label, just a scribble on the bottle that read *Take one pill every day for 30 days.*

"What's wrong?" Gerald asked as Martin sulked silently in his seat.

"It was hard, okay. You may all be trained to murder Sonya, but I love her. Saying goodbye wasn't easy."

"I'm sorry, Martin. It's not that I'm not sympathetic—please understand that. I feel for you, and under normal circumstances I'd say let's take a few days off and go drink at a bar. But we gotta get you and Brigham the hell out of here. It's not safe. They stole Web's laptop when they killed him. So it's only a matter of time before they break through his security and find out what we are doing here. They'll be back within the next few days, and it's best that none of us are around."

"I understand. We're all just doing our jobs."

Martin studied the pill bottle, his chest empty of emotion. Could this be the pain Chris was referring to? Was setting up his mother with Alzheimer's just a step to get him to this lovesick point of near depression? Chris was certainly crafty enough to orchestrate such a drawn-out plan.

He shook his head free of the thoughts, knowing they'd creep back in plenty of times over the next few days.

"When we get back to the hotel, we'll take about ten minutes to make sure all of our stuff is gathered, then we're leaving." Gerald spoke as he started driving, leaving Sonya and futuristic Denver in the rear view.

Martin leaned on the van door and wished nothing more than to go back to that day in 2018 when his mother asked him to take her to the new antique store in town. He rarely told her no, but it would have been worth every ounce of joy today. Would she have still developed Alzheimer's? Would he have eventually shot himself? Would Izzy's body ever have been found, sending Lela to prison?

It was impossible to answer these questions, so he had to trust that things worked out the way they were supposed to, regardless of what he actually wanted.

"Gerald, can I ask you something?" Martin spoke like a nervous child.

"Of course."

"Sonya said some things about me being considered for commander. Do you know anything about that?"

Gerald nodded. "It's true," he said, nonchalant.

"Were you going to tell me?"

"It's not for me to tell. I'm a soldier, Martin. I take orders. I was given strict orders to protect you at all costs, even sacrificing my life if need be. That type of protection is only given to the highest ranking Road Runners, mainly the commanders. They never told me directly that you're in consideration for the job, but the protection order speaks for itself."

"What am I supposed to do?"

"What do you mean? You run for Commander, win that election, and lead this organization. There's nothing else to do."

Gerald spoke of the situation as if it were a no-brainer type of decision. Was Martin the only person who didn't see himself as a commander? Sometimes people perceive you in a way that you never thought possible. But that doesn't make them right.

"Look, Martin, I can't tell you what to do. But if there are people higher up who believe you're fit for the job, then you're fit for the job. It's that simple. We've never even had a questionable candidate run for the position. There have been some with agendas we don't agree with, but never someone who we would ever question their ability to lead us toward an end to this war. You're not giving yourself enough credit."

Everyone keeps saying that.

Martin didn't respond, opting to gaze out the window as his unfamiliar hometown passed by in a blur. It seemed he didn't even have a say in the matter. When he arrived back to 2019, someone within the Road Runners' organization would be waiting with plans for him to run for commander, and he still didn't know why.

Gerald whistled a tune while they drove, clearly wanting Martin to have the moment to allow the reality of both the past and future to settle. When they pulled up to the hotel ten minutes later, Gerald spoke.

"Martin, one thing I want to be clear is that you're never alone when you're a Road Runner. Even if you're somebody like myself or Ralph. We may physically live by ourselves, but we're not alone. Thousands of Road Runners are ready to support and help with anything. Even more so when you enter a leadership position."

"Then why is Strike gone?" Martin asked coldly.

"Strike is gone because of her own recklessness. She should have gone home. But it shouldn't have been that easy for Chris to get to her, either. Something isn't adding up."

"And that's the position you expect me to welcome with open arms?"

"Nothing is guaranteed. You can't be forced into the position—it's an election, and you're not even well known around the community. At this point, I'd say you're a dark horse. Now, let's go inside and prepare to leave this place before we all end up dead."

Gerald killed the engine and stepped out of the van without another word. Martin followed him into the building and to their suite, where Brigham stood against the wall, sweat glistening on his skin, and four suitcases lined in front of him.

"I hope you guys don't mind," he said. "I packed all of your bags after I finished mine. I've had so much nervous energy all morning, I had to put it to use. I still feel like I could go on a 20 mile run and not bat an eye." Brigham spoke rapidly, like a teenage girl filling in her friends on the recent gossip from the high school hallways. "Let's just say I'm ready to go home. I almost drank my Juice and left a note for you, but I know that's not the way we do things."

He giggled at this last statement, like it had been an inside joke with himself.

"Well, thank you," Gerald said, stepping up to grab his bag. "I'm just gonna do a quick sweep of my room to make sure nothing got missed. Martin you should do the same."

"I've checked five times already," Brigham said. "But be my guest." He held out his arm toward Gerald's room, grinning madly at Martin, who returned a quick smile before turning to his room.

His bedroom was immaculate as he checked in the closet and under the bed for any straggling items. They had only been here a whole two days, so it was by no means an impossible task to have a clean sweep done within a few seconds.

Martin checked Web's room, also clear of any belongings, and wondered if packing up Web's things sent Brigham into the mental breakdown he seemed to be currently fighting. All three of them were still on edge about the situation, but Brigham had survived it, and had to listen to his friend get murdered in the living room. Brigham might never be the same, and Martin hoped the Road Runners had an extensive mental health team to help him recover from this tragedy.

Martin returned to the living room where Brigham had pulled the suitcases to the front door.

"I guess we're ready to go. Thank you for packing everything," Gerald said.

"Glad to help. It's the least I can do while you two are out saving the world. Did we get the medicine? I almost forgot that's what we came for."

"We have the medicine," Martin said, never releasing his death grip from the paper bag. "Our mission here is complete. Let's go home."

Brigham smiled like a surprised child and pulled open the front door. Martin expected something to go wrong. Sonya had handed over the medicine with no hesitation, and Gerald's voice kept shouting in his head that it was all a set up. Surely she had set him up to send an army of Revolters to their doorstep before they tried to leave.

But no one waited in the hallway as they made their way to the van and loaded the suitcases in the trunk. No guns fired as they pulled out of the parking lot. No bombs exploded as they turned onto the highway and headed east to the plains where they had arrived only two days earlier.

Martin leaned back in his seat, staring at the blue sky passing above as the rest of the world seemed to vanish into the background of his thoughts. His mind raced as quickly as the van blazing down I-70.

The truth he had longed for—and didn't know he'd learn on this trip—became clear. Sonya gave him the medicine with no strings attached, no hidden agenda. Even if she didn't say it, Martin knew that she loved him. And as they returned home to 2019, where a new chapter waited in his chaotic life as a Road Runner, the thought warmed his soul and provided him a fresh boost in confidence for whatever came next.

31

Chapter 31

Strike had a bit more strength the next morning. She managed to roll from side to side, but trying to pull herself up sent biting waves of pain from her abdomen to her neck.

Falling asleep the night before hadn't been too difficult, as she started snoring twenty minutes after Chris left her alone with Julian's corpse. Her mind and body were drained, having zero energy to even consider staying awake. They must have carried Julian out in the middle of the night, for he was gone by the morning when she woke up refreshed and mentally energetic.

The mansion had a relaxing mood about it, something she'd never admit. The couch, wide and soft, swallowed her in its comfort. The room temperature held at a consistent 72 degrees, perfect to sleep without a blanket. And lastly, all worries seemed to vanish overnight. She knew she was trapped in Chris's lair, a prisoner who would likely die in this same mansion, but none of that concerned her. Could Chris be pumping a sort of relaxant through the vents? It was possible, especially considering he was immune to just about everything as an immortal being. That could be why his soldiers obeyed him like desperate puppies.

Don't fall for any of his bullshit, she reminded herself. Years of studying Chris had led her to know that whenever the old bastard did any act of kindness, it was always motivated by slimy intent. She thought this as soon as the aroma of bacon, eggs, and waffles carried into the room. Footsteps followed shortly behind, before Chris swung the door open with a tray held in one skinny arm.

"Rise and shine, Commander," he greeted, both chipper and psychotic. "I've learned some exciting news this morning, and I couldn't wait to share it with you."

She tried willing herself to sit up, but only managed to roll onto her back with a drawn-out groan.

"What is it, Chris?" she asked, trying to sound uninterested despite the curiosity bubbling beneath her surface.

He placed the tray of food on his desk, clapped his hands, and skipped across the room, planting himself in the seat opposite the couch. "It appears my dearest Sonya has sided with Martin Briar. I've had my people following her since she moved to her newest location and she just happened to cross paths with Mr. Briar—total coincidence, from what we can tell—and has aided him."

Without him saying it, Strike knew what this all meant. She had authorized Martin's mission to go to 2064 for the Alzheimer's cure. What else would Sonya have aided him in doing?

"Why is this news? I'm here and can't do anything about it."

"I just thought you'd like to know since these are people you've been heavily invested in. They're still out there carrying on their lives. I don't suppose either of them even know about your disappearance, since they've been frolicking about in the future. How does that make you feel?"

He was clearly trying to bait her into a reaction, perhaps trying to set the tone for a rough day. But fuck him.

"It makes me proud to know that my Road Runners still care for each other and are willing to help each other. Even in the ugliest of places."

"Interesting take. It makes me quite disgusted, frankly. My own daughter betrayed my trust—"

"She hates you, you know. Wishes you would die without her having to die. She worked around the clock for two years trying to find a way to release this curse you've placed on her. *You* drove your own daughter to the brink of suicide, and *you're* the one disgusted?"

"Don't flatter me with these pity stories, Commander." Chris grinned as he slid a balled fist under his chin. "I made my daughter an offer to live under my protection, in a situation where she still didn't have to encounter me, and this is how she thanks me. It's a stab in the back."

"Like when you stabbed her mother in the back." Strike may have been relaxed, but her mind was quick and locked in, ready to dance with the devil.

"Ahhh, more nonsense to try and rattle me. It will never work."

"It'll work one day. We may not be able to get to you with words, but you've made enough people in this world furious. One day someone is going to wipe that stupid grin off your face and remove you from this world like the scum you are."

"Commander." Chris grinned even wider. "Please stop it, you're arousing me."

"You're sick. What is it you want from me?"

"Since we're growing our relationship and being so honest with each other, I suppose I can tell you. Martin has gotten away with too much. Yes, it's my mistake for not throwing him in the basement like I wanted—sometimes you gotta trust your instincts, right? I trusted him by giving him freedom within the mansion and on the property. You have to understand, from my point of view, he appeared ready to commit his life to the Revolution. He was either really smart and outplayed me, or too naive to know better. I say the latter, but it doesn't matter at this point."

"Get to the point, then."

"The point is he betrayed my trust. Used it against me for his own gain. Now, I'm equally as pissed at Sonya, but I can't do anything to her for obvious reasons. With Mr. Briar, though, I can make the next move in the war, and it won't be pretty. A violation of one of our unwritten rules, you could say."

"Don't you fucking dare," Strike snapped, and this time she was able to sit up a couple of inches before falling back into the couch.

"I absolutely dare, and I will. It's time to send a message, and I thought you should be the first to know, since there's nothing you can do about it from that couch. Do you care to watch, or shall I just fill you in on the juicy details when it's done?"

"You're sick. If you do this, we'll have no choice but to bomb the living hell out of every one of your hideouts."

"The only person with the balls to send the bombs was lying in this room with you last night. Where is he today?"

"You're a coward."

"Not the first time I've been called that, and not the last I'm sure." Chris giggled as he stood up. "I've brought you breakfast. Our cooks are some of the best. I'll send someone up to feed you."

"I'd rather starve to death than live another day in your shithole world."

"Well, I don't want you to die, Commander. If you refuse to eat, we'll just give you a new treatment in the electric chair and then force a tube into your stomach. Please don't make me do that, and just eat your breakfast like a good girl."

Condescending piece of shit, Strike thought, mentally lunging from the couch and squeezing the life out of the old man's throat.

Chris crossed the room to the door and turned around. "Don't worry, Commander. You and I will enjoy a front row seat to the madness. I gotta run, though – need to make sure everything has been settled for Martin's homecoming. Would hate to see his optimism run any higher than it already is."

He turned back and left the room, sure to slam the door shut behind him.

Strike thought she heard howling laughter coming from the hallway, but it might have been her imagination. Either way, she knew what Chris planned to do without him even saying it, and the thought disturbed her to the core as she lay on her back, staring at the ceiling.

Please don't let him do this.

32

Chapter 32

Martin woke up in 2019, his mind foggy and begging for actual sleep. They were still in the van, back in Watkins, in the middle of an open field beside a frontage road. Gerald mumbled, still coming to, and Brigham sat stiffly in the back seat, eyes bulging, grateful to be alive and far away from the year 2064.

While Gerald shook himself awake, Martin scanned the area, still half-expecting a group of Revolters waiting to execute them. "Coast is clear," he said, the spike of tension fading away.

"I just want to go home," Brigham said.

"We're on our way," Martin replied, nudging Gerald in the shoulder.

Gerald's eyes shot open and looked around the vehicle to gather his surroundings. "We all okay?"

"Yes. Let's get back to headquarters."

Gerald turned the van on without hesitation and reversed out of the field toward the frontage road. "Let me do all the talking when we get back. When I dropped off Web, I sort of left in a hurry; they're going to have hundreds of questions."

"Good with me, I'm gonna take a shot and go to sleep," Brigham said, no sign of joking in his voice.

That's all Martin wanted too. He hadn't had a solid night's sleep in a few days and it was starting to take a toll on his ability to think straight. One more skipped snooze session and he might grow crazy enough to run for Commander. He laughed, a bit slaphappy.

"What's so funny?" Gerald asked.

"Oh, nothing. Just can't believe how easily we got the medicine. It was supposed to be this big secret operation, and then someone just hands it over."

"I'm glad you think this is funny," Gerald snapped, clearly tired and cranky as well. They drove silently, thankful for the break in stress, enjoying a quiet morning into the city.

Within thirty minutes they pulled into downtown, working their way through the bustling traffic that was always present in 2019, regardless of the time of day. They pulled up to the marketing office, and Gerald let out a long sigh as he turned the engine off.

"We might have some visitors," he said, scanning the area.

"What do you mean?" Martin asked, reaching for a gun that wasn't on his waist, but packed somewhere in his suitcase.

"I think there are some high-ranking Road Runners in town, likely to see you, Martin."

Do these people not believe in resting? Martin wondered. *I just survived the future and want to go to bed. But all they want to talk about is what to do next.*

The fatigue created a short fuse for his irritability, but he understood the widespread panic across the organization with Strike being held hostage. He'd try to answer their questions, but if they wanted him to ever run for Commander they needed to respect his basic wishes of a private bed to sleep in.

Gerald kicked his door open and stepped outside, his back cracking as he stretched his beefy arms above his head. Martin joined him while Brigham pulled himself out of the back seat.

"It does feel good to be back in my city without worrying about stepping on a Revolter on the sidewalk," Martin said as he rounded the van to meet Gerald in front of the building.

"I've nearly forgotten the sensation," Gerald replied with a forced chuckle. "Shall we?"

Martin nodded and the three of them trudged up the steps and entered. The marketing office hummed with energy he hadn't seen before, and he wondered if everyone was actually working on their marketing projects, or looking for Strike. Eyes followed them as they passed through the hallway toward the back office.

No one said a word as they entered the manager's office where the secret staircase waited. A brief, sick thought popped into Martin's mind where he questioned the use of a basement as their hideout. Chris also used a basement for a hideout of Road Runners, and the connection made his mind spin.

As they descended the stairs, the sound of voices grew even louder than they had been in the marketing office. The Road Runners seemed to have doubled in population as dozens of people ran frantically through the office, papers in hand, phones to their ears, and not a soul paying attention to the three men who just returned from the future.

"Let's see if Tarik's in his office," Gerald said, and led the way toward his office where the door stood open. Tarik sat behind his desk, two other men standing along the walls in the middle of an intense conversation.

"Gentlemen!" Tarik said, standing up to meet them at the

door. "So glad you made it out of there alive. They bombed your hotel this morning, and we temporarily lost the signal on your tracking devices. Let's just say there was a good five minutes of complete panic until the signal came back and we saw you were safe."

Martin looked behind to see Brigham turn white as paper. Gerald stepped into the room, with Martin following. Brigham remained in the hallway, frozen as if he had just seen a ghost.

"I figured as much after they killed Web," Gerald said, unfazed by the news. "Have we learned anything more about his death?"

"I'm afraid not," Tarik said. "They didn't leave a trace beyond the bullet wound. It appears they never even touched him. We did learn his laptop was designed to self-destruct if any false attempts were made to access it, so they wouldn't have gained any information from that."

An older Asian man cleared his throat from the corner of the room.

"Gentlemen, this is Commander Quang, the leader of our Asia chapter," Tarik said. "And this is Commander Blair from Europe."

Commander Blair stepped forward and stuck out a hand to both Gerald and Martin. He appeared to be in his early 40's, with a head of light brown hair, and glowing white skin to complement a charming smile. "Always nice to meet a fellow Warm Soul," he said to Martin in a British accent.

Commander Quang followed suit, his bony hands fragile with age, but stern. He was bald and clean shaven, making him appear younger than he really was. "It's nice to meet you both," he said in a low raspy voice. "We have a lot to discuss, so if you wouldn't mind us beginning."

He directed this last statement to Tarik, who hurriedly escorted Gerald into the hallway and closed the office door. Tarik returned to his seat behind the desk and gestured for Martin to sit down.

This must be it, Martin thought, knowing what these Commanders wanted to discuss.

"Commander Iglesia was going to join us, but something came up in Argentina that he needed to tend to," Tarik explained.

Just cut to the chase already, Martin thought. *I need to get this medicine to my mom.* He had finally released his death grip on the pill bottle when they entered the office, trusting his back pocket to keep it safe while these men tried to convince him to run for the Commandership.

"Mr. Briar," Quang said. "Commander Strike thought very highly of you. Her reports call you a perfect fit for a future commander position within our organization. We're close to calling her rescue mission a failure, and need to have certain plans in place before that decision is announced."

Martin decided to play dumb.

"I'm sorry, did you say you want *me* to be a commander?" he asked, placing an open hand across his chest.

"Yes, sir," Commander Blair added. "You've progressed quickly through our training program, and now have a futuristic mission under your belt. We assume you have the medicine you sought to get, yes?"

"I have it, sure, but that doesn't mean I'm a commander."

"Not yet," Quang continued. "It's an election, and sure to be a crowded one. But an endorsement from each of us can basically guarantee your election. Is this something you're interested in?"

"Honestly, no," Martin said sternly. "I don't want to be responsible for people's lives. I don't even want to deal with time travel anymore."

"With all due respect, Mr. Briar," Blair said. "We are beyond that point. You're in this life until you die, especially now that Chris has a target on your back, but I'm sure you already know that by now."

Martin's face flushed, the inevitable gnawing at his soul no matter how badly he wanted to refuse. He now realized that stepping out of Chris's mansion both simultaneously liberated and trapped him.

"I haven't even been a Road Runner for a year – why would anyone take me seriously?"

Blair nodded. "Same scenario as me. I was a Road Runner for six weeks when the election came up. They asked me, endorsed me, and I won. Now I've been the Commander for a little under a year. It's very much a job you learn on the fly, not much any one can do to prepare you for it."

"I just don't understand why *I'm* the one you want out of all the people who are surely more qualified."

Tarik pulled open a drawer and dropped a file on the desk. "This is Commander Strike's report on you. We've had eyes on you since the very first time you took the pill from Chris and traveled two hours back in time at his store."

Martin peered at the file, bloated with an inch thick of papers.

Commander Quang stepped forward. "Chris doesn't know that we follow everyone he brings into this world of time travel—at least in recent years since we've started doing so. You were followed during your attempt at Columbine, saving your daughter, and all the way up to your trip to 1919. We look for people who have a natural feel for adapting to different eras, finding ways to survive, and you passed every test. You're a natural time traveler."

"But I'm not a leader."

"Wrong. You don't have leadership experience. There is a big difference. Your raw ability to adapt and strategize will translate into strong leadership qualities. You'll never grow into a leader without trying."

"And putting me in charge of the entire organization is the best option to do that?"

Quang smiled, the wisdom of thousands of years swimming behind his eyes. "We like to move quickly and boldly."

The room fell silent, waiting for Martin to make the next move, but all he did was look from Tarik to Quang to Blair, then back to his twiddling thumbs. After two minutes, he realized they had dug their feet in and wouldn't say a word until he did, the medicine burning a hole in his back pocket.

"I don't have much of a say in this, do I?" he finally asked.

"Anyone in the organization can nominate anyone for the position," Blair said. "I guess you could say we're seeking your blessing before doing so. But we have every intent of nominating you unless you give us a compelling reason as to why we shouldn't."

Blair crossed his arms and leaned against the wall. Martin felt Quang's eyes burning into his soul. His Warm Soul. The damned reason he was in this mess to begin with.

"I suppose the fact that I don't want to do it isn't compelling enough?"

Blair shook his head, grinning as if he knew he had won this debate. Which he had. They had him backed into a corner with no way out. Martin Briar was going to be a nominee to lead the North American Road Runners, and had endorsements in place from the commanders around the globe.

He wanted to start laughing at the thought, growing more punchy by the second, but the tension in the room was ready to burst at the seams. He was pretty sure Quang was trying to hypnotize him, as the old Asian man had still refused to break his glare toward him.

Martin's mind raced for something—anything—to say that would make them leave him alone, but there was nothing.

"Okay. So what happens next?"

33

Chapter 33

Martin wasted no time bolting out of the office. He promised the Commanders to return as soon as he delivered the medicine to his mother. And yes, he would bring a pill back for them to reverse engineer.

His car waited outside, and he jumped in, speeding off like he had just robbed a bank. His mind kept trying to tug him to sleep, but it had no chance against the anticipation of saving his mother's ailing brain. Martin drove like a maniac, weaving through traffic, honking at anyone who dared touch their brakes. By habit, he reached into his pocket for his cell phone, but it wasn't there. He didn't remember where he left the damn thing, or if it was even in the correct year. He wanted to call his mom and let her know that he was on the way with the medicine in hand.

"I'm coming!" he barked into the empty car.

He briefly wondered how painful it was for Sonya to cut the tracking device out of her arm. Any amount of pain would be worth the freedom of getting his mother and disappearing to an island in the Caribbean with his millions, never to be seen again. Sooner or later, the Revolters and Road Runners would give up searching and move on to the next schmuck they learned had a special ability.

He rolled down the windows on the freeway, the day's warmth magnified in the enclosed car. The wind ripped through the car, splaying his hair in a wild mess, and drowning out the silence with the whipping white noise that accompanied driving 75 miles per hour with the windows down.

As much as he hated traffic, Martin was relieved to see other cars on the road, driving slowly without a care in the world. The way it should be. Even the bustle of life could be taken for granted when you saw the darkness of the future where zero traffic existed because everyone was dead.

Martin brought his mind back from that dismal setting, taking his exit that faced the stunning Rockies in the near distance. As he weaved down the side streets and toward his neighborhood, butterflies started to flutter in his stomach. He had subconsciously accepted his death on the journey to the future, and never expected to be driving home right now with the medicine.

He turned into his driveway, heart thumping as he parked and jumped out, hands flailing for the medicine bottle in his pocket as he rushed to the front door and burst inside.

"Mom!" he shouted. "I did it. I have your medicine!" The house was silent. Too silent, he thought. "Mom?"

She could just be napping.

He dashed down the hallway to her bedroom and flung open the door. Martin gasped and sprung back, tumbling across the hall and banging into the wall as all feeling drained out of his legs, causing him to collapse to the ground. The door banged against the inside of her bedroom and swung back toward its closed position, stopping ajar with a three-inch gap of visibility. Martin saw his mother lying in bed, her throat slashed in the shape of a red smiley face, her intestines oozing out of her stomach like a gutted deer.

The room spun around Martin as his mind worked in overdrive to make sense of what his eyes were seeing. His entire body trembled as his throat swelled like it had an inflated balloon inside.

You're dreaming, he told himself. *You've done too much time traveling and your brain doesn't know what's what any more. You're asleep and will wake up soon, back in bed with Sonya, because none of this has actually happened.*

The lie to himself gave him enough strength to rise to his feet and step toward his mom's room. No, he didn't actually believe he was dreaming, but wasn't that how dreams normally worked? His body shuddered when he entered the room, the stillness of death thick in the air. He glanced around, looking for anything to keep his eyes from returning to his torn open mother. She kept a table by the window, stacks of her puzzle books and novels standing neatly on the edge. A single sheet of paper in the center caught his attention.

Martin forced his legs to cross the room, Marilyn to his left where the darkness of blood soaking into the sheets was impossible to ignore. He cleared his throat and gulped as he leaned over the table to read the paper:

Hello old friend,

I thought we had an agreement after I saved you from the Road Runners. I brought you into my home, my private domain, and you betrayed my trust by running away a few hours later. I'll admit, it's my own fault for not being more cautious, and thanks to you, future residents will have zero privileges as far as roaming the house and the grounds.

We could've made a great team. I had a grand vision for how to use your special ability to make the world a better place, but it appears you've fallen into the familiar trap laid out by the Road Runners. It's a shame, because now our relationship can only end with your death.

I was ready to let it all go since I had only myself to blame. But then I heard you used Sonya to get the medicine to cure your mother. How dare you try to find a workaround to our deal. I exchanged a lifetime supply of the Juice (which you still have) for your pain. By avoiding the pain of watching your mother fade into a shell of her former self, you violated our agreement.

I'm sure you understand why I had to carry out this drastic action. If it puts your mind at ease, she was sleeping when we did this, so she shouldn't have felt a thing.

I'm not a monster, just a man of my word. Until next time.

Your friend,

Chris

Martin's lips quivered as he read the note, clenching the paper tighter in his grip with each passing line. Tears spilled down his face onto the paper, blotting parts of the handwritten ink. Reality sunk in that this was no dream.

I can go back in time and stop this from happening.

The thought jumped into Martin's head with such fierceness that he sprinted out of the bedroom in search of his bottle of Juice. He couldn't remember if he had left it hidden in the basement bar or somewhere in his bedroom, sprinting to the basement first since it was the closest door.

But like most ideas that come to fruition in the middle of panic, the possibility quickly faded, taking along every ounce of hope with it. There was nothing he could do about his mother's death—Chris would never allow it. If he had gone through this much trouble to prove a point, anything further would only result in Martin's own demise.

That doesn't sound so awful right now, Martin thought, memories of his mother flooding his mind. It had been a while since he contemplated taking his own life, and much had happened since that last time at his old apartment in Larkwood. But the temptation always stood silently in the corner of his thoughts, in case he needed an easy way out.

He had left his suitcase in the car, containing his flask and pistol. He debated running to the car and flipping open the suitcase in dramatic fashion, to face the ultimate crossroads of his life within the same bag. Drink the Juice to go back and save his mother, or slide the pistol between his teeth and squeeze the trigger, once and for all.

The days of flirting with suicide were behind him, though. If there was anything Chris had done, it was reform Martin into a person who longer toyed with the idea of ending his own life. He now tried to contribute to the world after coming out of Izzy's death a changed man. Even if Sonya and the Road Runners were the ones who *actually* reformed him, it was Chris who had given him the opportunity to ever meet them.

Chris had indirectly saved his life—something he would never admit out loud. Before he met Chris, his life had dragged through the shambled mess it had always been since Izzy's death. Even after learning the gruesome truth of what had happened to his daughter, Martin found peace in the closure he had received.

Defeated, Martin returned upstairs with his head hung low, reality's cold and unforgiving grasp squeezing his heart. For the moment, his past with Chris was forgotten, his future with the Road Runners buried in his thoughts. All he cared about was the present.

When he reached the landing at the top of the stairs, he looked into the living room, spinning around to admire the mansion he was able to buy with hopes of starting a new life with his mother and Sonya. A steady breeze howled outside, providing the only sound in the silent house.

He shuffled across the living room, looking to what could have been. It seemed like yesterday when his mother was boiling water in the kitchen, wanting to make noodles they didn't have. Martin sunk into the couch and gazed to the dining room where he had sat with his mom and told her the truth about his unique opportunity to travel through time. It was the same table where he and Sonya had scarfed down lunch before beginning their journey to 1919, the same trip that had led him to becoming a Road Runner and to this very moment.

"You win, Sonya," he said, his voice echoing off the vaulted ceiling above. "Your mission is complete."

Sonya was gone. His mother was dead. The future waited, whether he liked it or not.

Martin Briar had been delivered to the Road Runners exactly as planned. They expected him to lead, to change the future for an entire organization working around the clock to defeat their nemesis who had, in some way, hurt each individual person, whether physically or emotionally.

He hadn't yet processed everything that had happened since Sonya led him into a trap. And he'd be damned if he'd miss the opportunity to grieve his mother's death. Grateful to be alone, disconnected from the world and any technology in it, Martin buried his face into his open hands and cried.

34

Chapter 34

Martin later found his cellphone in his bedroom, waiting peacefully on his nightstand as if he had never taken a dangerous trip into the future. He called Tarik and explained the scene at the house, the words causing fresh outbursts of tears.

It felt good to cry, relieving. Ever since he had gone back to 1996 and followed Lela to the lake where she threw Izzy's body, Martin hadn't had a chance to sit in solitude and grieve. This particular afternoon served as the perfect time to catch up while he shed tears for Izzy, the hundreds of lives lost in the Columbine High School fire, Sonya, and now Marilyn.

It wasn't the fact that his mother had died that bothered him—he had mentally prepared for that inevitability at the end of a painful Alzheimer's tunnel. It was the gruesome nature in which she had been murdered that sent shockwaves of pain throughout his body. Even though he had only caught a glimpse, it was enough to burn the image of her bloodied and mutilated body into his memory forever. Perhaps that was a good thing. Being motivated by such a disturbing memory would surely end Chris one day, but now wasn't the time to plot revenge. There was plenty of time for that.

Tarik sent a squad of Road Runners to clean up the mess in Martin's house, and offered to handle the burial arrangement and services. There were a few relatives Martin had to inform of Marilyn's death, but he needed to brainstorm a cover-up story first.

The crew Tarik had sent worked quietly and respectfully, as if this was something they had done hundreds of times. A morbid thought popped into Martin's mind as he wondered if these were the same men who would have come to clean him up if something went terribly wrong.

Tarik joined the crew and stood outside Martin's house, pacing while he spoke on his cell phone. Martin pulled himself off the couch and joined him after he hung up.

"How are you doing?" Tarik asked, slinging an arm around Martin's shoulders.

"Aside from regretting every decision I've ever made, I feel okay." Mucus clogged his nose and throat, prompting him to clear it out after every sentence he spoke.

"Look, Martin, we want you to do whatever you need, take your time recovering from this. The Road Runners will be here for you every step of the way."

"I appreciate that. What about the election?"

"We're delaying the special election, until you're ready. Technically we can because Commander Strike is still alive; we know that much."

Martin nodded, knowing there was no way out of it now. They wanted him in that position, and went as far as postponing the election to let him grieve.

"What am I supposed to do until then?" Martin asked.

"Whatever you want. Take a trip, get out of town. Go do

whatever makes you happy and helps you find yourself."

"Will I be followed?"

"Of course. Chris is too busy with Commander Strike at the moment, but he still wants you. You'll have eyes on you at all times, and a couple of our soldiers within close proximity no matter where you go. Carry on as if we're not there. We'll only intervene should something arise."

The thought of not having any true privacy would have normally bothered Martin, but he had no more emotional energy to give a shit. The Road Runners were going to do as they saw fit.

"I just want my mom situated, and then I'll worry about what to do with my time."

"Of course. Commanders Quang and Blair send their condolences; they had to return home, but look forward to meeting with you again in the future."

"Are we still trying to save Commander Strike?"

"We're exploring all options, but it's not looking good. The attack that Julian authorized on Chris's mansion didn't even leave a dent. He's clearly using some sort of steel from the future—it's indestructible. There's not much we can do if we can't even penetrate his fort. We're looking into tunnels, but are hesitant because we don't know what we'll run into as we start digging toward the mansion."

Deep down, Martin wished they would rescue Strike and let him off the hook for this damned election, at least for the immediate future.

"I don't want you to worry about these things right now," Tarik said. "Worry about yourself, we'll be just fine when you're ready to come back. Give me a call if you need anything at all."

Tarik offered his hand, and Martin shook it. "Thank you. I'll be in touch."

Tarik nodded before turning back down the driveway where his car waited, leaving Martin as the crew worked as silently as mice in his mother's bedroom. They would have everything cleaned up within two hours.

Martin needed to get out of the house, wanting to get far away from his life as a Road Runner. He wanted to remember what a normal life felt like. A life where there was no secretive global war. No Chris hunting him down like a prized animal. No Road Runners forcing him into a leadership position he didn't want.

Let them follow me. I'm getting the hell out of town.

Without a word to the crew down the hallway, Martin swiped his keys off the kitchen counter and bolted out of the house.

He slid behind his steering wheel, reaching over the suitcase in the passenger seat, and opened it, rummaging through the layers of clothes until his fingers grasped his flask of Juice.

With the Juice in his possession, Martin wasted no time turning on the car and pulling out of the driveway. He stopped before driving away, taking one last look at the house he had purchased thanks to his time travel capabilities. The ghosts of his lost future cried for him to stay, but he couldn't. Not right now.

He nodded to the house, genuinely unsure if he would ever return to see it. He had no plans for where he'd go, but would travel as far as he could until he found somewhere that called to him. The tank was full, so he had plenty of hours ahead.

The spontaneity made his heart race in a way he didn't remember. Time traveling gave him a rush, sure, but nothing compared to diving into an unknown adventure.

Martin drove away, leaving his life in the rear view mirror. It would always be there, and he could always return to it. For now, all he cared about was the future and honoring his mother's life. He requested they cremate her remains, and have them deliver those remains to wherever he ended up.

Maybe I'll finally go to a beach and drink fruity drinks all day.

Martin grinned as he pulled out of his neighborhood and made his way toward the freeway. He drove quickly, the freedom of the open road ahead. Headlights appeared behind him in the distance. They may have been random, or possibly the Road Runners keeping their invisible hand over him.

He didn't care. Let them follow. He had plenty to contemplate and would take his time doing so. The future, much like the past, wasn't going anywhere. And much like he'd done since meeting Chris, Martin kept moving forward, waiting for what would come next.

Pre-Order Keeper of Time

Keeper of Time is the fourth installation of the Wealth of Time series. This book will continue the story from where Bad Faith ended, as well as take a deep dive into Chris Speidel's past in a first-ever look at his rise as the Keeper of Time.

The book is slated for a release in Summer 2020.

You can pre-order your copy for only 99 cents by CLICKING HERE!

GET EXCLUSIVE BONUS STORIES!

Connecting with readers is the best part of this job. Releasing a book into the world is a truly frightening moment every time it happens! Hearing your feedback, whether good or bad, goes a long in shaping future projects and helping me grow as a writer. I also like to take readers behind the scenes on occasion and share what is happening in my wild world of writing. If you're interested, please consider joining my mailing list. If you do so, I'll send you the following as a thank you:

1. A free copy of *Revolution*, a prequel story that goes back in time before Chris Speidel ever knew about the mysterious world of time travel.
2. A free copy of *Road Runners*, a prequel story that visits the origination of the Road Runners organization.

You can get your content **for free,** by signing up HERE.
https://www.andregonzalez.net/Wealth-Of-Time-Bonus

Acknowledgments

I can't believe this is already my eighth book since starting this journey back in October 2016. Back then I had clue what to expect. If you told me I'd be eight books in before the turn of the decade, I probably wouldn't have believed you. But here we are. This whole career is sort of like jumping off a cliff and hoping for the best, much like Mike in *Stranger Things*, taking that leap of faith and trusting that Eleven would save him.

My Eleven is very much you, the readers. With every new release I get to connect with old fans and new fans alike, slowly accumulating a following as we move along, and seeing this career really being to flourish. I still connect—quite often—with those loyal readers who have been with me since that October of 2016, and seeing them excited for each new book keeps the fire roaring within. If you've ever left a review or messaged me about your enjoyment of a book, please know it goes noticed and helps this author maintain that trust each time I jump off a new cliff.

Bad Faith wraps up the most recent installment of this *Wealth of Time* series, and I'm blown away at the positive reception this series has received. Please know that I have many plans (in a steel-trap box in my head) for this series. It has endless possibilities with both Martin's main story line and so many potential spinoffs.

I'd like to first thank my editor, Stephanie Cohen. She is just as vested in this series as me, and her hard-work and timely deliver helps keep me on an aggressive release schedule. I hope she doesn't mind me bragging for her, but she just landed a big editing job for a major publisher in NYC. Congrats, and I can't wait to keep working with you!

Thank you to Dane Low at EbookLaunch. As always, you have the perfect vision for these covers. Keep them coming!

Thank you to the Dizzy Dragons. It's so much fun "working" with others with the same drive and vision.

Arielle, Felix, and Selena for providing that constant motivation to keep going and never settle.

And as always, thank you to my wife, Natasha. I know you sacrifice a bit for this dream, I'm just glad to have you in my corner. I love you.

Andre Gonzalez

Denver, CO

11/14/18-10/31/19

Enjoy this book?

You can make a difference!

Reviews are the most helpful tools in getting new readers for any books. I don't have the financial backing of a New York publishing house and can't afford to blast my book on billboards or bus stops.

(Not yet!)

That said, your honest review can go a long way in helping me reach new readers. If you've enjoyed this book, I'd be forever grateful if you could spend a couple minutes leaving it a review (it can be as short as you like) on the Amazon page. You can jump right to the page by clicking below:

US - mybook.to/BadFaith

UK - mybook.to/BadFaith

Thank you so much!

Also by Andre Gonzalez

Wealth of Time Series:

Keeper of Time (Wealth of Time Series, Book #4)
Bad Faith (Wealth of Time Series, Book #3)
Warm Souls (Wealth of Time Series, Book #2)
Wealth of Time (Wealth of Time Series, Book #1)
Road Runners (Wealth of Time Series, Short Story)
Revolution (Wealth of Time Series, Short Story)

Insanity Series:

The Insanity Series (Books 1-3)
Replicate (Insanity Series, Book #3)
The Burden (Insanity Series, Book #2)
Insanity (Insanity Series, Book #1)
Erased (Insanity Series, Prequel) (Short Story)

The Exalls Attacks:

Followed Home
A Poisoned Mind (Short Story)

Standalone books:

Snowball: A Christmas Horror Story

About the Author

Born in Denver, CO, Andre Gonzalez has always had a fascination with horror and the supernatural starting at a young age. He spent many nights wide-eyed and awake, his mind racing with the many images of terror he witnessed in books and movies. Ideas of his own morphed out of movies like *Halloween* and books such as *Pet Sematary* by Stephen King. These thoughts eventually made their way to paper, as he always wrote dark stories for school assignments or just for fun. Followed Home is his debut novel based off of a terrifying dream he had many years ago at the age of 12. His reading and writing of horror stories evolved into a pursuit of a career as an author, where Andre hopes to keep others awake at night with his frightening tales. The world we live in today is filled with horror stories, and he looks forward to capturing the raw emotion of these events, twisting them into new tales, and preserving a legacy in between the crisp bindings of novels.

Andre graduated from Metropolitan State University of Denver with a degree in business in 2011. During his free time, he enjoys baseball, poker, golf, and traveling the world with his family. He believes that seeing the world is the only true way to stretch the imagination by experiencing new cultures and meeting new people.

Andre still lives in Denver with his wife, Natasha, and their three kids.

You can connect with me on:

- https://andregonzalez.net
- https://twitter.com/monito0408
- http://facebook.com/AndreGonzalezAuthor
- http://instagram.com/monito0408

Subscribe to my newsletter:

- https://andregonzalez.net

Printed in Great Britain
by Amazon